FRANCES BRODY

A Murder Inside

A BRACKERLEY PRISON MYSTERY

D0332840

PIATKUS

PIATKUS

First published in Great Britain in 2021 by Piatkus

1 3 5 7 9 10 8 6 4 2

A CIP catalogue record for this book
is available from the British Library.

ISBN 978-0-349-42310-4

Typeset in Perpetua by M Rules
Printed and bound in Great Britain by
Clays Ltd, Elcograf S.p.A.

Papers used by Piatkus are from well-managed forests
and other responsible sources.

Piatkus
An imprint of
Little, Brown Book Group
Carmelite House
50 Victoria Embankment
London EC4Y 0DZ

An Hachette UK Company
www.hachette.co.uk

www.littlebrown.co.uk

Frances Brody is the author of twelve Kate Shackleton mysteries and three historical novels. Frances began her writing career in radio and has also written for theatre and television. Her novel *Sisters on Bread Street* won the HarperCollins Elizabeth Elgin Award. *A Woman Unknown* was shortlisted for the Mary Higgins Clark Award. Her stage plays have been toured by several theatre companies and produced at Manchester Library Theatre, the Gate and Nottingham Playhouse. *Jehad* was nominated for a Time Out Award.

Frances lived in New York for a time before studying at Ruskin College, Oxford, and reading English Literature and History at York University.

A Murder Inside is the first mystery in the Brackerley Prison series.

Visit Frances Brody online:

www.francesbrody.com
www.facebook.com/FrancesBrody
www.twitter.com/FrancesBrody

Praise for Frances Brody:

'Frances Brody has made it to the top rank of crime writers'
Daily Mail

'Witty, acerbic and very, very perceptive'

Ann Cleeves

'Delightful'

People's Friend

'A fascinating and under-used period for new crime fiction'
Ann Granger

To Veronica Bird OBE

The law condemns the man or woman
Who steals the goose from off the common
But leaves the greater villain loose
Who steals the common from the goose.

ANON

One

Nell Lewis was five foot six inches tall, but the bottom of the heavily barred, high window was above her head. The window had sixteen panes of glass. Cold seeped from the soles of her feet. She sat on the narrow iron bed with its thin mattress, stuffed with something spiky and uncomfortable – coir, she found out later, coconut husk fibre. She took a mental inventory: washstand with an enamel basin and jug, a chair and table and a little shelf. The prison rule book lay on the table. Feeling the need to move, she stood and pressed her palms against the whitewashed wall. She had seen a horror film in which the walls of a room closed in and crushed the occupant. She felt the sudden need for a pee. All control vanished once a person stepped through that door. A prison officer could look in at any moment, like a window shopper, like a visitor to the zoo.

Just as Nell thought the mad officer had forgotten about her and gone off duty, the key turned in the lock. Like a school bully, the officer stood in the doorway, blocking Nell's path. Her eyes glinted, waiting for some sign of weakness. 'What did you think?'

After two years in the police force, Nell did not suffer fools or give way to bullies. Showing round a trainee had gone to the officer's head. Nell said, 'If I'd known this was on the timetable, I'd have worn a cardigan under my overall.' She shrugged. 'It's a cell, and I don't believe that locking me in is on the syllabus. If it is, I shall suggest its removal, miss.'

The answer took Nell's would-be captor by surprise. 'Some trainees will never imagine what it's like to be a prisoner. Now you know.'

The officer was wrong. While Nell did not know what it was like to be a prisoner, she did know the feeling of seeing no way out of an impossible dilemma. What she had known by the age of seventeen was the ripping away of the life she dared to imagine.

After her baptism of fire, her experience as a trainee at Risley and Holloway prison, Nell attended college. She realised that the powers-that-be would not waste a thorough and costly training course on those not cut out for the job. That explained why trainees were sent to work in the worst prisons before starting at the residential college in Wakefield.

Nell gave up her rented room in order to save money. At weekends, she was the only student with nowhere to go. She studied regulations, answering mock questions, testing herself. She played against herself on the netball pitch, aiming the ball into the net until her arms ached. She walked in the surrounding countryside, learning to read the finer points of a map and to use a compass. In orienteering and in every test, she came out on top.

Each week at college, there would be someone who was present on Friday but absent on Monday. It turned out that

not all trainees could turn a key to lock a cell door on someone. They might say the lock stuck, or there was something
the matter with the key. They would try again. 'It just won't
work. Is there a knack to it?' A person without the knack of
locking a cell would be gone, as would those who failed the
written tests.

Nell could not afford to lose her chosen future. She had
lost too much already. Being pregnant at sixteen was seen by
her family as a calamity to be kept secret. When Nell's baby
was weaned, Nell's sister Sheila made it clear that Nell must
begin to think about getting a job. She need not move out yet.
Not that Sheila was rushing Nell, she explained, but Roxana
needed only one mother.

Sometimes, during those days, Nell did not know whether
she slept or woke. She would take the baby from her cot in the
night and hold her and never want to let her go. Her breasts
ached. Her whole body ached. Sometimes she felt she would
float away; other times she knew she had turned to stone.

Roxana will always be mine, Nell told herself. But it was
too late for that. On Roxana's birth certificate, Sheila and
her husband Wilf were named as parents, to avoid disgrace.

Nell had handed over her daughter like a little parcel. It was
for the best, she was told. Roxana had a mother, a father, a
sister and a brother. Nell could contribute towards Roxana's
upkeep, Sheila said, but if Nell bought presents, it must be for
all the children, so Roxy would not be singled out.

Wilf proved sympathetic and helpful to his young sister-
in-law. He was a police constable, studying for his sergeant's
exam. 'There's a job for a clerk in the office at our nick. When
you're twenty-one, you can join the force. You're bound to
meet someone.'

Sheila gave Nell tablets so that she would not burst into tears at the job interview. Nell flung them back at her. She was seventeen and felt as old as she would ever be. She took the job at Wilf's police station and learned to type.

When the others at the station said to her, 'Cheer up, it may never happen,' she learned to pull the right sort of funny face. Never again would anyone ride roughshod over her.

She stayed on and joined the force at twenty-one. WPC Nell Lewis opened two Post Office savings accounts, one for herself and one for her daughter, Roxana. It gave Nell a secret delight that Roxana's hair had stayed blond, like her father's. Sheila did not like that. 'What did you expect?' Nell asked. 'My hair's red, Roland's was fair. Tell her the truth and give her back to me.'

Eighteen years had passed since Nell left the police force, age twenty-three, and joined the Prison Service. She served her time in five prisons, taking on new responsibilities, dealing with everything that was thrown at her, by prisoners and by management. Climbing through the ranks, sticking to the rules, she never received less than a glowing report. She had been at HMP Armley for three years. Tomorrow, she had an interview.

After work, she drove to London and booked into a small hotel overnight. She arrived late at the hotel, but not too late to borrow an iron and press her skirt.

Roxana joined her Auntie Nell for breakfast. She had a job working as secretary to an elderly American journalist with an office on Fleet Street. Roxy felt she had more in common with the office cleaner than she had with him. Part of her job was to take cuttings from all the newspapers, go to the British

Library to do research for his articles that she then typed and he sent to New York. She had a room in a shared house off the King's Road but hardly saw the others.

Underneath it all, Roxy was admitting that she had moved to the big city with great expectations and not made friends, except for another secretary in the building.

'Well that's a start,' Nell said. 'It's not always easy to make friends. Just remember other people can be shy or self-conscious.'

Suddenly, it was time for Roxy to go and for Nell to get herself ready, and for them to agree that next time they would spend longer together.

As she stood, Roxy snapped her fingers. 'Mam said you chose my name and she doesn't know what made you pick it.'

Nell was quick off the mark, because Sheila had mentioned that Roxy might ask this. 'It's a Persian name, and it means light of dawn. You were born at dawn.'

'I'm glad to have an unusual name. Thank you!' She kissed Nell on the cheek and was off, waving at the door.

Nell took the tube to Prison Service HQ for the interview. There was the familiar building. A passer-by would not give it a second glance. Nameplates informed Nell that Akbar Ltd took up the first two floors. The Association of Tile Contractors occupied the top floors, leaving the two middle floors for Prison Service headquarters.

The brass nameplates being sufficiently polished to provide a reflection, Nell took a look at herself, and passed muster. Her smooth light red hair was styled in a bob, cut by a hairdresser near her prison who had trained with Vidal Sassoon but could not afford city-centre premises. She wore her smart navy-blue suit and carried her hand-crafted leather shoulder bag. The unlucky pickpocket who once tried to dip into that bag had been surprised by her swift judo move. When she'd released his arm, she was left holding the folded raincoat used to disguise his pickpocketing activities. Only lack of time had prevented her from marching him to the nearest nick.

When no voice crackled through the slatted grille of Prison Service HQ in answer to her ringing the bell, Nell pushed open the door, stepped onto a soggy doormat and into a hallway sorely in need of a coat of paint. She climbed the stairs – fifteen minutes early.

From previous visits, Nell remembered the secretary, Miss Wilson, and that she was allowed to bring in her elderly cocker spaniel who would sleep under the desk. Miss Wilson greeted Nell warmly and asked about her journey.

'It was straightforward. There were the usual old bangers on the M1 hard shoulder, flat tyres or bonnets open and steam coming out, a motorist scratching his head.'

'Rather you than me, Miss Lewis.'

Nell sniffed the air. There was no scent of wet dog. She decided not to enquire. It would be a sad story.

Miss Wilson led Nell into a corridor. 'I'll show you to the waiting room.'

'Who is on the interviewing panel?'

'We have a deputy director, Jackson; a retired governor, Mansfield, as chair; and Trimble from admin.'

There would be one familiar face. Greg Jackson was now at HQ. He had been on the staff at the Wakefield college when Nell did her training.

Nell was up for the job of deputy governor at a new open prison for women. The place was currently a borstal, but about to have a change of use. The existing borstal governor was still there. Once he left, whoever was appointed deputy would become governor

Nell opened the door on to a room, dense with smoke and resembling a doctor's waiting room for men in fair to middling health, all well turned out in smart suits and highly polished shoes. Neatly folded raincoats were placed under chairs, several with a trilby resting on top. She did a quick count. There were seven men and nine chairs. She wondered whether another woman might be up for promotion. One of the two ashtrays on the low table in the centre of the room was already overflowing.

Nell made her way to an empty chair.

There were one or two nods, but no one spoke.

One man went to look out of the window.

Nell ignored them. She let a stillness come over her, a readiness. The times were a-changing. Nell felt ready for change. Just let them know how good you are.

With a rise in salary, Nell could give Roxy the deposit for a flat. Don't think about that, she told herself. Focus on the interview. You want this job.

No candidate was in for long. The interviewers would have everyone's paperwork, their progress reports and histories. This exercise was to ensure that candidates still had their marbles in place, could walk a straight line across a room and had not grown cynical or exhausted.

Nell's turn came. She entered the room and crossed the worn carpet to face three men on the other side of the table.

The chairman, Roger Mansfield, looked pleased with the world. He introduced himself and his fellow interviewers. Nell's old tutor Greg Jackson gave her a friendly smile. John

Trimble, from admin, wore fashionable round gold-rimmed spectacles.

The moment came when Nell was asked how she would go about turning a former borstal into an open prison for women.

'I would start from the sure knowledge that an open prison, a prison with rules and a routine but without bars, is the most efficient and humane way of ensuring that a prisoner will not re-offend. A woman deemed fit for open conditions is ready for rehabilitation that allows her to develop her skills, find voluntary and then paid work in the community so that she again becomes part of the world outside, to take her place as your neighbour, as the woman you see walking her child to school or managing your local launderette. It will require superb organisational skills, a dedicated staff and hard work. Open prisons are a well-kept secret. I would love what we do to be more widely known. We could be an antidote to the sensational stories in the press.'

Nell had expected the reminder of tight budgets. It came from John Trimble.

Nell said, 'I've visited Brackerley.' She did not say she was part of the Armley darts team that wiped the floor with the Brackerley team at a match in the Hare and Hounds. 'The grounds are superb, the farm allows the prison to be almost self-sufficient in food. Much more could be made of the premises. I would encourage links with the community that would foster good relations and produce revenue. With the right staff, I would work wonders.'

The chairman spoke. 'Change of use from a borstal only took effect last week. It was decided, after a recent inspection, to transfer inmates, except for a few boys close to their parole date. The deputy governor will have a free hand. The borstal governor, Major Harding, is three months away from retiring. Currently he is convalescing after a spell in hospital, and remains in the governor's cottage.' He looked to his colleagues and some prearranged signal seemed to take place. 'Do you have any questions, Miss Lewis?'

'I know that Governor Harding has been in post for several years, about ten?'

She did not mention the most recent inspection report.

The chairman scratched his cheek. 'Yes, that is correct.' Nell could hear the cogs of logic turning in manly brains. Closure following an inspection report could mean that the institution was deemed unsatisfactory for the boys. Let's send in the women.

This would be promotion to a setting that boasted an excellent football pitch, lots of urinals and a borstal governor unwilling or unable to pack his bags and drive into the sunset, but with seniority and perfectly able to interfere for three long months.

She had met Governor Harding. He came to watch the darts match at the Hare and Hounds, sat in the corner and drank beer with a whisky chaser. He had struck her as affable, someone who got by on his personality, war record and a good staff to fall back on.

The major must have holiday entitlement due. If he took it, perhaps he could be gone by the end of the week. Nell sensed that the job was hers, but she also had a feeling of an uphill battle ahead, as long as Governor Harding was in place.

'Do you have any final questions?'

Nell had several. She left until last the one that seemed most vague, sparked by a feeling that something had been unsaid.

'Is there anything else a prospective deputy governor ought to know?'

The panel exchanged looks. Nell realised they had not intended to say, unless asked.

'This is completely confidential,' the chairman said. 'We had a bad apple. That bad apple has been dealt with. We have closed the door on the episode. Existing staff are utterly trustworthy. The deputy governor would start with a clean slate.'

They were unwilling to say more. Nell wanted the job. If they would not tell her, she would find out. The small voice in her head said, There is never just one bad apple. I've been warned.

Two

A person in a cell has time to think, if her brain will let her. Linda could still feel the weight of the suitcase and the swing of her arm. Everything she had needed for her new life was in that suitcase.

The clothes hung loose on her now. She never had a lot of flesh on her bones but everyone on Holloway food lost weight. Her striped towel had a hole in it. But the square-faced travel clock still kept good time.

Linda lived by prison time now. They told her when to get up and when to lie down and go to sleep, but she always knew the time. It was a game she played when she woke in the night. What time is it? Her luminescent clock told her she always guessed right.

Her university place probably went to waste. They would have shut up the room where it happened until enough time went by that people forgot the details.

What should have been the first day of the rest of her life turned into her last day of freedom. When the spiteful warder left on the light in the prison corridor at night, the light spread, brightening the never quite dark cell. Sometimes the past came to her as a flickering film. Some nights, lying half asleep and half awake, a series of pictures popped up on the ceiling. She knew this must be a dream or a hallucination. That did not stop her trying to erase some images and repaint the others.

She saw her younger self in the railway station, at the ticket barrier, fumbling for her train ticket in the wrong pocket of her gaberdine raincoat. The man at the barrier was patient. 'Big day, eh lass?' Perhaps she mumbled a reply.

'York, platform three,' he said. 'Good luck.'

A fellow passenger held the carriage door open for her. He asked if he could help with her suitcase. She could manage, thank you.

At York station, the same young chap who had held the door asked would she share a taxi to the university. That was where she was going? No, thank you, she would not share a taxi. In a burst of familiarity that surprised her, she told him the number of the bus and where to catch it.

The campus was set around a lake. She had been to look one quiet Sunday and to locate the building where all information would be given. Now the place was thronged. She saw the great big room through a fog, and so many people. A shining girl looked as if she might burst with the urge to make friends and had already gathered a group of admirers. The shy types who flocked to the shining girl would be relieved to find someone with the ability to pour out words to strangers. A boy who had enough spots to count as measles said sorry when he brushed against Linda. He looked as useless at making friends as Linda was. For the first time, it came to her that 'make friends' was something people did as a particular thing.

Nobody had ever mentioned that. It was one of those pieces of information you either knew or didn't know.

There were tables, and signs, and her name to be ticked off and sheets of paper that would tell her all she needed to know and where she must go next and where she must go after that, and the name of the girl who would be her roommate.

What no one could have told her was that by the end of that day she would no longer be Linda the student. She would be Linda the killer, the student who murdered her roommate's father.

It was 7 a.m. Linda, up and dressed, heard the footsteps. The grille shutter on the cell door shot back. 'Rise and shine!' The key turned.

This was the guard with the task of paying special attention to Linda, her personal officer. At first her voice had grated so that Linda wanted to stuff her ears with the flocks that she could pull from the hole in her mattress. But there was a motherly kindness too, giving Linda the feeling that Officer Friel would really like to be saying, 'Now here's a nice cup of tea and a slice of apple pie.'

Linda knew everything about Betsy Friel. She spoke as no other guard did, revealing too much about her family life. Mrs Friel was waiting for one of her married children to produce a grandchild; either sex would do nicely, as long as it came out healthy. Last week, she had a wisdom tooth removed, and oh didn't it just give her gyp. Linda wanted to tell her to be careful, just as she had been advised on her first night. Keep your head down. Keep your own counsel. Blend in. Don't lend, don't borrow. Don't confide. Yesterday's friend becomes tomorrow's enemy.

Linda expected a report on the absence of tooth or the absence of grandchild, but no, that wasn't it.

The words came out in a rush, too much of a rush. 'Linda, you know how it is here that all of a sudden someone who is nicely settled will have their cell door opened one morning and they'll hear the words, "Get yerself moving, you'll be off on the ghost train." And that girl is whipped away without a by your leave, no notion of where she's bound, no time for goodbyes. Well, such suddenness doesn't suit everyone, even if the move is to make that person crisp and ready for the big wide outside.'

'Am I to be moved?' Linda asked. A rumour started yesterday. Some people were to be moved to another prison. Fear gripped her bowels. In here, she was safe. Out there lived people who would murder her to stop her tongue.

'All I'm after telling you is there are some surprises no one at first likes the thought of. It's the same for officers, moved about like pawns on a chessboard.'

'Are you to be moved?' Linda bent her knees slightly, feeling they might otherwise give way. She wanted the answer to be no.

'No person who comes into the Prison Service on my terms, with a home and family, is forced to move. We're called "temporary", unless we change the situation of our own volition. And would I be able to tell you off my own bat if you were to be moved or if I were? No is the answer. But it's always best to have a variety of possibilities in mind.'

Linda felt every sinew in her body tighten. She clenched her fists.

Mrs Friel, having no idea she had given Linda a fright, said, 'Shake a leg or you'll miss your breakfast.'

14

People talked too much. Linda wanted merely to serve out her time without interruption and then serve it again. There was nowhere to go, nowhere she could imagine herself living and breathing. She had already died. People in here did not notice that. They simply thought that she was quiet.

The worrying moment passed. No sane person would move a trusted prisoner who worked in the library, a quiet and compliant murderer who had given not a moment's trouble since stabbing a stranger, her roommate's father, in the eye, because he put his hand on her shoulder. She did not tell them about that hand and the tattoo of an eye on his middle finger. He was no stranger, but she did not say so. Shame and guilt overwhelmed her. She pleaded guilty and put up no defence, except to say that she did not know what came over her. It was true that her reaction was automatic when he touched her. She went for his balls with her knee, grabbed the paperknife and thrust it through his eye.

She knew what came over her afterwards. A great wave of relief. She thought she might float up through the ceiling and into the clouds, holding a beautiful balloon.

And then a girl came into the room, and screamed. That first day as a student had begun so well for Linda. She did not know that by the end of the day she would be a killer.

Three

Nell drove back up the M1, arriving home in time to call an estate agent and put her flat up for sale, including furniture.

That night, she found it hard to sleep. It had taken her eighteen years to reach what might be the top of her tree. Life had been more simple when she started out. As a young WPC, Nell was first choice as a decoy for pickpockets and for arresting shoplifters. Once she had them in her grip, they never got away. She never lost a prisoner. Lose a prisoner, lose your job, the unwritten rule in a world bounded by rules. How would that work out in a prison with no bars, where gates were locked to keep people out rather than in and the main door would be locked only at night? The words 'deemed suitable for an open prison' took on a new weight. The women coming to Brackerley had better be 'suitable'!

As a WPC, Nell had looked after lost children, taken down details of lost dogs, walked her beat until her shoes nipped, her feet swelled and her legs ached. In winter, chilblains drove her mad.

She might have been doing that work still, but she felt

which way the wind blew. Julian McHale, a PC who joined a little while after Nell, was clearly set for promotion. He was given challenging jobs. He socialised with CID officers.

When a poster appeared on the station noticeboard announcing that the Prison Service was recruiting women at double her rate of pay, accommodation provided, Nell applied. Nell had good reason for wanting to start again, just as she had a good reason for needing more money. She saw Roxy only once a month. She would buy a car to make that easier from wherever she was posted.

At her first interview for the Prison Service, Nell said that she wanted to help people who were worse off than herself. Her face burned, her neck blotched and she thought sweat marks must show on her blouse. If she failed this interview she could not face going back on the beat, could not face the I-told-you-so, the rented room, the feeling of being surplus to requirements in the family.

Nell cleared her desk at HMP Armley. She went round saying her goodbyes to her close colleagues and fellow members of the darts team. Bert Hastings, who ran the prison workshops, had worked at Brackerley. 'You've a beautiful building there. The stained-glass windows at the top of the stairs are stunning. I hope they haven't damaged the wooden panels in the hall. I'll tell you what you need first thing.'

'What's that?' Nell expected some tips about security.

'There are some lovely old floors. The hallway is tiled. I called in to see the major. They've kept it clean, but it could be beautiful. I'll loan you the machines and you can show your lassies how to use them. Anything you need, just let me know.'

'Thanks, Bert.'

'Tell you what, I'll come across with a work party.'

In the Malt Shovel, Nell was given a send-off and presented with gifts, including a dartboard. She was taken for a Chinese meal. It made her feel quite tearful and also delighted at all the good wishes and demands that she keep in touch and to just ask if anyone could be of help.

Nell didn't drink and so gave Bert Hastings a lift home. It was on her way. He had been around a long time, and must surely be due for retirement soon. As she reached his house, he gave her a good-luck kiss on the cheek. Nell said, 'Tell me who was the bad apple at Brackerley?'

'Officer Horace Thompson. He minded stolen jewellery for his mate, who was the dad of one of the borstal boys. On visiting day, the mate would bring his sparkles to leave in a prearranged place. What did for him was bringing in ciga-rettes for that same lad to sell on. You've nothing to worry about, Nell. Horace was banged up.'

Nell's windscreen wipers squeaked, fighting a losing battle with April showers. The straight-ahead sign read 'Brackerley Village', the right turn 'HMP Brackerley'.

She turned onto the lane, startling a rabbit that disappeared into the hedgerow.

Rounding a bend, she caught sight of tall iron gates and high red-brick walls. She pulled up short of the gates. Spotting a bell with a rope attached, she was about to get out of the car when a uniformed officer emerged from the gatehouse. He glanced at the car's number plate and then opened the gates.

He was in his mid thirties, with thick dark hair cut in a

straight fringe, good-looking. Nell had a memory for faces. When she was at HQ, in the waiting room for the promotions board, he had been sitting by the window. She had seen him somewhere else, too. Now she remembered.

Nell drove in. She rolled down the car window. 'Good morning.'

He leaned down, bringing his head level with hers. 'Miss Lewis?'

'Yes. I'm early.'

He beamed what might be the warmest greeting she had ever had. 'Welcome to Brackerley, ma'am. I'm Derek Jeffrey.' He gave a salute. 'Everyone calls me Jeff.'

'Thank you, Jeff. I'm glad to be here.' Glad was an understatement. She would transform this place. People would say, This is how a prison ought to be run.

When he turned to close the gates, Nell got out of the car to stretch her legs and look around.

At the other end of the wide drive stood Brackerley House. Nell remembered it from her brief visit on the day of the darts match. This former nineteenth-century residence of a wealthy manufacturer looked to Nell like a cross between a stately home and a gingerbread house. It was of red brick with gabled attic windows and tall chimneys. Neatly trimmed ivy edged the ground-floor bay windows. On the floors above were multi-paned windows, framed in stone surrounds. The porch and front door were wide enough for someone to glide through wearing a crinoline. Brackerley was one of those buildings the Prison Service bought after the Second World War. A time of national plans for a better future coincided with once-wealthy families being no longer able to bear leaking roofs, draughty rooms and death duties. It was the sort of place that prompted the mock recruitment line, *Join the Prison Service and Live in a Country House.*

Jeff was back by her side. 'I'm standing in for the gate man so as to greet you. We'd normally slide the gate-book through the window, but this is a historic moment. Will you step in and sign, ma'am?' He opened the door with a flourish.

Nell smiled. 'With my fountain pen!' She took the pen from her bag.

He opened the book. She wrote the date, 28 April 1969, 0715 hours. Helen Lewis, Deputy Governor.

If the gateman was on the six until two shift, he may not have appreciated being sent for a walk so soon.

There was a line for *purpose of visit.* She left that blank. Her title spoke for itself. 'We were both at HQ for interview,' she said to Jeff. 'And you're on the darts team.'

'Yes! You were the only female in the room. I knew you had to be coming here. They didn't give you a lot of time to pack up and move on.'

'True, but we're all used to that.' Might as well get the awkwardness out of the way now. 'Were you up for this job?' According to her information from Bert Hastings at Armley, versatile Derek Jeffrey was ambitious. He was a training officer in mechanics as well as a qualified PE officer who boxed, played football and shone with energy and light-the-blue-touchpaper enthusiasm.

'I told everyone that the job ought to go to a woman. I'm moving to Durham. I start there a week next Monday, as principal officer. I'm booked on an induction course there. It's on the timetable.'

'Congratulations.' Nell offered her hand.

'Thanks, ma'am.' His handshake was less of a greeting and

more a test of her bone density. 'Any job at all that you want me and Crofty to do during the time I'm still here, just say. Otherwise, I'll be helping Mr Ramsden at the farm.'

'I'm early. I asked the admin officer to set up a meeting at eight thirty. I'll drive round the grounds, check the boundaries. Will you let the duty officer know I'm here?'

'Of course!' They stepped outside. 'Oh, and there are two borstal lads still in residence, ma'am. They'll be paroled on Friday. The Probation Service couldn't change arrangements. I've told them they must stay up the farm end, make themselves useful. Mrs Ramsden, the farmer's wife, made up beds for them.'

'What are their names? I might bump into them.'

'Mick Edwards and Dave Carson, regulation short back and sides and wearing bib overalls.'

'I'll look out for them. Governor Harding gave permission for them to stay?'

'He wasn't well that day. It was one of those situations where someone had to make a decision.'

'Sometimes that happens. You have a chief officer – Miss Markham?'

'It was her day off.'

Nell left it there for now. Given the failings pointed out in the report, Nell had the feeling that Jeff had placed himself in charge with good reason.

From the space between the gatehouse and the visitors' block, the gateman appeared.

Nell paused for a word, wanting to meet all the staff and learn their names. He was Sam Reeves, a man with a plump, round face and cautious eyes, quick to tell her that he had lived all his life in the village.

'I'm pleased to meet you, Sam. I want everyone to feel part of what we'll do here. This is to be an open prison for women, a halfway house between serving a sentence in a closed prison and going back into society better prepared to tackle what surprises life has in store. We're using the term residents, not prisoners. Everyone has good ideas. If you want to talk to me, or have suggestions, arrange a time with the admin officer, or catch me as you see me passing.' She would say this many times over the coming weeks.

He nodded. 'Summer fayres was always popular, in the old days, and produce shows.'

She took out her notebook and jotted down his idea. 'Thank you, Sam. That's a good idea.'

He made no move to go, but there was clearly something else he wanted to say. She prompted.

'My neighbour, she says this place will be a glorified holiday camp, gratis bed and board for women who break the law and then have free run of our village.'

'Contrary to your neighbour's ideas, this is no holiday camp. If an inmate puts a foot wrong, is tempted to wander out of the grounds, that can put her release date back by four years. She'll be sent back to Holloway or Risley. No one wants that. If she misbehaves, visits are shortened, home leave and parole stopped. The residents will take responsibility for themselves and others. They are here to make progress towards release. If monthly reports reveal behaviour is not up to the expected standard, or progress is not happening, then she will be sent back to a closed prison.'

'Right then, I'll tell my neighbour that.'

'Good. The more people know about us, the better. Is there anything else, Sam?'

'There is. The thing is, ma'am, I am responsible for the gate-book, me and the two-to-ten keeper. There is someone on the premises who has not signed. He came in by the farm but did not stay up that end. He visited the governor. I saw him.'

'Do you know who he is?'

'No, because he did not sign.'

'I'll look into it.'

After her brief tour of the grounds and boundaries, Nell parked her car by the main door. Jeff was there, ready to assist, offering to take her cases in. She hesitated, and then thought it would be churlish to refuse. She opened the boot of her car. 'Thanks, just by the office door.' By the time she had locked the car and gone inside, he was at the top of a broad flight of stairs. 'I'll put them on your landing.'

So, he was one of those men who went the extra mile. Or, he did what he thought best rather than what he was asked to do.

The place was grand but shabby. She had expected this from reading the latest inspection report. First impressions would be important. With a little care and attention, the tiled floor could be brought back to its former glory. The newel on a wide oak staircase had lost its cap. Wallpaper peeled. Fortunately, no one had desecrated the oak doors with paint, only with discreet signs. To the left of the entrance was the Administration Office and Governor's Office. To the right of the entrance was a door marked Reception. Jeff followed her in. 'That's where we receive our inmates, ma'am.'

'Residents, Jeff.'

'Residents it will be, ma'am.' She thought he suppressed a

smile. 'There's a secure cell in the basement, for any resident who absconds or attempts to.'

Nell turned to Jeffrey. 'Yes, I do know of it. I have the plans. Thanks, Jeff. I'll see you at eight thirty.' He has grown unused to taking orders, Nell thought. He knows he's good-looking, has charisma, wants to be seen as the perfect gentleman and carry my suitcases to the flat. He made no mention of Governor Harding giving permission for the borstal boys to stay on. Perhaps the staff had given up on expecting leadership from the governor and were no longer willing to cover for him.

The door marked Administration opened. A blond head appeared, followed by a slim young woman in uniform. 'I thought I heard voices. Miss Lewis?'

'Yes.'

'Jenny Meadowcroft, your admin officer, known to all as Daisy. Welcome to Brackerley, ma'am.'

'Thank you.' They shook hands. 'Pleased to meet you, Daisy.' Nell did not ask why Jenny was Daisy, sure that all would become clear.

Daisy unlocked the door marked Governor and handed Nell the key. 'The kettle's on. Would you like tea or coffee?'

'Thanks. Coffee would go down well, but I want to take a quick look round first.'

'Right you are, ma'am. Ready when you are. I've set out the chairs in your office as you requested.'

'Good.'

Nell stepped inside the oak-panelled office with the baize-covered desk and swivel leather chair. She did not mind that it smelled of pipe tobacco and coal dust and that the windows were hung with wartime blackout curtains in a place where no bomb ever fell. The view from the window was of a too immaculate lawn and trees. Nell had never had the time for gardening, but it struck her that a little anarchy would not go amiss out there. A low fire burned in the grate. A black metal safe with brass trimmings stood in the corner. Filing cabinets lined one wall.

Five chairs faced her desk in readiness for the 8.30 meeting.

Nell took out her notes. She had drafted a residents' time-table for her admin officer to type.

7.00	Morning bell
8.00	Breakfast
8.30	Go to work*
10.45	Ten minutes break for cocoa
12.30	Lunch
1.30	Back to work
4.30	Tea
5.00	Walking in the garden/Association
6.00	Classes
8.00	Supper, bathing, radio/TV
10.00	In room
11.00	Lights out

*Work parties: cleaning; laundry; farm; garden

There were two pieces of paper in the tray marked 'In'. The first was a copy of the week's staff roster, bearing Derek Jeffrey's initials. The other was a telephone message:

Jane Gardner, journalist, Harrogate paper, would like to interview you about your first day here.

There was a telephone number.

The door between Nell's office and the admin office was open. She called Mrs Meadowcroft and gave her the timetable. 'For typing, please, with copies on the women's dormitory door, on the noticeboard and in the staffroom. Oh, and add a note that I'll be available in my office between five and six p.m., Monday to Saturday.'

'Yes, ma'am. Erm, we don't have a staffroom.'

'Where do you have your breaks?'

'I have mine here. The others, wherever they happen to be, or in the dining room or kitchen.'

'You must have a staffroom. Let's have that on our list, to pick a room.' Nell made her own note.

'And what about the journalist, ma'am?'

'It's a little soon for me to be talking to a journalist when I've just taken off my coat. Lead me on the guided tour, Daisy. Shall we start at the top? I want to see the residents' accommodation.'

'This way, ma'am. I should tell you that we all have nicknames. As I've told you, I'm Jenny but my nickname is Daisy.' She blushed slightly as if her nickname suddenly sounded ridiculous. 'It's because of the Meadow in Meadowcroft, Daisy in the meadow. My husband, Paul, he's Crofty. He's the only one who understands the intricacies of the boiler.'

The Meadowcrofts were 'temporary' staff. Nell thought that the boast of Paul Meadowcroft's skill with the boiler might be Daisy's way of putting in an early plea. If, because of the change of use, only one male officer was needed, could it please be her husband, Crofty. The plea surprised Nell. Derek Jeffrey was the only other male officer, set for his transfer to Durham. She only had to look at him to see he was waiting to climb the ladder. Crofty was works department. He was the one male officer who could remain on staff.

Nell had thought she might be the first to set a precedent as a woman governor with a house provided, the governor's cottage. Instead, she had the usual female governor entitlement to a 'suite of rooms'. Well, that would do nicely until Governor Harding packed his bags. Had he not been here, she might have moved into the cottage, and had the argument as a sitting tenant. Now HQ might say, 'Oh, you have your suite of rooms. Perhaps the cottage can have another use.'

Daisy showed Nell round the building, opening doors and apologising. The rooms were spartan, with a look of having been abandoned years ago.

'It's a bit grim,' Nell said. The accommodation would be a step up for someone who had shared a cell in Holloway or suffered the anguished cries of other prisoners along the corridor at grisly Risley. Yet this was not what Nell envisaged for her model open prison. She did not expect the Ritz. A clean and basic boarding house standard would do. 'Daisy, how did the house come to be so neglected?'

'We haven't had time, you see, ma'am. The lads slept in the dormitory block, like an army barracks, not in this building. What took precedence for the major – Governor Harding – was keeping the barracks ship-shape, work on the farm, training and sports. The boys came in here for meals and indoor association. After the inspection, we thought we were going to be closed down, mothballed.'

'Well, we're open for business, Daisy. Women serving their time here need to keep their spirits up, make friends, look forward to a fresh start. Coming from a closed prison, being locked in a cell, to an open prison with more freedom of movement will take a bit of getting used to. My governor at Armley told me that the original owner of Brackerley House was an admirer of William Morris and followed his ideas. He wanted nothing in the house that was not beautiful or useful. I want this to be the kind of place where transformations happen.'

'I think that, too,' Daisy said. 'We're the ones who can make a difference to a person's life. We've done what we can to make the place suitable.' She opened a door. 'We got the message that you'd want small dormitories for the new arrivals, so this is what we did.'

The large room with big windows had been recently wallpapered. There was a smell of paste. The iron bedsteads were covered with bright counterpanes. There were chests of drawers, each with a vase and paper flowers, two wardrobes and a hanging rail.

'This is perfect, Daisy.'

'We made sure it was nice and welcoming,' Daisy said.

'What a fabulous job you've done.'

'There was a jumble sale in the village.'

'You've made it look bright and cheerful. Who did the papering?'

'I did,' Daisy said. 'Crofty painted the ceiling. Chief Officer Markham insisted on removing the paint to take the woodwork back to its original state. She's been doing that in her spare time for weeks. I had the chimney sweeper in before we started, and in your suite of rooms.' She glanced towards the hanging rail. 'There is one thing you should know, ma'am, perhaps before the meeting.'

'Go on.'

'We have no women's clothing in the building. I put in a

request as soon as I knew of the change of use, but nothing has arrived.'

'There'll be the clothing allowance for two outfits per woman, but meanwhile, what do we have?'

'Bib overalls and boiler suits, which I suppose may be suitable for outdoor work, but demoralising if it's all we have. There are mixed size boots and gaiters for the farm work and gardens. All the boots have been cleaned.'

'We'd better get moving on that. Ring HQ and see what they can find for us. Do we have contact with the Women's Voluntary Service?'

'No.'

'Find out who's the local WVS president. I'll talk to her.'

Daisy nodded. 'Will do. And I'm a member of the local Women's Institute. The WI ladies were kind to the boys, baked cakes, did a sale of work for an outing, raised funds for a wood saw for the workshop.'

'Good to have the WI onside. We'll need nightwear.'

Daisy blushed. 'What I did was—'

'What?'

'My next-door neighbour runs a catalogue. When it looked as if we had a problem, I ordered four winceyette nightgowns in different sizes, different colours, crossing my fingers, four flannel dressing gowns and four pairs of felt slippers. Of course, being a catalogue and weekly terms, it's top whack, but I'll take care of that.'

'That was kind and thoughtful. I'll make sure you're not out of pocket.'

'And I spoke to the admin clerk at Holloway, to let her know the women must bring nightwear and footwear, even if we need to return them at a later date. I hope that was all right.'

Nell thought for a moment. Two miles outside of Brackerley, no one would know of HMP Brackerley Women's Open Prison.

'On second thoughts, Daisy, I will talk to that journalist. We're going to need all the help we can get. Explain that I'm pushed for time on my first day, she'll understand that, but I'd be happy to talk to her.'

'She wants to bring a photographer.' Daisy sounded uncertain.

'Good. People have an outdated view of prison warders. Let them see I'm not an ogress.'

Nell sat at her desk, facing her members of staff. The four women sat together, Daisy nearest the window with a notebook and pencil. Next to her was young Miss Kitteringham, a training officer and recent arrival, qualified in housecraft and cookery. In this prison of nicknames, Miss Kitteringham was already Kit. She had a wide, pretty face, chin-length light brown curly hair and blue eyes that appeared only slightly troubled. Kit had taken charge of the old-fashioned kitchen. Nurse Theresa Carreras, nicknamed 'Florence', after Florence Nightingale, looked glum but attentive.

Miss Markham, chief officer, grey hair permed into a tight bubble style, wore sensible tweeds, pristine white shirt, bootlace tie and brown brogues that would last a lifetime. Being 'Chief', she needed no nickname. Nell knew, without sight of the place, that Miss Markham's domain, the education block, would be pristine and ready for use.

Jeff sat close to the door. Paul Meadowcroft, Crofty, sat beside him. Crofty, a Viking of a man, took his heritage seriously. Nell had seen that his interests included historical re-enactments in the village pageant.

The thing about pep talks was that they must be short and not sound like a pep talk. She addressed each of them by name. 'I'm delighted to be here and to be working with you. This is Brackerley's first day as an open prison for female offenders, and we're the ones who will make this place the best it can be, where we'll all be proud to work. You've all worked in closed prisons. Even enlightened regimes can sap energy, leave prisoners institutionalised, despairing and unprepared for life outside so that high iron gates become a revolving door.

'We'll do things differently here. HMP Brackerley must work for our residents, and it must work for us too. But for the first month we make absolutely sure no one has the opportunity to leg it. We supervise residents at all times.' She paused, took a breath and let her shoulders drop a little. They were all listening. They were with her. She knew this was going to work. 'I've seen the effort that has gone into making a dormitory for our residents that will be comfortable and homely.' She turned to the men. 'Crofty, we'll talk about what we need to improve our surroundings. Jeff, we'll be losing you but, before you go, we'll need the benefit of your experience on the farm and in the gardens.' She addressed them all. 'Let's put that same effort into making this a pleasant place for you to work. You need a staffroom. Perhaps the room opposite the library? We could see about having the snooker table re-covered and putting in a dartboard.

'We all know what to do when residents arrive. I want Brackerley residents to know the rules and understand the penalties and rewards. It will be the responsibility of the personal officer to ensure her appointed resident understands the rules. Let's have a signature on the first month's report, acknowledging that understanding of the rules, along with awareness of rewards for complying and sanctions for failure to comply.

'Daisy will set up times for me to talk to each one of you.' She passed round copies of her plan. 'The gist is that within twenty-four hours of arrival, each woman will be interviewed, her literacy and numeracy assessed, and a case file opened – to which they will have access. Each resident will have a personal officer. Progress will be monitored, and officers' monthly reports completed. During the first month, residents' work will be within the prison, buildings and grounds, moving on to voluntary work in the community when appropriate, with the aim of progressing to paid work. The personal officer, education officer and each resident will discuss what educational or training course is appropriate for the prisoner to follow. Wherever possible, families and a home probation officer should be involved.'

She paused. 'Any questions so far?'

Florence leaned forward. 'I tried to get an anatomical drawing of a female body for my consulting room. HQ sent a drawing of a male body. Again. It seems that's all they have.'

Nell turned to Daisy. 'Follow that up please, Daisy. Make sure Florence has what she needs.'

'I have a point, ma'am.' Chief Officer Jean Markham was five years older than Nell. She must have made the decision not to seek further promotion. If she had wanted, that cut-glass accent of hers would have taken her to the top. 'As I've

32

said to Jeff and Crofty, who moved the machines from the workshop, I want the fly press back. It was taken without my permission. The work is repetitive and mind-numbing, but no worse than putting ice cream tub spoons into little bags, and it pays better.'

Jeff shook his head. 'Crossed lines, the order came from the governor when we had donations of desks and typewriters an issue of space.'

Nell said, 'We can't let something go that will provide paid work. Crofty, you're works department. Have the fly press brought back today.'

Crofty looked dismayed. 'It took three of us to move everything, ma'am.'

The chief cleared her throat. Nell nodded to her.

The chief said, 'The top two sections are detachable.'

Jeff reached out and gave Crofty a reassuring nudge. 'We'll do it. I'll get the farm foreman to give us a hand.'

That's why Jeff has been made principal officer, Nell thought. He's someone who can do things, not the one who stands on the sidelines shaking his head. She waited for a moment. 'Any questions?' There were no questions. 'We're expecting three arrivals from Holloway and one from Low Newton. You all know what to do, so let's get to it.'

There was a shuffling of chairs as people rose to leave. Daisy carried two chairs back into her office. Chief Officer Markham lingered. 'You'll come and see the education block, ma'am?'

The telephone rang.

'I will, very soon.' Nell sensed there was more her chief wanted to say. Daisy would answer the telephone. Nell gave Jean Markham an opening. 'You were in the forces?'

Markham remained standing. 'Auxiliary Territorial Service, ma'am. That's where I met the governor, when he was Major Harding. He would not have overruled me regarding the fly press.'

Four

As the chief officer left, Daisy opened the communicating door. 'That was Mrs Grieves, ma'am, the chaplain's wife. He's on his way up to greet you. He won't take up a lot of your time. He's here now. I just spotted him through the window.'

'That's good of him. He's vicar of . . . ?' Nell had forgotten the name of the church.

'He's Father James Grieves, vicar of St Michael and All Angels.'

When Nell was growing up, everyone knew what a clergyman would look like. Times were changing. Now one never knew what to expect from clerics. They were just as likely to roll up their shirtsleeves and play a guitar as walk the aisle in a cloud of incense.

Father James was a tall, slightly stooped man in a black suit and dog collar, carrying a bunch of red and yellow tulips wrapped in brown paper and a brown oddly shaped pottery vase. 'Miss Lewis, welcome. Compliments of my wife. She made the vase herself.'

They shook hands. 'How kind. Please thank Mrs Grieves for me. Do sit down. Do you want a cup of something?'

'I'm not going to take up your time. I know you have a lot to do.'

Nell, who had intended to call on the governor, watched Father James settle himself on a chair as if he were here for the duration.

'This arrived yesterday from the chaplaincy at Holloway. They say it ought to be dealt with here because the prisoner is being transferred. I know Linda Rogers hasn't arrived yet, but I thought you ought to see this letter sooner rather than later because it's the sort of thing that you may need to let percolate.' He took an envelope from his pocket and handed it to her.

Nell took a sheet of notepaper from the envelope. The address was Norwich. The letter was written in a careful copperplate in black ink.

> Dear Chaplain of Holloway,
>
> I am advised by my vicar that you are the person to whom I should write. I request a visit with my husband's killer, Linda Rogers. Never a day goes by that I do not think of Simon's last day on earth when, so full of hopes and excitement, we delivered our daughter to university. I have tried to understand why Linda Rogers killed my husband when he was taking our daughter's additional suitcase to her room and inadvertently found himself on the wrong floor. Is Miss Rogers bad or mad? If bad, is she fit ever to be released? If mad, should she not be in an asylum? Surely during her time in prison someone has tried to find out why she acted as she did. Simon was the kindest of men

who would not have hurt anyone. Indeed, he had employed ex-prisoners saying that everyone deserved a chance. Yet this young woman caused his death, and admitted it, without explanation. I want to know why. I want to know what happened while Annette and I were exploring the grounds and then waited for her father to return. Linda Rogers said nothing in court either in her own defence or by way of mitigation or explanation. Surely, unless she does so, she ought never to be let out into the world.

Since confidentiality and secrecy surrounds her existence behind bars, the only way of finding answers will be to talk to her. I feel that I have a right to know what she has to say for herself and, as a Christian, to try and find forgiveness. My anger and distress still burn. I am told there is such a thing as closure. I do not believe that. However, I do believe there is such a thing as understanding and the mental peace and quiet that may come when the whirling of questions stops. I should like to try and understand why Miss Rogers acted as she did. Only she has the answer. I wish her no harm. In an odd way, I pity her. Our daughter postponed her university course for a year but in the end graduated with distinction, while Miss Rogers remains behind bars. She will be released quietly, I suppose. Perhaps she will assume a new identity. Before that happens, I want to look her in the eye and ask why.

Yours faithfully,
Marian Saunders

Nell set the letter on the centre of her blotter. It lay very still, this mysterious object that seemed to look back at her, as if knowing its contents presented one conundrum and its perfect handwriting another. *I deserve an answer from Linda*, it said. *I require acknowledgement of this careful letter.*

Nell let out a breath. There may not be an answer. 'I don't know what to say.'

Like Nell, the chaplain fixed his gaze on the object. 'This took me by surprise as well.' He scratched his eyebrow. 'I've never had a request such as this.'

'The transfer from Holloway is today. I'll need to read Linda Rogers's file, get to know her, and consider what to do for the best. Leave it with me.'

'Yes, of course.'

'Will you acknowledge?'

'There would have been a formal acknowledgement from the Holloway chaplaincy. That should satisfy for now.'

'Thank you, Father James. I am not obliged to pass this on to Linda since it's not addressed to her. We'll talk again.'

Lacking a file for Linda Rogers, Nell put Mrs Saunders's letter in the safe. While the safe was open, Nell checked the key rings.

Nell opened the door to the admin office. 'Daisy, how poorly is Governor Harding?'

'I'm not sure,' Daisy scratched her ear. She blushed slightly.

You're lying, Nell thought. You don't want to say. 'He does know that I'm here?'

'Oh yes. He had a memo and a telephone call. He is looking forward to meeting you, ma'am, but there's his foot, you know.' Daisy shook her head sadly.

'What about his foot?' Nell's imagination ran to foot rot or gangrene. 'What ails him and how is he?'

'He broke the metatarsal bone, tripping over a kerb outside the Horse and Hounds. The foot is on the mend, but the mental exhaustion got to him, and the shock of the closure.'

'When was his injury?'

'The day before the inspection.' She sighed. 'One can only do so much.'

Nell knew that a foot injury could take a long time mending, but it ought not to have got in the way of Governor Harding leaving her a message. She gave him the benefit of the doubt. 'Give him a ring, Daisy. Say that Deputy Governor Lewis has arrived, is taking a look around the grounds and will knock on his door to say hello.'

'You'll like the governor, ma'am. He's a perfect gentleman, so charming. In his younger days he played rugby for his college and his county. They broke the mould when they made him.'

Nell kept to herself the thought that breaking moulds could be a good idea. The inspection report had criticised the leadership in the mildest terms, and recommended security improvements. There had been neglect of the fabric of the building, a complaint of bullying and a lack of variety in work experience. Not all departing boys were ready for the outside world. Nell suspected that the boy with the jewellery thief father might have had to take over the business.

Nell said, 'I don't see any padlock keys for the outbuildings. Where are they?'

'Crofty and Jeff have them. They check regularly.'

Nell went back into her office, picked up the phone and dialled the Armley workshop number. She gave her name and asked to speak to Mr Hastings.

Bert picked up the phone. 'Problems already?'

'Not at all. Everything is running smoothly. But a favour.'

'Go on.'

'When you come with your floor-cleaning machines, will you bring a bolt cutter and padlocks. I want to change the locks on the outhouses.'

Five

As Nell walked up the drive, she saw Chief Officer Markham scattering a handful of corn to a gaggle of ducks.

'Popular job,' the chief said. We've always had a duck lad. Soon we'll have a duck lass, meanwhile it's yours truly.' She pointed to some water lilies near the edge of the pond. 'See there?' She bobbed down, dipped her hand into the water and withdrew a bottle of whisky. 'We keep an eye on all the spots where some chum from the outside can leave a gift.'

'Whisky, for the borstal boys?'

The chief shook her head. 'That I couldn't say. Of course the boys are gone now, all but two.'

'Any big hauls?'

'Only once.' She took the top off the bottle and poured the contents onto the grass. 'I spotted a velvet pouch containing jewellery. It had been hidden in the hedge but some animal or bird must have scratched around and moved it into view. I took it to the major and he reported it to our area officer, who came to collect it.'

'Was that connected with the recent bad apple?' Nell spoke as if she knew all about it.

'It may have been, ma'am. It was about the right time for it. I wondered afterwards whether it was intended as a bribe for a vigilant officer, or a trap.'

Passing the whitewashed governor's cottage on her right and the walled garden to her left, Nell walked up to the farm to take a look around. It would not be a good idea to knock on the governor's door five minutes after Daisy's call. He might need time to shed his pyjamas.

Mrs Ramsden, a woman with wild white hair, spotted Nell approaching and waved through the window. Mrs Ramsden flung open the farmhouse door and invited her in. 'You must be Miss Lewis.'

'And you must be Mrs Ramsden.'

'I am, and the kettle's just boiled.' She insisted on making a fresh pot of tea and produced a plate of scones. Nell suddenly realised she was hungry, having eaten only an apple before setting off this morning.

'Have you come far?' Mrs Ramsden asked.

'From Leeds. I was at Armley Prison yesterday, signing off on my final reports and handing over.'

'No bit of a holiday then?'

'Later in the year, perhaps.'

'Oliver will be sorry to have missed you. Him and Eddie, our foreman, are in fields with the two lads who are waiting to be paroled. We'll right miss them when they go.' Mrs Ramsden poured tea the colour of iodine. 'We have a very good worker who turns up every now and then and to help out. He's doing some muck-spreading. Oliver's worrying about being short of labour. I said to him, don't forget I was a land girl during the war – that's how we met. And there's no need to suppose women prisoners won't turn their hands to the plough.'

'Absolutely,' Nell said, holding back for now, not knowing the first thing about farming. 'As I've said to the gateman and I'll be saying over and over, we're using the term "residents". This is to be an open prison, a halfway house between serving a sentence in a closed prison and going back into society better prepared to tackle whatever surprises life has in store.'

'Oh aye?' Mrs Ramsden went to the cupboard. 'I didn't give you the jam. It's strawberry. Now, tell me something.' Mrs Ramsden pushed the jar of jam across the table. 'The lads were marched about like soldiers, never left alone. Parade drill, running, jumping, boxing, kicking balls about till they fell into their beds exhausted. For some of them, driving a tractor was a bigger pleasure than bloodying someone's nose. That won't suit women. What's to stop them from hopping it?'

Good question, Nell thought. For her own comfort, she now had several answers. First and foremost among these: the women would know that Brackerley was a better alternative to almost any other punishment the courts might mete out. They would not risk being returned to a closed prison.

Instead, she replied as she had to Sam the gateman, adding, 'The women will have been assessed for their suitability for an open prison.' Let Mrs Ramsden take that back to her friends in the village. 'Did the borstal have any absconders, Mrs Ramsden?'

'Oh yes, every now and again, even though the lads were under supervision at all times. The governor went after them and brought them back. They didn't get far.'

Well, they wouldn't, Nell thought, not lads in borstal overalls or bib and braces with a platoon of ex-army prison officers keeping them in line. Motorists would know where they were from, recognise the uniform.

Women wearing their own clothes would just need to stand by the side of the road, show a leg, thumb a lift, they'd be off.

As she left, Nell thanked Mrs Ramsden for the tea and scones. 'I look forward to meeting Mr Ramsden. I'll talk to my officers about setting up the farm working party and arrange for the officers to have a demonstration of the work. We're starting with a small intake of residents for the first four to six weeks.'

'And big changes, eh? You'll have a lot on your plate.'

The governor's cottage was brick-built, with a small flower garden in front. A dense and carefully tended hedge grew on either side of the wooden gate. Nell recognised hawthorn, berberis and gorse. She walked up the crazy-paving path and raised the door knocker, which was the carved head of a green man, crowned with laurels.

A dog yapped.

It was a couple of years since they'd met briefly in the Hare and Hounds after the darts match. As soon as the door opened, Nell noticed the change in the governor. He was upright and well-scrubbed but looked gaunt. His hair had thinned and his deep-set eyes were bloodshot.

'Miss Lewis!'

'Good morning, sir.'

'Do come in. Pleasure to see you again, and do call me Major.' An elderly Jack Russell eyed Nell for several seconds before deciding to wag its tail.

Nell stepped into the porch. Crutches were propped by

the wall under coat hooks hung with a Barbour jacket and a checked cap. There were wellingtons and stout boots in a straight line. Ahead, steep stairs led to the floor above, with a newish-looking rail fixed on the wall. Was the rail because of his injury, Nell wondered, or was it there to help him up and down the stairs when drunk?

Not everyone would recognise the signs. Nell did, from the days when she and her older sister had to put their mother to bed, then tip her booze down the sink.

Wearing one shoe, one slipper and leaning on a walking stick, Harding moved carefully. His twill trousers and check shirt were loose on him. He had lost weight and looked unwell. His convalescence for whatever ailed him must have pre-dated his fall. Nell followed him into the sitting room. A low fire burned in the black lead grate. On the mantelshelf stood a wedding photo of a younger, dark-haired Mr Harding and his bride, both in tailored suits, she carrying a nosegay and wearing a felt hat with the veil turned back, he with a carnation buttonhole.

He waved Nell to a low chair and took the higher one himself. On the table beside him was a copy of *The Times*, the crossword puzzle half completed. He pointed to his bandaged foot. 'The pot's off but it's still slowing me down. I expect Daisy told you about my fall and where it took place.'

'She did.'

'Daisy is a devil for detail. Yes, I tripped outside the Hare and Hounds. No, I was not drunk.'

He protested too much, too soon. Nell smiled. 'I'm not here to enquire about your sobriety. The change at Brackerley has happened very quickly. You've been here a long time. I'm the new girl.'

'The new broom.'

'That too. But give me the benefit of your experience. Tell me what I need to know, the arrangement with the farm, for instance. Anyone or anything I need to watch out for, any hidden boobytraps?'

Nell had expected a bit of waffle, a lack of clarity, but he answered like a man on top of his game. 'Watch out for the courts landing someone on you without asking whether you've a bed. As to the farm, we take rent partly in kind. The pigs are ours. We share piglets with our tenant farmer, Oliver Ramsden. They have hens, we have hens. You could bring our hens down this end. Chief Officer Markham can tell the birds apart. Oh, and we've never been short of milk. Ramsden delivers only as far as the village. Does he tip the balance in his favour when it comes to crops? I've no reason to think so. We've enough veg to see us through. It's not a bad deal and I was never inclined to haggle.'

'Right. Thanks. I'll talk to Mr Ramsden soon.'

'We taught basic mechanics to the lads. The machinery and tools have been moved to one of the barns. They ought to fetch a bob or two if HQ wants to flog them.'

'Was that your decision, Major?'

A brief look of puzzlement crossed his face. He did not remember. 'I believe we talked it over, Jeff, Crofty and Miss Markham and I, what work would be suitable for women.'

'The more choice of paid work, the better. Are the barns secure?'

'As secure as can be.' His right hand began to shake. He held the wrist with his other hand. 'There's sherry. Shall we toast your future here, Miss Lewis?'

'You can toast me, Major. I'll toast you when I'm off duty.' She decided against saying she was teetotal.

He reached for his stick. Nell sprang up. 'I've two good feet. Let me.'

He gave a slight bow of agreement.

As Nell poured, he said, 'As to your politely unasked question, I shall vacate the cottage as soon as I'm well enough.'

That could be a long time, Nell thought. 'Do you have leave entitlement? If you don't take it now, you never will.'

'Good point. I shall be heading for the seaside as soon as I can put one foot before the other without too much pain, eh Pip?'

The dog wagged its tail.

'You have family or friends there?'

'A sister and brother-in-law in Filey. Meg is looking out for a place for me.'

He raised his glass. 'Good luck to you, Deputy Governor Lewis.'

'And to you, Governor Harding.'

'What are your first impressions of Brackerley?'

'Beautiful grounds, amazing house, but how did it become so run-down?' She almost regretted the question straight away. It felt like putting the boot in.

He shrugged. 'A year ago, word was we were to be closed down and the property sold. Now it's change of use. We're army men, not house renovators. Crofty keeps an eye on things not deteriorating too much. Daisy is superb.'

'She decorated one of the rooms.'

'That sounds like Daisy.'

'You have reservations about her husband, Officer Meadowcroft?'

'He has taken to doing plumbing jobs on the side. Keep your eye on Crafty Crofty.'

'You haven't spoken to him about it?'

He shook his head. 'I should have. My energy fled. Daisy covered up for me before I admitted the seriousness of my condition. The Meadowcrofts have been good to me. But if you ever hear that Crofty has gone for a part for the boiler, keep an eye on how long he takes and whether he comes back with a part.'

The major took a gulp of sherry. Nell refilled his glass. At this rate, she ought to give him the bottle and a straw. When he put down his glass, the dog jumped onto his lap. He scratched its ears. 'I'll let you out in a minute, Pip.' He smiled. 'He's getting his walks. One of our old boys called to see me. Arthur Burnett. Ramsden's given him casual work on the farm. Arthur took Pip round the wood. He gave me his hand-knitted Hull City scarf because I was feeling a chill. It's hanging by the front door. I didn't like to tell him I have a drawerful of scarves. My sister Meg sends me one every Christmas.'

Another person might have taken this as a cue to ask about the major's sister, but Nell thought back to earlier in the day when she'd signed the visitor's book. There was no Arthur Burnett in the gate-book. Officially, he was not on the premises.

'Did Arthur do well after leaving here?'

'He went from borstal into the navy.'

'As a career?'

'Just national service.'

'You were pleased he came to see you.'

'I was. I've had the occasional letter from a lad who's made good, but rarely a visit. We did our best for Arthur here, but sometimes a young person's taken too much of a battering from life ever to fully set himself straight.'

'You obviously did something right since he likes coming back here.' Nell paused, as if the thought had only just occurred to her. 'I signed the gate-book this morning. Arthur's name wasn't there.'

'He'll have walked up to the farm gates.'

'Major, if Arthur Burnett could come strolling in, so could anyone else. Let's find time for a chat. You can give me your thoughts on security. It's unlikely we can do anything about the public footpath by the church, but I'll want other holes plugging. I also want to know about the bad apple and how you uncovered him. He's serving time?'

'That was thanks to a whistle-blower who spotted that suddenly half the borstal lads had more cigarettes than they could smoke.' He began to cough and took out a handker-chief. When the cough subsided, he reached for the tiny glass of sherry. 'Sherry doesn't quite cut it, but it's smooth and my wife and I always had a sherry. But, Miss Lewis, before we talk about plugging holes, there's something I want to tell you. I'd better say it before I lose my nerve. I can see you're keen as mustard, and that's good. In many ways, I've been fortunate. I was born into interesting times. Certain things have gone wrong on my watch and I take the blame. There's no reason why you shouldn't have a straight run. I won't stand in your way, but before I go, I'll give you chapter and verse on what you ought to know. What you do with that knowledge will be up to you. See that table?' He pointed to a drop leaf dining table by the wall. 'There's a cupboard in the leg of the drop leaf table. Inside are my borstal diaries, all the things I didn't put in the official records. There's no need to plough through them. I'd rather tell you than give you written evidence, but I'm better in the evening, when

I've had a snooze in the afternoon. And I'd rather we talk somewhere else. People drop in on me. They mean well, but it's tiring.'

'Of course. Thank you for your confidence. I appreciate that you believe me the right person to pick up the baton. When shall we meet?'

'Let me give you supper at the Hare and Hounds. There's a little room where we can be private. Daisy is keeping my diary and she'll be keeping yours.'

'Yes.'

'She'll fix a date.'

The telephone rang. Nell had arrived ready to spit feathers at Governor Harding for letting such a beautiful building deteriorate. Now she felt pity. He probably had not much more of a budget than her own. He was a sick man, with much more wrong with him than a damaged foot. He ought to be in a convalescent home, or a retirement home. Daisy must know the situation but had kept her counsel.

She heard the major say, 'Yes she's here, just a moment.' He turned to Nell. 'Daisy says the journalist is here and a photographer.'

'That was quick.' Nell took the phone and covered the mouthpiece. 'Major, where's a good place for a photograph? I want to make this snappy.'

'The walled garden opposite.'

'Daisy, bring them to the walled garden. Make it clear that the photographer is not to take any other photographs.' She replaced the phone.

The major had sat down again. Now he rose to see her out. 'There you are, you see, people are already asking for you. The camellia is in flower. Pose by that.'

Nell laughed. 'You're trying to catch me out. Lady Deputy Governor of the Camellias graces the pages of the *Harrogate Advertiser*.'

'Go for an evergreen then.'

What Nell wanted to say next called for tact. The cottage hadn't been cleaned. There was dust on the shelves, ash on the hearth rug.

As he saw her to the door, she said, 'Our residents will be doing regular cleaning tasks. You'd be doing us a favour if we can bring them here on a day that suits you.'

'Thank you. I won't say no to that. Daisy will tell you a good day.' He stepped onto the path. 'I can give you one tip that might come in handy.'

'What's that?'

'If you have a difficult person to talk to, try and do it outside. I always found a lad was more ready to open up if you were both doing something – planting potatoes or sweeping up leaves.'

'I'll remember that.'

As she walked away, he called to her, 'Miss Lewis! If I were a well man, I'd come and have a photograph with me shaking your hand.'

'Then wait by the gate. I'll bring the photographer across.'

Daisy was walking a woman and man up the drive. He carried a camera and tripod, she a shoulder bag. Nell waved. She crossed from the cottage to the archway that led to the walled garden. Daisy waved and turned back.

As they drew closer, Nell saw that the reporter was in her mid-twenties. She wore a navy dress with a broad band of white at the hem, and a boxy jacket. Her hair was smooth and cut in a thick fringe. Nell felt a brief pang as she thought, you're the same age as my daughter. That was something she could never say aloud.

They shook hands. The reporter's name was Jane Gardner. She introduced the photographer, Joe Wood.

'Mr Wood, the gentleman at the gate—'

'Governor Harding,' he said. 'I've taken his picture before.'

'Would you take a shot of us together? We'd like that.'

'Of course.'

Nell went back to the major while the photographer took the camera from its case. The major held onto the gate-post. He said, 'When I saw you coming down the path, you reminded me of my wife. She was always smartly turned out and the full box of matches.'

They gave their best smiles. The major shook hands with the photographer and hobbled back indoors. Nell and the photographer crossed to the garden.

Even the most modest of walled gardens had something magical about them. This one was just as Nell expected it would be. Small red bricks formed a high straight wall creating an oblong enclosure. Jane made noises of delight, as if Nell had put on a show especially for them. Two tortoiseshell butterflies hovered over a bed of wild flowers. On the opposite bed was a magnolia tree. During her time as a WPC and as prison officer in some of the bleakest prisons, Nell had found little time to appreciate nature.

The photographer asked to take Nell's photograph by the magnolia tree. And why not, she thought. He took several pictures and then left his camera case with them – to prove he was sticking to the rules of no more photographs. He went to explore the vegetable garden.

Nell and Jane sat on a bench. Jane took out a shorthand notebook and jotted down Nell's brief biography.

'What do you hope to achieve here?' she asked.

'I want this to be a place of reform and rehabilitation, a place of hope. A person takes a wrong step, makes a mistake, falls into bad company, commits a crime sometimes out of weakness or desperation. The courts sentence her to prison. Women who have served time in a closed prison, and who are deemed suitable for an open prison, may be sent here. They will have sufficient time left on their sentence to use the time productively. We will encourage them to stay in close contact with family and friends, have visits, perhaps home leave as they near the end of their sentence. People may think being in a place like this is a soft option. It's not. I want to be sure that while a woman is here, she will learn to hope and plan for a better future, learn a new skill, have work experience, find employment. I hope that we'll have the support of the community and that our presence here will be of mutual benefit.'

Nell walked back with them to their car.

Jane said, 'My uncle is a prison officer. He says they're a mixed bunch, as everywhere, but mostly they do their best. I know how much training they do – no one ever talks of that.'

'For every grade, there are courses and an examination,' Nell said. 'The learning never stops.'

'How long have you been doing this, Miss Lewis?'

'Eighteen years.'

Jane said, 'Thank you for seeing me on your first day. I admire you for what you're taking on and I wish you luck. It's great that you're here to give women a second chance. If there's ever anything I can do, just give me a call.'

'I will.'

Six

Nell watched the reporter and photographer leave.

Another car was leaving at the same time. It was a Mercedes, the Prison Service's preferred choice for transporting a single prisoner.

Daisy looked up as Nell entered the admin office. 'You'll have seen the transfer vehicle, ma'am?'

'Yes.'

'Her name's Diane Redmond. She looks utterly bewildered. She's in reception with the chief and the nurse. I took plimsolls in. She's wearing high heels and a smart skirt and jacket, fretting because they belong to her sister and she was going to put them back in the wardrobe after the court appearance. She'd gone to court with change in her purse for the fare home, and got two years starting with the week's remand at Low Newton.'

Nell took out the file. Diane Redmond had been convicted of handling stolen goods. It was her third offence, and her first prison sentence. She would have been warned that she would face a prison term if there was a next time.

'The chief will put Diane straight about the sentence. She'll settle down.'

'Yes, ma'am. I think Diane's genuine about her misunderstanding.'

'People hear what they want to hear. Thanks, Daisy.'

Diane was thirty-four years old and from Hull. She had been widowed five years earlier, her trawlerman husband lost at sea after a storm. Her children were seven and five when they lost their dad.

Diane had two part-time jobs, as a cleaner and a barmaid.

Living near Hull docks and working in a pub must carry the hazard of helping out when someone needed extra storage space for contraband goods. Diane had not 'snitched' on anyone. She had probably been doing paid favours for a family member or friend. She was fortunate in one respect. She lived on the same Hull street as her mother and sister, who were taking care of the children.

The chief came in to report. 'Diane has settled down, ma'am. She didn't know where she was. I showed her on the atlas that she'd gone from Hull to Durham and then here. I pointed out that there are trains and buses. Her family will be able to visit.'

In Holloway, Linda listened as her property list was read to her. She signed to say her goods had been returned. The once familiar brown suitcase now looked strange. Linda opened it and transferred her cell belongings, folding the paper carrier bag carefully and placing it on top.

Everyone at reception was friendly, now that they were leaving. They sat on a wooden bench in a waiting room. Cherry humoured Olga by playing I Spy. Sometimes Cherry whispered her guesses and Olga laughed. They were being funny about the guards, or about Linda, who wouldn't join in but went on reading her library book. She resisted the urge to flip to the end.

Transport had been delayed. Having been signed out, they could not go back into the canteen. An officer with a boil on her cheek brought them Kit-Kats and cups of tea.

The moment came. Betsy Friel appeared. 'Come along, girls, it's time.'

Linda had finished her book. She handed it over. 'Are you coming with us, miss?'

Betsy Friel beamed. 'Coming with you and stopping with you. I'll see the three of you to your new abode and, when your sentences are up, I shall be there to wave you goodbye, God willing.'

Officer Friel tucked a newspaper in her bag, well out of sight.

Linda watched Miss Friel's deft movement as she concealed the newspaper. There's something in there about one of us, Linda thought. It won't be me. People have forgotten about me. It'll be Cherry, who's good-looking and had a career ahead of her and her photograph in a magazine. 'Young designer of the year'.

Or it'll be Olga. There'll be a picture of her looking like a witch. 'Fortune teller failed to foresee her future in jail.'

Linda could read Miss Friel's discomfort and something else that the guard did not usually display. Self-importance.

They were escorted to the yard. Miss Friel said, 'Smartly does it, girls. Your Pixie awaits.'

Linda read the van's numberplate, with the letters PXE. Add an 'I' and another 'I' and off go three pixies and their minder.

Linda waited until they were settled in the back of the van. The engine came to life.

'May I look at your newspaper, miss?'

'Ah no, not just now, Linda. Reading while in motion can make you sick.' The offending paragraph was on page four. Killer Student To Be Set Free? Someone had tipped off the press that the 'teenage killer of blameless dad of three' was being released from Holloway. There was a grainy rogue's gallery arrest photograph of Linda, her face a mask of misery. Some copper had earned himself a bob or two for providing the mugshot.

Nell went into the admin office, watching through the window for a first glimpse of her new charges from Holloway.

The driver's mate was opening the passenger doors. First out was the officer, smart in her uniform, putting on her cap before holding out a hand to assist a tall, thin woman in a black dress whose grey hair was pinned up in double plaits so that it looked like a telephonist's earphones. One of the other women passed her a walking stick.

The next person out, leaving by the opposite door, was dressed in knee-length velvet trousers, a matching bolero and an Indian cotton blouse. She kept a distance between herself and her companions, turning aside either to avoid a bad smell or assess her surroundings. That must be Cherry Davenport, drugs runner and fashion designer. Her tap, tapping foot gave away her impatience or irritation.

One more to go. The officer went to the van door, opened it, and waited.

Linda Rogers emerged slowly. Nell knew her age to be twenty-six, but she moved awkwardly, as if walking was something to be re-learned after the sunless confines of the Holloway exercise yard.

Olga Tagney looked an elderly sixty. She walked sufficiently upright to balance a book on her head and strode so briskly that her stick might have been a stage prop.

Cherry Davenport was at the main door in no time, moving as if impatiently dodging rush hour traffic on Oxford Street.

Linda, with a shock of short dark wavy hair, wore a green skirt and yellow blouse that might pass as school uniform. She moved with the caution of a person needing to avoid landmines. Her slight stoop and her way of suddenly shifting her weight forward gave Nell the impression that Linda might roll herself into a tiny ball and disappear down a hill.

Chief Officer Markham and Diane, until now the only resident, stepped forward. They formed the welcoming party. Nell did not want her new arrivals to be overwhelmed.

Nell moved away from the window. She knew instinctively that she must pay close attention to Linda. Something about her cried out, At Risk. She was here because no one knew what to do with her.

Nell listened as the footsteps crossed the hall. After such a journey, they were to have a meal first.

When they had gone past, led by Diane to the dining room, Nell opened her door.

The London officer stood at attention, cap in hand. 'Ma'am.'

'Mrs Friel.' Nell extended her hand. 'Come in and sit down. Did you have a good journey?'

'We did, ma'am. The girls were made up with the bacon sandwiches. We had a long debate over the preference for brown sauce or tomato ketchup.'

'What was the verdict?'

'Ketchup, three to one. Linda doesn't like the colour red.'

Daisy brought in tea and biscuits. Nell introduced Betsy Friel to Jenny Meadowcroft, not forgetting to add that Jenny's nickname was Daisy.

'It's because of my surname,' Daisy explained. 'Daisy in the meadow. My husband is Crofty. Anything at all, just ask.' She went back to her office.

Betsy Friel took several drinks of tea before producing a newspaper, opened at the offending article. She handed the paper to Nell. 'I'm sorry to bring this news, but some toerag has put Linda Rogers in the paper. I hope that no dratted newspaperman or photographer will find out where she's come, or you might have them trying to take a picture of her.'

'Has Linda seen this?'

'No, and if it's within my power she won't. She's a very private girl.' She placed the paper on the desk.

KILLER STUDENT TO BE SET FREE?

Linda Rogers, age twenty-five, pictured on the day of her arrest seven years ago for the brutal unprovoked murder of businessman, blameless father of three Simon Saunders, has left Holloway. The girl dubbed 'teenage killer' departed under conditions of stringent secrecy for an unknown destination.

Nell said, 'This is today's paper?'

'Yes, ma'am.'

'So when it went to print, Linda hadn't left Holloway.'

'No, ma'am.'

'I'm wondering about the source. Do you have any thoughts about that?'

'None whatsoever, ma'am, some scurrilous fellow with a tip-off.'

'If that's so, all he knew about was the move, not the date, not the place and he was a year wrong with her age. Perhaps he overheard something, loose talk, and made a connection.'

'That could well be, ma'am.'

'Right, leave this with me.'

'Something else, ma'am.'

'Yes?'

'Two things. She perked up today.'

Nell felt pleased at the thought a change might already be taking place in Linda, but Friel was talking as if Linda was the only person in the van who mattered. 'She perked up at the thought of coming here?'

'Not until the driver's mate – don't ask me how he knows – told the girls that there is a farm here, and a walled garden.'

'Is Linda interested in farm work?'

'I doubt she's ever seen a farm. It was the garden. As a child, she read a book called *The Secret Garden*. She'll hope to find it – the secret garden, I mean, not the book. Though either of them I suppose would do.' She paused for breath. 'There's something else you ought to know, ma'am. It's noted in her file.'

'Go on.'

'Yesterday, I had to break the news of her mother's letter. Linda's father is gravely ill in St Luke's Hospital. She said she wouldn't go see him. Now there may be a good reason she doesn't want to see him. I have my own thoughts. But today, as we walked from the transport café back to the Pixie, Linda said that the hospital wouldn't be so far from Brackerley. It wouldn't be a train journey.'

'So, she may have changed her mind about visiting her father?'

'That's what I'm thinking, ma'am. She couldn't face going on the train all the way from London and the risk of being recognised, but a car journey would be different.'

'Thank you. Now, pop back to reception. The chief or the nurse will take you to meet Miss Kitteringham – Kit. She'll show you round and give you a meal. I hope you'll be comfortable.'

'Thank you, ma'am.'

Nell could see that Mrs Friel was disappointed at the dismissal. Friel ought not to have been transferred. She had grown too close to Linda.

Nell opened the adjoining door. 'Daisy, an urgent one.' Nell gave her Linda Rogers's details. 'We have the parents' names and address. Telephone St Luke's Hospital. Find out whether Mr Rogers is still a patient there. If yes, speak to the matron about arranging a confidential visit, outside of visiting hours, for an accompanied prisoner. We will ring back to confirm.'

Nell closed the door. She took out Linda's file and began to read, then picked up the telephone and dialled T5's number. The call was answered on the second ring.

'Hello, Helen Lewis at Brackerley.' She listened as the person at the other end asked how things were going. 'Everything is going well thanks, but there's been a bit of a slip-up. An officer has transferred from Holloway, escorting three prisoners. They arrived today.' Nell listened again. 'Yes that's right, Officer Betsy Friel. I have no complaint about Friel. The difficulty is that she knows all three prisoners well, was personal officer to one of them, and has grown too close.

61

Would you please ensure she is transferred and that I have a replacement officer.'

There was a tap on the adjoining door. Daisy popped her head round. 'I've spoken to the hospital. Linda can visit her father as soon as convenient. She will be taken to the ward by a side staircase. Mr Rogers is on a small ward with an entrance near the staircase. The nurse will close the curtains for privacy.'

'Thanks, Daisy. Will you bring her along, just say I want a word.'

When Nell put down the phone, she turned her attention to Linda's bulky file.

Nell had learned to skim-read and to make a short summary for her own reference. This sometimes allowed a fact or an idea to jump out at her. She did that now.

Linda Rogers, aged eighteen, murdered a stranger. Came to trial at nineteen, pleaded guilty. Now twenty-six years of age, served seven years of a life sentence for the murder of Simon Saunders, age forty-eight. Murder took place in university accommodation block – enrolment day. Linda alone in allocated twin room when Mr Saunders brought up daughter's additional suitcase while his wife and daughter explored campus. Rogers admitted stabbing Mr Saunders in the eye with a paperknife when he 'put his hand on my shoulder'. Offered no defence or explanation except 'my mind went blank'.

Assessed during remand: in her right mind; cognisant of actions.

Holloway: further psychiatric tests, individual & group counselling.

During group counselling showed interest in others &

contributed. Rogers 'addressed her offending' and 'showed remorse'. Trusted prisoner, worked in library – passed library assistant qualification – helped teach literacy.

According to Personal Officer Friel, 'Linda feels safe in her cell.'

Additional note from leader of counselling session: 'intelligent – institutionalised – at a standstill – consider transfer'.

Nell returned Linda's file to the drawer and locked it. She noted that it was only after Linda had attended group counselling that she 'addressed her offending' and 'showed remorse'. The thought occurred to Nell that through listening to other prisoners during group counselling sessions, Linda had learned what to say, and that she learned what to say so that she would be left alone. It seemed to Nell that Linda, gaining a qualification, being a trusted prisoner, teaching reading, was not in the least at a standstill, except perhaps in being able to say what triggered her violent attack on a stranger.

Seven

Linda did not expect anything to happen so soon and so suddenly. They were taken through reception, saw the nurse, had their belongings logged and their money counted. An admin officer gave them a talk and so did a chief officer, but they kept it short, dished out an advance against wages to Olga, and told them when it would be teatime. Another prisoner, Diane, who had come out to meet them, showed them to the dormitory to unpack. She offered roll-ups, which Cherry and Olga took. Unpacking did not take long.

Linda was finished first. She went out onto the landing, thinking she would go downstairs and look at the library. But on the stairs, an officer said, 'Hello, you're Linda.'

'Yes.'

'I'm Officer Meadowcroft. The governor would like a private word with you in her office.'

Linda did not like the unexpected and so she felt as if she walked through a blur, a fear of what might come next at being summoned by the governor. It would be to do with a mistake. She should not have been sent here. Or, it would be to do with her father.

This summons to the governor was not to tell her that sadly she was too late to see him. If he had died, she would be seeing the chaplain.

The admin officer tapped on the governor's door. 'Here's Linda Rogers, ma'am.'

'Come and sit down, Linda.' The governor smiled in a way that made Linda feel she was the only person the governor wanted to see that day. That was a knack some of them had.

Linda sat down.

'I hope you had a good journey.'

'Yes thank you, ma'am.'

'I'm very sorry to hear that your father is critically ill.'

'Yes, ma'am.' Too much whirled in Linda's brain. Her body felt as hard as iron. She ached from holding herself together, wondering what was coming now.

Linda knew that they all shared information. This governor would know that her parents stayed away from court. By pleading guilty, Linda had not given them the satisfaction or inconvenience of a trial. Her mother visited once, when Linda was on remand, brought by a good neighbour. She had said, 'Your father has washed his hands of you.'

Linda wished he had washed his hands of her a long time ago. She could never wash him away.

The governor started to speak again. She said, 'You may wish to see your father, Linda. Given the seriousness of his condition, an officer will take you there this evening. But if you would rather not go, just tell me. Whatever decision you make will be respected.'

Linda could not think. She was obliged to say yes or no. This was not a situation in which to say, I'll think about it.

Linda heard herself say, 'I'll go.'

'Then your personal officer will come and find you when it's time to go.'

Linda wondered whether Officer Friel had passed her driving test. She only ever mentioned buses and the tube.

The governor must be a mind reader because she straight away said, 'Your personal officer at Brackerley will be Chief Officer Markham.'

'Thank you, ma'am. I'll get my coat.'

Miss Lewis stood and opened the door for her.

Linda's heart raced so fast as she went upstairs that she thought she must be going to have a heart attack and drop down dead. Her face was hot. There was a kind of trembling that she couldn't stop. She had to sit on the bed and calm her breath. Going back downstairs she thought she might trip and had to hold onto the banister.

She could not face another journey. Coming up the Great North Road had been overwhelming enough, all that life going on, worlds and worlds of it. All the while in Holloway, the centre of her universe, she knew that everything outside would still be there but there was no shape to the thought, nothing definite attached to it. And now she was going to see him. She did not know why she had said yes. And then she did know. All those talking sessions alone and with the groups where women might speak in fits and starts, suddenly burst into tears, or shout and scream, had given her new ways and new words, almost a new language. She had a sudden glimpse of why she had said yes, and then that glimpse vanished. It came down to this. He thinks he got away with it.

Chief Officer Markham was brisk, that was the word, and well-spoken and no-nonsense. Linda knew that the minute Miss Markham opened the car door and said, 'Hop in!'

The guard must know that to be sentimental and sympathetic wouldn't do.

On the way, she pointed out landmarks or told Linda how far there was to go, but she asked no questions. Linda was glad.

Warder Markham drove straight up to the hospital entrance. She stepped out of the car, saying, 'I'll let them know we're here. Back in two shakes of a sheep's shimmy.'

She locked the car door. Linda picked up a newspaper from the dashboard. She opened it, so as to screen herself from view. A prisoner is a passenger in a car. A passenger in a car is a prisoner.

The words on the newspaper page meant nothing to her. They were shapes, that's all. Her mind would not let her read.

Her warder appeared at the main doors and came towards the car.

Linda wondered whether Miss Markham expected her to make a run for it. Perhaps she had gone inside first to say, 'Is Mr Rogers still alive?'

She unlocked the door. 'Come along, Linda.'

The nurse in the doorway did not stare or give Linda a sly look. She led them up flights of stairs and onto a landing and to the double doors of a ward. 'Will you both go in?'

Miss Markham said, 'I'll wait here.'

And then the nurse did look at Linda, and she looked at her kindly, and said, 'Your father is awake and is able to speak.'

She pushed the door open, held it, and when Linda went through, the nurse picked up a chair and walked quickly along the ward. Linda knew this was how people moved, people who had jobs to do, places to go, people to see.

Linda did not know how to hurry. She followed at her own pace, her breathing shallow, wondering what to expect, not wanting to be here. She was aware of men in beds on either side but kept her head down.

The nurse stood by the chair. 'Sit down. Here's a clean beaker. Pour a glass of water if you want.'

'Thank you.'

'Take your time. When you are ready to leave, go back to the landing.' She straightened the already straight sheet that was folded over a blanket. He wore striped pyjamas. His arms lay on top of the bedding. 'Your daughter is here, Mr Rogers.'

The nurse pulled the curtains closed, the rings making a clicking sound.

He wore an oxygen mask. There was a drip in his arm. It took her a few moments to see that it was him behind the sagging, sallow skin. When she did see it was really him, her stomach churned. His hands that once had fat fingers were monkey paws. Yet the tattoo of a red eye on his poison finger was still visible.

He had heard her footsteps and the scrape of the chair. His voice was still his voice. 'They sent for you because I'm dying.'

She looked at where the drip entered his arm. She had not known that he would one day look like this. She could pull the drip from his arm, take off his mask, put a pillow over his face.

He opened his eyes. 'They said you were coming.' It was his voice still, the tobacco rasp, but weak and a gasp below each syllable. 'Have they set you free?'

'I'll never be free.'

He looked at her. 'This is a terrible way to die.'

'My life as a girl was a terrible way to live.' She had not known what, if anything, she would say, or if he would hear. People thought she was quiet. She was. But in her cell she had spat words at the wall. They were spat at him, and the others. Now the words welled up and came out without her help.

'Did you go on abusing other girls?'

'Don't know what you're talking about.'

'Your friend had a girl same age as me. Did you do the same things to her?'

'I'm tired.'

'Did you know we would go to the same university? Did you know someone there allocated us the same room? The long dirty arm of coincidence.'

That was the part she could not understand.

'Don't know what you're talking about.'

'Did it make you feel powerful?'

'You're mad.'

'I might be mad. But I have a better chance than you of being alive in the morning.'

He waggled his poison finger with its obscene red eye tattoo. 'Some life, eh?'

She could have grabbed and broken that finger, bent it back until it snapped, but to touch him would make her skin crawl. 'Are you sorry for what you did?'

'You're the one who brought shame on us.' He turned his head away and closed his eyes.

Linda stood. She looked down at him, helpless, useless, and then she walked away. What made her angry, what made her want to scream was this: she was shaking. She could not stop shaking.

Linda had wanted an answer of some kind, an explanation, an apology, a reason. There was a pattern to what had been done to her and what made her kill. It was not the kind of pattern nature makes.

Eight

Nell needed more hours in the day for planning, paperwork, listing jobs, calling in favours and listening to what her officers had to say and reading reports. She could almost have imagined herself in one of those old films where days fly from a calendar to mark the passage of time. Chief Officer Markham had reported on Linda's visit to her father. Linda seemed to have coped but did not want to talk about it. The chief also reported that Diane had come to an arrangement with her sister, who would ring the residents' call box from the private phone at the pub where Diane had been a barmaid. Miss Markham was also glad to have her fly press back. It was being put to good use.

The cleaning of the governor's cottage came up on the list on the day that Nell was to meet the major for supper. The residents in Kit's cleaning party would be Linda and Diane. Kit visited the cottage in advance, to assess what work was needed. She was sorry to say that it would be impractical and embarrassing to gather up the major's empty bottles. She would tell Diane and Linda where not to clean, and under no circumstances open the garden shed.

A little after six, Nell went upstairs to wash and comb her hair, and kick off her shoes for half an hour before going to supper with the major.

Nell had been perfectly satisfied with her clean but slightly shabby second-floor flat. Now she was on the point of falling in love with the governor's whitewashed cottage. It was every inch his, from the air freshener intended to dispel the scent of whisky to the dog hairs on the cushions. The cleaning party would have made an impression today but that would not last long. She was keen to know what revelations were in store. Was the whistle-blower still here? If the major was as good as his word, Nell would be able to govern with a clean slate. No one liked a scandal. The major would be allowed to retire quietly. He had hinted that Crofty was the one to watch. Since Daisy was the perfect officer, it was a shame that her husband didn't match up. Perhaps, over supper, once he got the past misdeeds off his chest, he would give some hint about a retirement date. According to Daisy, he had thirty-five days' leave due.

She decided to drive up and call for him. Otherwise, being an upright old soldier, he might set off hobbling to Brackerley House.

At five to seven, she drew up in line with the front door, so as to be seen. At seven, she went to the door and knocked. Pip's bark was muffled, as if the dog must be in another part of the cottage. There was no other sound.

She followed the flagged path that led round the side of the cottage. The major was sitting outside in a deckchair, a fringed tartan blanket tucked across his knees, a newspaper shielding his face. Had he forgotten she was coming, or lost track of time? He would be embarrassed.

Nell heard Pip whimpering behind the kitchen door. Someone who had complained of rarely going out ought not to have forgotten, especially a trip to his local pub.

'Governor Harding!' she called.

He did not answer. As Nell came a little closer, she realised he had fallen asleep. That was annoying. He might have kept off the bottle until they got to the Hare and Hounds, but he had gone to some trouble. His one shoe was highly polished. He wore a tartan slipper on his bandaged foot. His trousers held a sharp crease.

And then she saw that his right arm dangled. Below his hand, a revolver lay on the grass. She stopped dead. What was he doing with a revolver outside? If this was a practical joke, it was in bad taste.

The newspaper moved in the breeze. The sudden screech of crows from an old oak beyond the shrubbery startled her. As the crows swooped, Nell clapped her hands and shouted. She picked up a stone and threw it at the birds. All but one of the crows flew off. The major did not move. A chill ran through her as she realised why the crows were here. Carefully, she picked up the tartan blanket from the major's knees, ready to flap it at the crows if they returned, to cover him with it if her worst fear was true. Nell saw that the newspaper was spattered with blood. She touched the corner. The paper stayed stuck to his face because blood had dried. A couple of pages of the broadsheet had blown across the garden. The major's neatly combed white hair was darkly stained with blood from a hole in the side of his head. Blood stained the shoulders of his dark jacket and the collar of his white shirt.

Oh God, she thought. This is my fault. In a moment of weakness, he decided to tell all. He ran out of courage. He didn't want to leave this place. I insisted on turfing him out. Did Daisy tell him that I asked how much leave he was due?

Nell tried to place the newspaper back on his face, intending to put the blanket on top. A breeze blew up. The pages of *The Times* fluttered, black on white with red spots of blood. She looked for a heavy stone, put the newspaper under the chair and placed the stone on it. She reached for his left hand, knowing the right must have held the gun. His hand was cold, and now so was hers. Two governors holding hands, the living and the dead. Shivering uncontrollably, she picked up the blanket and placed it over the major's head, adjusting it to ensure that his head and shoulders were fully covered. She stood still and took deep breaths. Take a hold of yourself, said that logical part of her that had been trained to respond professionally, who knew what to do in the face of death.

She did not want to leave him. A single stubborn crow watched from a branch. Nell looked at the major's highly polished shoes, the socks with a diamond pattern. The voice in her head asked him, What were you thinking? Why this? You would have been all right, got better by the sea, you and Pip.

There was a feeling she ought to do something, even if that were only to keep watch until someone came. But she was that someone. Had he shot himself, knowing that she would be the one to find him? An old hand, she would know what to do.

She ran to the rockery, picked up two large stones and aimed one and then the other at the crow, screaming rage as she did so, blaming the bird. The crow flew away.

No one heard her rage. No one came.

It's up to you now, she told herself. Deal with it. Think.

He would not have locked the back door, not while sitting in the garden. If she opened it, she might disturb something — a note he had left. Certainly, she would disturb that dog. It would come rushing out, leaping up at its master.

Nell hurried back to her car.

She drove the few yards to the house. This time of the evening, between six and eight, was for 'classes', she had written on the optimistic timetable. Of course, there were no classes yet. There had not been time to plan them. Residents would be in the sitting room, watching television. Kit was on duty. She would be with them.

Nell unlocked her office door. She locked it behind her and then picked up the telephone and dialled 999.

'Police, ambulance, fire brigade?' the voice at the end of the line asked.

'Police.'

Nell waited to be put through. In the days when she was a WPC, Nell would have taken such a call as this. She pictured herself sitting at the desk in her old station, pen in hand, incident book at the ready. She had only twice responded to a caller who reported a death.

'Connecting you now, caller.'

Nell was reconnected. A male voice, young she thought, said, 'Police,' with such a light-hearted tone of voice that she felt slightly sick, and somehow guilty about what she had to say.

Words refused her. Instead of tripping off her tongue, they slid down her gullet. She took a breath. 'I am calling to report a sudden death.'

Why am I not saying suicide, she asked herself?

'Your name, please.'

'Nell Lewis, deputy governor of HMP Brackerley, formerly the borstal. The borstal governor, Major Harding—' Her mouth went suddenly dry. 'He didn't answer his door. I walked through the garden. I found him sitting in a deckchair, a revolver beside him.'

'What time was this?'

'Shortly after seven. We were to have supper together.'

'Are you sure he is dead?'

'Yes.'

'Was there anyone in the house, or nearby?'

'Not that I saw. I heard his dog whining behind the door.'

'Did you try the door?'

'Neither that nor the front door.' Nell pictured the officer, writing her words. 'I'm going back to stand by the body. There were crows circling. I covered him.'

'We'll send someone right away, Miss Lewis. Who will open the prison gates?'

'The gateman is on duty until ten.'

'Anything else we need to know?'

'If you use a car with a siren, will you turn off the siren when you reach the village, please. I don't want to alarm our neighbours, and I have residents who have only just transferred here.'

'I'll pass that on. Have you told your colleagues, or anyone else?'

'Not yet. I'll tell the chaplain and I need to report to HQ.'

'Tell no one else until we arrive.'

'Where will you be coming from, officer?'

'Harrogate, North Yorkshire Police, ma'am.'

'Thank you.' Nell clicked off the call.

There was a leather-covered pad with alphabetical pages by the telephone. She opened it at C for Chaplain and dialled. The chaplain shared her responsibility for the well-being of everyone connected with this place, and if there was a time for needing a helping hand, this was it.

While she waited for an answer, Nell looked at the duty roster. Kit would be with the residents in the TV room. Officer Friel would be on telephone duty in the reception area. Chief Officer Markham, Daisy, Crofty, and Jeff were off duty and would have to come from the village if the police needed them here. Whether the police did need them or not, they must be told. Daisy seemed to Nell to be half in love with the major. 'They broke the mould when they made him,' she had said. The last thing Nell needed was someone who might weep and wail, but Daisy would step up to the mark. They all would.

A woman answered the telephone, squeezing great friendliness into the word, 'Vicarage.'

'Hello, Nell Lewis, governor. I need to speak to the chaplain urgently.'

'Putting him on, Miss Lewis.'

'Hello, Miss Lewis.' The chaplain's telephone voice seemed to emerge from a tomb.

'Father James, I need you to come over now.'

'What's wrong?'

'Sorry to break the news so abruptly, but Governor Harding is dead.'

There was a brief pause. 'I'm on my way.'

76

'I'll be at the cottage.'

It was long past time for Chief Markham to have locked up the education block and gone home. On a hunch, Nell dialled the number.

'Brackerley Education Block, Chief Officer Markham,' came the clipped reply.

Nell felt a huge relief that Miss Markham hadn't gone home. 'Chief, Governor here. There's been an incident. Would you please alert the gatehouse to expect the police and direct them to the governor's cottage. That's where I'll be. And would you come to the house and take over from Friel as duty officer?'

There was a pause during which another person might have asked for more information. 'I'll get my coat, ma'am.'

Nell felt the ludicrousness of her situation, making telephone calls while the dead man waited patiently for her in his garden. It was her responsibility to keep HQ informed of everything that happened in the prison. This was too important to leave until later. Day staff would already be off duty, but there would be a deputy director on call.

She dialled T5's number. The phone was answered immediately. 'Deputy Director Barnes.'

'Mr Barnes, Nell Lewis, deputy governor of HMP Brackerley.'

'I'm listening, Miss Lewis.'

'I have tragic news. Governor Harding is dead from a gunshot wound.'

'How shocking. So sorry to hear that, Miss Lewis.' He spoke so calmly that, in spite of his 'shocking', Nell wondered had he heard right. 'Let me pull out the file. I'm stretching the telephone cord.'

How long would this take? Nell wanted to say, never mind the file, just take down the information.

'Got it. Go ahead, Miss Lewis.'

'I called for the major at seven. We were to have supper. He was dressed to go out, sitting in the deckchair in the back garden of his cottage, a gun on the ground and a gunshot to his head. I've telephoned the police. Officers are coming from Harrogate. The chaplain will be here shortly.'

'Is there anything you need from me immediately, any back-up?'

'No. I'm going back to the cottage right now, to wait for the police. I'll report to you again when the police have been.'

'It's going to be a long night for you. I'm looking at your complement of officers and prisoners. Let me arrange for an officer trained in counselling to be with you.'

Nell's first thought was, Where will I put her? Before she had time to answer, Barnes said, 'I'll make all the arrangements. She'll ensure that you, your staff and inmates and their relatives have the right support.'

Nell realised this was not an offer. It was procedure. 'Very well.'

'Keep us informed. I'm so sorry to hear this.'

Nell went to the safe. What was the combination number? Daisy had reeled it off. Her Co-op dividend number in reverse order, she had said, assuring Nell that it was secure because only she knew it. 'We'll change it,' Nell had said. Of course other people would know the number, including the manager and staff of the Co-operative store. Reversing a number was not a stroke of genius.

Nell felt under the flat surface between the drawers on

either side. The major hadn't remembered the number. It was taped underneath the desk.

Nell opened the safe, took out the set of keys marked 'Cottage' and added them to her pouch.

Nine

Nell drove back to the cottage. This time, she parked by the entrance to the walled garden, leaving space for the police by the cottage gate.

Wishing she could be starting again, she walked towards the cottage, imagining she might see the major by the window and raise her hand in greeting. It was impossible to fool herself. Her feet dragged. A heavy sense of dread and doom propelled her to the gate.

How long had the major remained cold and still in the deckchair, she wondered. Had Officer Friel and the girls been in the garden when the gun went off?

The crazy-paving flagstones that led to the back of the cottage took on the look of flat gravestones waiting for names, dates, relationships. The breeze had dropped. Clouds were darkening. The blue of the sky was fading with just one bright spot that seemed to shrink as she looked at it. Silence hung heavy. A flock of doves suddenly appeared, circled and flew away.

The dog began to bark, and then to whine. Nell spoke to

the back door. 'There's no one else to hear you, Pip. I can't let you out yet.'

The dog would race up the garden to his master, and wail for the moon. Did Pip know something? Would it be one of these extraordinary situations where the dog went to a certain person, the killer, and began to bark, to bite, to accuse in dog language, 'murderer'.

Why do I think he was murdered? Nell asked herself. It was because the major was dressed and ready to go out. Or, had he suddenly been unable to face going into his local with her? It would be an announcement that he was done here, like saying, Meet my replacement. Time's up for me.

She stood at a distance from the back door. There might be footprints, fingerprints on the door handle, but not if this death was as it appeared. Suicide.

She then made herself walk back to Governor Harding. The blanket was as she had left it, the crows defeated. The blanket's fringe covered his top pocket and the neatly folded hanky she had seen. Without needed to lift the blanket, she saw him in her mind's eye. He wore a blue silk tie with a Windsor knot. He was expecting to eat steak pie and chips in the Hare and Hounds, talk about his life and times, and advise the new girl on how to be a governor.

How long would it take the police to come from Harrogate? Perhaps CID had already gone home or were on another job. Nell's stomach rumbled. She had not eaten since breakfast, forgetting the time, focusing on the paperwork spreading across her desk, spending too long on the telephone.

Retreating from the major, she would keep watch from the corner of the cottage. From there, she could keep an eye on the garden and look out for a car.

The suddenness of the voice made her jump. 'Hey up!' someone called, loudly enough to wake the dead. 'Anybody home?'

The voice came from the front of the cottage. Nell hurried round to see who was there.

A stout figure, bending at a ninety-degree angle, shouted through the letter box, the peak of his cap pressed against the door. 'Major! It's Oliver!' He straightened and was just about to turn the door handle when Nell called to him.

'Mr Ramsden?'

He swivelled round. The farmer was wearing a blue striped collarless shirt and brown suit trousers that must have fitted him when he was thirty.

'Ah, you must be Miss Lewis. The wife said you called.' He extended his pork chop of a hand, grasping her hand, shaking it thoroughly, looking into her eyes. 'I am very pleased to meet you, ma'am.'

'How do you do, Mr Ramsden.'

'How do, and where's himself?'

Nell said, 'You won't get an answer.'

Ramsden knew the answer to his own question. 'He'll be round back. He sometimes sits out of a fine evening.'

Nell cut off his path to the rear of the cottage.

Ramsden made a sideways move. Nell countered his move. For a moment it looked as if they might dance.

Nell held her ground. 'He's indisposed.'

'What's up?'

'We were to have gone to the Hare and Hounds for supper, but that's off. He has some business with the chaplain.' She raised her forefinger skywards, as if listening for footsteps, aware that the gesture could mean she was pointing towards

82

the major's bedroom, or heaven. 'Let me drive you back to the farm.'

'No need. I have legs.' He spoke with a mild tone of rebuke. 'If the major is *indisposed*' – he made the word sound like the lie it was – 'I'll wait and see if he wants summat.'

'He doesn't.'

'There was summat he wanted me to look at in't garden.'

'Leave it for this evening, Mr Ramsden.'

Driving Ramsden back to his farm would take a few minutes. 'My car's just there, and there's something I want to ask you.'

'Something I want to ask you, too,' he said. He stayed where he was, ready to chat.

Nell walked across and opened the car door.

She watched as he decided to be glad of a lift. He would enjoy the opportunity to report on her bossiness and comment on her driving.

She got in the car, opened the passenger door and then started the engine.

Mr Ramsden lumbered onto the passenger seat and settled himself.

Nell thought of the police arriving. They would want information, reports, facts. She had no facts, except that the major had been hounded by his successor to clear out, had a seemingly limitless supply of whisky, and a visitor whose name did not appear in the gate-book.

'Governor Harding was telling me about one of his former borstal residents who called to see him.'

'Residents? We used to call them inmates,' Ramsden said. 'They preferred to call themselves prisoners. A spade is a spade.'

'Arthur Burnett.'

'Arthur turned up asking did we need an extra pair of hands. Well of course we do, with all the lads leaving. He's a good worker.'

'He's still here?'

'He's bunking in the barn. I've got the two lads in the house until they're paroled. But I think Arthur likes being in the barn. He's a big kid really. He would've made a good countryman if he'd been steadier.'

'So the major was telling me,' Nell said. At least Arthur Burnett wasn't a figment of the old governor's imagination.

'What brings this up?' Ramsden asked.

'I like to know who's coming and going. His name isn't in the gate-book.'

'This is my telling off then, is it?'

'I do need to know who is on the premises, either up at the farm or anywhere else.'

'I'll see to it in future.'

'Good.' Nell drove round a fearless pheasant as Ramsden shouted, 'Gerrout the way, you daft blighter!'

'Arthur went straight from his stint in borstal to do his national service, I believe.'

'A lot of them did. If you ask me, it was a bad day when national service ended.'

'They say it was the making of some young men.'

'Not for Arthur. Hated it. And he finished on a low.' Ramsden took out a large hanky and blew his nose. 'That Nasser feller took over the Suez Canal. I blame Anthony Eden.'

'Arthur was at Suez?'

'By his own account he was.'

Nell had the information she wanted. Suez was 1956.

Arthur must have left the borstal sometime in 1953 to put in his three years' service. He must not have made much of a fist of his life, or he would not be back looking for work all these years on, not unless he was running away from something or someone, or he had a powerful reason for wanting to see his old governor. As a former borstal inmate, he should have known better than to come onto the premises without signing in.

'All right if I let you out here, Mr Ramsden?'

'Yes. Thanks for the ride.' He climbed out, but then remembered that he had a question too. He held the door and leaned forward into the car. 'Tell me, ma'am, were any of your lot land girls?'

'Only one resident would have been of working age during the war.' That one was Olga. Nell tried to picture a younger Olga, striding across a ploughed field carrying a hoe. It was possible to create the image, but Olga was more likely to have worked on the London buses.

'Let's arrange a time. I'll bring the girls to the farm and you can show us around. We'll see what we can do.'

'Only there aren't enough schoolkids round here for the potato picking and the strawberries, and there's plenty to be getting on with meanwhile.'

'We have just four residents today, but in a month we'll have four times that number and by harvest time we'll have a regiment.'

This was something of an exaggeration, but Nell wanted him to go home happy and stay there until the police arrived.

Farmer Ramsden's eyes lit up at the thought of a regiment of women gathering crops.

'Of course,' Nell said, 'I'll be wanting to find paid work

for at least a third of my residents, to prepare them for the outside world.'

Ramsden made cherub lips and sent a sigh to the heavens. 'We've tight margins on the farm.'

'Mr Ramsden, we all want the farm to do well. I'll be with you every step of the way.'

Ten

After Nell had dropped off the farmer and returned to the cottage, a sudden mad fear came over her as she walked along the path at the side of the house. The major might have been whisked away. She paused, half-expecting to hear someone or something.

She had forgotten how quiet the countryside could be. There was little birdsong now. What birds? Blackbirds, thrushes? She did not know. The major would have known. She felt absurdly sure of that.

The dog whined behind the kitchen door. Perhaps it had been silent, only to start again at the sound of her footsteps. What had the dog seen, or heard? Suddenly, he howled. She made herself continue along the path. There was the body, as she left it. There was the dog, raising objections, voicing desperation from his place on the mat behind the door.

'I'm here, Pip.'

She stood sentry by the back door, looking beyond the hedge to the trees, gazing at streaks of pink in the darkening sky.

Her skin prickled. It was a comfort to lean against the bricks of the cottage wall that had been warmed by the sun. She took deep breaths. Having this happen on her watch felt like an enormous failure. For years she had made sure that all went well and better than well, and now this.

Nell, she lectured herself, this is not about your brilliant career. This is about the ignominious end of a man's life, an empty chair in the Hare and Hounds. For his sister, there will be a hole in the world, marking the spot where someone she loved has gone for ever.

The police must be here soon, she told herself. This was the North Riding of Yorkshire. The police became so bored of hearing about stray sheep, city slicker trespassers, wealthy housewife shoplifters and speeding motorists that answering a call from a prison and hearing the word death would send eager officers into a scramble for attendance.

By the time a sudden sound intruded on her thoughts, she had stopped listening. The dog's change of yap alerted her. She walked round to the front of the cottage.

The chaplain had come on his bicycle. He wheeled the bike up the path and leaned it against the side wall of the cottage.

'I'm glad you could come so quickly, Chaplain.'

'What a shock for you, Miss Lewis. What happened?' He had come prepared and took a small bag from his handlebars.

He was waiting for her to open the cottage door. 'Shall we go in?'

Did he expect to walk up a narrow flight of stairs to a neat bedroom where Governor P. W. Harding, MBE, would be lying with his head on a white pillow? People would be able to say, He died peacefully.

'He isn't in the house.'

'Oh, I imagined a fall down the stairs. That new banister didn't look safe.'

'This will be a shock to you, too, Father James. The major is in the garden.' She led the way. 'I covered him because there were crows. I didn't go in the cottage, so as not to disturb anything. The police are on their way.'

The black Ford Consul stopped by the gate. Both rear passenger doors opened. A man's head seemed to appear first, as sometimes happens when the occupant is too tall for the car. The head shone bald on top. On either side of the smooth round bald patch was an abundance of fair, waving hair, giving the bald pate the appearance of a clearing on top of a woodland mound. The man who stretched himself out, wearing shoes that needed a polish, was familiar.

It was Julian McHale. She couldn't be mistaken, could she? He was the same beanpole height, the same slight stoop.

He remembered her. She saw the flicker of surprise and something else she could not name. Might it be suspicion?

'DCI McHale, Miss Lewis. You made the call.'

'I did.'

They shook hands. 'We meet again,' he said quietly.

He introduced his colleagues. 'Detective Inspector Ian Dennis and Sergeant Angela Ambrose. A constable is on his way.'

'Nell Lewis,' she said. 'I took up my post as deputy governor on Monday.' She hesitated. Now was not the time to go into this, that and the other. 'The borstal governor, Major P. W. Harding, we were to have had supper. He's in the garden. The chaplain is with him.'

Sergeant Ambrose stayed by the front door.

Nell led the way around the side of the house, telling Julian, 'As soon as I'd telephoned the police, I rang the chaplain to let him know that the major was dead. I also informed Prison Service HQ.'

Julian took long strides across the lawn. The chaplain stood sentry by the deckchair. He had folded the tartan blanket and placed it on the shrubbery. Nell introduced Julian and his DI to the chaplain.

Julian shook hands with Father James, saying, 'Detective Inspector Dennis will take your statement, Father.'

DI Dennis took out his pocket notebook. They walked towards the cottage.

Julian took out a polaroid camera. 'The photographer will be here shortly. These are for me.'

He bobbed down beside the body, taking photographs of the major, and of his arm and hand, and of the gun that lay on the ground.

As Nell watched, she saw the scene differently. Yes, it looked like suicide, but was it too neat? The deckchair, the sort you might hire for the day at the beach, had stayed firmly in place. The major's head lolled, but his body was upright. Had the chaplain straightened him up? She hoped not. He was right-handed. A man weakened by ill-health might have been expected to grasp his right forearm with his left hand so as to keep his hand steady for the shot.

Having Julian here was reassuring. It was years since they had worked together as constables at the same police station. Nell joined the force after working as a clerk in the station office. Julian joined after completing his national service. During his first week as a constable, she helped Julian find his way through the forms and paperwork. They walked the beat together. They were the same age, and shared a birthday. Shortly after Nell left to join the Prison Service, she heard that Julian had moved over to CID. That had always been his ambition.

'It's been a shock for you,' Julian said. 'Have someone make you a cup of tea.'

'But first tell you what happened?'

'Yes. And who else knows of the death.' Julian took out his notebook.

'As I said, the chaplain, you and Prison HQ.'

They moved away from the scene, towards the garden shed. The sergeant brought round a photographer. As Nell spoke to Julian, she was aware of the sergeant taking measurements of the gun's distance from the chair before placing the gun in an evidence bag. She also bagged the blanket. A cover was placed over the major.

Nell continued answering the DCI's questions. 'When I spoke to the chaplain, I simply said the major was dead. I believe Father James arrived thinking there might have been an accident in the house.'

'Why might he have thought that?'

'When I called on Monday, I noticed a handrail on the stairs that looks new. The stairs are right opposite the front door, and they're steep. The major had broken a bone in his foot.' She hesitated. 'It crossed my mind, and must have occurred to the chaplain, that the governor liked a tipple.'

'A serious tipple?'

'According to the officer who brought a cleaning party to the cottage today, you'll see a lot of empties.'

Julian made another note. 'Anyone else aware that there's been an incident?'

'Chief Officer Miss Markham. I rang the education block, on a hunch she might be working late. I asked her to go to the house. I meant to ask her to take over the phone but she'll do that anyway. The officer on duty is new. I told the chief there had been an incident and to ask the gateman to direct you to the cottage. She'll know this is serious.'

'Who else is in the house?'

'Officer Kitteringham, in her first post, and Officer Friel, transferred from Holloway. This is our first week. We have four residents. A person who might suspect something odd going on is the farmer, Oliver Ramsden. He knocked on the front door and called for the major through the letter box. He was reluctant to give up, said there was something he was supposed to look at in the garden. I drove him back to the farm, just to be sure he was out of the way.'

'Thanks, Nell. I'll need your officers to come in. I want to talk to everyone who's had some connection to him.'

'I'll open the visitors' block for you.'

'You've mentioned Markham, Kitteringham and Friel. Who are the others?'

'We're a small team at present. Derek Jeffrey, senior officer, just promoted to principal officer and soon to be transferred; Nurse Theresa Carreras, who has a flat above the hospital wing. The Meadowcrofts live in the village: Jenny is admin officer, Paul is works department. Since the changeover, Officer Jeffrey is the sole occupant in the male quarters. Everyone else has been transferred. Then of course there's the farm.'

'I'll send the sergeant up to the farm.'

'A former borstal boy is working there, on a casual basis. He was at Brackerley in the 1950s, Arthur Burnett. There are two borstal boys due for parole staying in the farmhouse, Michael and Dave.'

Julian made a note. 'And tell me, did you touch anything?'

'Apart from covering the major with the blanket, no.'

Nell took the cottage keys from her bag and handed them to him. 'You'll want these, front and back door.'

DI Dennis had reappeared, without the chaplain. Julian beckoned the DI and handed him the keys. 'See what you can find inside.' Julian turned back to Nell. 'What do we do about the dog?'

'I'll take him.'

Julian called to the sergeant. 'Give us a few minutes and then bring the dog out the front.'

It was not that Nell was going to cry, but her nose felt suddenly damp. Her jacket pockets were still sewn up from when she bought the suit. There was no hanky up her sleeve.

Julian said, 'I'll need a statement, but tell me briefly about finding the body.'

'It was so strange. When I saw him from the corner of the cottage, I thought at first he was reading his paper. As I came closer, I could see he was dressed to go out. I couldn't take it in, and then the crows appeared and that brought me back to earth. I threw a stone at them.'

'What else can you tell me? Might the major have had any visitors today?'

'I don't know about any visitors. One of my officers, Miss Kitteringham, brought two residents to the cottage to clean.'

'Their names?'

'Linda Rogers and Diane Redmond.' Nell held her breath, expecting the next question.

'Linda Rogers who was all over the papers some years back?'

'Yes.'

'I'll need to talk to them.'

'The prisoners would have been under supervision at all times. I realise this is important, but they've barely had time to settle in. Linda Rogers's father is critically ill.'

Julian raised an eyebrow. Nell guessed what he was thinking. Some other young woman's father is dead because of Rogers. The police would be unlikely to overlook two prisoners, one a convicted murderer, being in a house with a man who is found dead a few hours later.

He said, 'Let me see what Miss Kitteringham has to say. If she assures me she never took her eyes off them, that might be sufficient.'

It was what Nell expected. She would have done the same in his place. Nell hoped that Linda and Diane would escape questioning. Nell felt as if her breath was suddenly sucked out. She needed air. The prison reins, her prison reins, were being snatched away. By opening the visitors' centre, at least she would keep police out of the house.

'How do we go on from here?' she asked.

'Bring your officers, security and the people from the farm together in the visitors' centre. I'll say that Governor Harding is dead and that the death is being treated as suicide. We'll set up interviews. Some will be very brief. You'll be there to support your staff.'

'What time?'

He looked at his watch. 'Let's go for nine o'clock.'

'I'll make a start.'

'Tell me, how open is this open prison of yours?'

'Residents know the boundaries. Anyone familiar with the area could find a way in. I started on a plan to tighten security

94

but haven't had a chance to implement that yet. There's a path from the church – the chaplain will have cycled here along it.'

She felt a wave of sympathy from him. He gave a sad, wry smile. 'We'll be as tactful as possible. I'm sorry you have this to cope with in your first week.'

'The staff will want to pay their respects. Will you let me know when the ambulance arrives, or when it's ready to leave? They can gather by the gate.'

'Of course.'

In that moment, he seemed like the old Julian. They had been the two new kids at the station, finding their way, having a laugh together. There would be another way of interpreting his apparent sympathy. Deputy governor arrives to take up her new post. She finds the old governor digging in his heels. What's the quickest way to get rid of him?

Nell knew that everybody, including herself, would be a potential suspect.

She suddenly remembered the reason why she and the major were to have dined out.

'You've thought of something,' Julian said.

'The major had things to tell me. He wanted me to get off to a good start. Did you know about what went on here, and that a whistle-blower plucked a bad apple?'

Julian said, 'I heard a whisper, but you know that the Prison Service likes to take care of its own dirty laundry.'

'According to the major that business – and I don't have inside information – was more extensive than anyone knew. This sounds cloak-and-dagger, but he kept diaries. He told me where he hid them but said that he would tell me the story himself this evening in a private room at the Hare and Hounds.'

Eleven

The chaplain was waiting for Nell at the front gate of the cottage. 'How can I help?' he sighed.

'I'm going to open up the visitors' block for the police interviews. They want to talk to all of us.'

The chaplain frowned. 'In that case, I ought to alert the nurse, Theresa Carreras, or Florence as they all call her.'

'Why Florence especially?' Nell asked.

'She and the major had grown close.'

'No alerts, Father James. The DCI will make an announcement.'

DI Dennis came from the front door, with something stuffed under his coat and Pip on a lead. Pip's ears and tail were down. He came quietly, walking between Nell and DI Dennis, looking up at Nell every few strides, giving the occasional whine. 'I'll come back for the car,' Nell said. 'The dog's been cooped up too long.'

'How long?' DI Dennis asked, in what Nell thought a reasonably good imitation of an artless television detective trying to trip up a guilty party. He was one of those comfortable-looking men who no doubt insisted on proper dinners.

'Good question,' Nell said. 'We'll know how long the dog has been whining when someone tells us when Governor Harding was last seen alive.'

'Any clues?' the sergeant asked.

'Officer Kitteringham will be able to tell you what time she left the cottage. She would have spoken to the major before leaving.'

Walking the short distance back took longer than it should because Pip wanted to sniff his way there.

The inspector veered towards the house. 'And what's the procedure for locking up your main building? It's my first visit to an open prison.'

'This way, Inspector. The visitors' block is behind the gatehouse. I have the keys. To answer your question, we lock up at suppertime, eight o'clock. We unlock just before the morning bell, at seven.'

They walked the next few yards in silence. Nell took her bunch of keys and looked for the right one. She was still getting used to them.

As she opened the door, the sergeant put his hand inside his jacket and withdrew a tin of dog food. 'I took the liberty when I went into the cottage. We have a dog at home. This is what she eats: PAL – prolongs active life.' He gave a little chuckle, as if about to tell a joke. He then thought better of it and turned the chuckle into a cough.

Nell switched on the lights. The room was spartan and gloomy. She had until a week on Saturday to make the place look welcoming for visiting day.

In spite of the tables, set out at a distance from each other, the room seemed empty. Chairs had been left standing on the tables. Walls were plain white, with no decoration. Light shades were black metal. At the top end of the room was a partitioned kitchen, the louvred half-doors open.

The whole place gave off an air of depression and left-over anxiety.

The DI said, 'You'll have a tin opener, ma'am?'

The chaplain came into his own. He reached for the tin. 'I'll take that. Thank you. I know my way around the kitchen. Come on, Pip!'

'There's a telephone in there,' Nell told the DI. 'Telephone numbers are on the kitchen wall, so ring across if you need anything.'

The DI cleared his throat. 'If you and I have a chat now, Miss Lewis, that will leave you free to support your staff.'

'Yes, I'm glad you thought of that. I'll be with you in a minute. I think I saw an emergency box of tissues on my look round the kitchen, and I'll let my chief officer know I haven't abandoned ship.'

Nell did want to wipe her nose, but this walk to the kitchen also gave her time to think. The DI might be interviewing her because he and she had not met before today. Nell did not have much history with Julian, but it was there.

Nell dialled the house. Jean Markham picked up the phone on the first ring.

'Chief, I'm in the visitors' block.'

'What's happened, ma'am? I've been watching from the window and checking with the gateman. Police, and a pho-tographer. It's the governor?'

'Yes. Once the officers have gathered, DCI McHale will make an announcement. The police want to talk to us. This is a clumsy way for you to hear sad news. I'm sorry about that. An ambulance will come for the governor. I've asked the DCI to let me know when, so that we can gather by the gate.'

It took Markham a few seconds to speak. 'The Meadowcrofts and Jeff are on their way.'

'Send Officer Friel across. She can be interviewed and then be available to hold the fort.'

'I'll do that now. Kit is with the residents in the sitting room. I'll stay by the phone until I hear from you.'

Nell returned to the table where Inspector Dennis was waiting, pocket notebook at the ready.

The chaplain went round the room taking chairs off tables and placing them neatly.

Inspector Dennis jotted down what Nell had told the DCI about finding the body, and then pressed for a little more information about the major.

Nell was grateful for the chaplain's presence. 'Ask the chaplain, Father James Grieves. He and Chief Officer Markham know the major well. I met him only once, apart from being introduced a few years ago when I was at the Hare and Hounds with friends from Armley. This may have no relevance to what has happened, but he was a sick man and an alcoholic. I believe he relied heavily on his loyal staff.'

The inspector made a note. 'How do you know he was an alcoholic after meeting him once?'

'I recognise the signs. I set up a group for recovering alcoholics at Armley.' Nell would not say that she knew all the signs because her mother was an alcoholic. It was Nell's sister Sheila, seven years older, who at age nineteen took charge and kept their lives ticking over.

'Anything else?'

'When we did talk, he was very frank. I know he would have given me helpful background information that would save me time in getting to grips with the job. I asked him about the bad apple that was caught out. He was willing to talk. I had the distinct impression that the line under that business was drawn prematurely but we'd deal with that ourselves in the Prison Service. I'm telling you so that you'll have a full picture.'

The DI looked suddenly interested, but then made himself draw back. 'Perhaps it was a bluff, trying to impress you.'

'That's possible, but I think unlikely. Not talking to him will be a big regret, a lost opportunity.'

The DI looked thoughtful. He made a note.

'How did you pick on this particular evening to have your supper, and your chat?'

'The admin officer checked diaries. She would have quite rightly thought I wouldn't want to go out on the evening of my first day. The major had a hospital appointment on Tuesday, and that usually left him feeling tired the day after.'

Giving this explanation, Nell felt a sense of deep unease. Yes, the death looked like suicide. It would be treated as suicide unless a post-mortem revealed otherwise. But was there a connection between the major's willingness to talk and his sudden death? The major had warned her about Crofty not being trustworthy. Daisy might have mentioned the supper arrangement to her husband. If Crofty had something to hide—

No, Nell told herself. Don't jump to conclusions.

'If you think of anything else, no matter how small, just tell me,' said DI Dennis.

There was a tap on the door. Officer Friel opened the door

and stepped inside. Nell beckoned her and met her halfway across the room.

'I'm glad you could come across so quickly. I'd like you to talk to DI Dennis. I'm sorry to tell you we have had a tragic incident on the grounds today. The police are talking to all of us. This is entirely routine, just answer the DI's questions.'

'Of course, ma'am Anything to help.'

'When you have finished, go take over from Kit so that she can come across. The DCI will be making an announcement and I'll pass on what he says when we get back.'

'Very good, ma'am.'

'Come and take a seat and I'll introduce you.'

Nell led Friel to the table. 'Inspector Dennis, this is Officer Friel, our newest officer. If you'll interview Officer Friel first, she can then go back on duty.'

The DCI smiled. 'Thank you for coming across, Officer Friel.'

Nell had been on the verge of saying something else to the DI. Now she was glad of Friel's arrival.

It would be absurd and old-fashioned to voice her thoughts aloud to the DI. As well as being an amiable alcoholic no longer up to his job, the major was a gentleman of the old school who would keep up appearances. Nell would not have expected him to leave her to find him like that. Yet who better to find a suicide than a tough prison officer, a former policewoman? The woman who was to step into the job of governor might have been his choice as the first person to know.

If the major had been driven to take his own life, he may

101

have convinced himself that the world and everyone in it would be better off without him. Perhaps talking to his successor did not enter his mind on the day he died.

Nell was on her way out of the building when she practically bumped into a young constable who had let himself in and was waiting in the entrance. 'Miss Lewis?'

'Yes.'

'Constable Mudie, ma'am. I'm asked to tell you that the ambulance will be later than expected, ma'am, due to a road traffic accident. Also, two of us will be keeping an eye on the cottage and the grounds overnight.'

'Would you kindly go to the main door and tell Chief Officer Markham. She's in the reception office just to the right of the door. She'll be able to pass the word.'

'I'll do that now, ma'am.'

The chaplain was hovering outside. Nell stepped out to join him. 'Father James, did you manage to see Theresa?' Nell asked.

'I'll go now. I'll see if I can prepare her without giving her the full weight of news.'

'Yes, I can see that could be a difficult balance. If anyone can do it, you can. The ambulance is delayed, but I think things will happen quickly.'

Nell saw Sergeant Ambrose approaching. 'Theresa ought to be here for the announcement and the interviews.'

'You're right. I'll go now.'

It was a relief to Nell to be out of the building for a breath of fresh air. The windows must not have been opened for weeks. There was still a touch of blue in the sky, in spite of darkening clouds.

The gateman came out and walked towards her. 'I knew

something was amiss when I saw you and a plain-clothes man and the chaplain with the governor's dog, ma'am.'

'Sam, I thought you were on the six-to-two shift today.'

'We did a switch. I took my wife to the dentist this morning, so I'm two till ten.'

'You'll have gathered there's been an incident. I can't say more at present. Come into the visitors' block when the detective chief inspector arrives to makes his announcement. The police want to speak to all of us.'

She did not have the full measure of this place yet and how news travelled. Had the governor mentioned his planned supper to whoever did his shopping, and had that person mentioned it to Mrs Ramsden, who told Crofty when he came to clear out the pond?

Sam said, 'I'm the wise monkey, ma'am. See nowt, hear nowt, say nowt – unless you ask me.'

'Is there anything in particular I should ask you? About security, about signing in, or hiding places for contraband?' She did not want to play guessing games.

'Would you be interested to know who came in a few weeks ago, without signing, over the Easter weekend?'

'I would, because we will be having a meeting about security and I value your contribution.' Sam meant well, but could be exasperating.

'Well, I can't tell you because they didn't sign. No gateman was on duty over Easter. The gates stayed locked.'

'So how do you know?'

'There was a band playing in the grounds on Easter Sunday. It wasn't the village band. I heard it as we laid flowers in the churchyard for the wife's family.'

'Did you ask when you came back to work?'

'No, ma'am. I made an official note of it in the book, to be read and commented on. It was initialled as an acknowledgement but without explanation.'

'I'll look at it when we have our meeting. Tell the inspector what you've told me. He'll want to talk to you. Let him see the gate-book.'

Nell felt a wave of dismay. A whole band had been let in to play on Easter Sunday? She was beginning to feel she had arrived not in a prison but at a circus.

Twelve

Nell left the dog with DI Dennis and went back to the house. Chief Officer Markham spotted her coming and opened the door. 'Ma'am.'

The chief indicated the door to reception that she had left open. 'I was sitting in reception, ma'am. It gives a view of comings and goings and there's a cup of tea there for you. Poured it as I saw you coming.'

'Thanks.' Nell took a drink of tea. A sandwich might stick in her throat. She took one. This could be a long night.

The chief squeezed the bridge of her nose and screwed up her eyes. 'Ma'am, this morning, I called at the cottage with a pie from the butcher and a marrow bone for Pip. The major was looking forward to having supper with you this evening. What exactly happened? You wouldn't have police on the premises unless there had been a crime. Why the secrecy? Why the silence?'

Nell met the chief's gaze. 'Chief Inspector McHale will be making an announcement.'

The chief took a deep slow breath and let out a sigh. 'Of

course he will. This is a notable death. The DCI will do everything by the book.'

'I'm so sorry for the loss of your old friend and comrade, and for not telling you as soon as I would have liked. You and he went through a lot together. You've known him a long time.'

'We went through experiences that I'll never forget. That's history now.'

Through the window, Nell saw the chaplain and Nurse Carreras walking towards the visitors' block.

The chief stood and buttoned her jacket. She was watching Father James and the nurse. 'Florence Nightingale is going to take this hard.'

'The major and Florence?' Nell made this a question, not wanting to say that the chaplain had already told her.

Markham picked up her cap. 'The major and I had a high regard for each other, shared some of the same experiences, but that didn't mean I put on blinkers.'

'I don't follow.'

'He was used to being looked after. When a man gets to his age, he wonders who will take care of him. He was never less than charming.'

Nell was taken aback. Was this cynicism or insight? 'The major wasn't on his uppers. He could afford to pay for care.'

'He was never wise about money – had a weakness for horse racing and a profligate son. Florence is a good nurse with an urge for self-sacrifice, but I'm not sure she knew what she was letting herself in for. I think she has a bit in the bank, and he would have gone through that. It's cruel to say this of my old comrade-in-arms, and I would have done anything for this not to have happened, but she will be better off without him. She would have been second fiddle.'

'And the first fiddle was . . . ?'

'The major would never forget Felicity. I was friends with both of them. She had a great circle of friends. He had none. His forces pals were scattered. We joked about it. I said I would be his friend when he was old.' She sighed. 'I would have too, but not if it meant early retirement to the seaside, or being best buddy with Florence Nightingale.'

'Thanks for telling me.' Nell checked her watch. 'Here's Officer Fricl on her way back. Please fetch Kit. We need to be on the move.'

Nell combed her hair, put on some lipstick. What lay ahead called for a brave face and best foot forward. She watched as a white Rover pulled up by the gatehouse. Crofty and Daisy got out. The car moved on and turned left to park. The driver got out. It was Jeff. She was glad to see him. He was straightforward, reliable. Nell had a feeling Jeff was the whistle-blower who reported the bad apple. That must have helped towards his promotion.

Nell joined her officers near the entrance. Julian was walking down the drive towards them. She made the introductions and was proud of her officers, smart in their uniforms.

Julian gave her a small, sad smile of encouragement as they went inside. Tables and chairs had been arranged around the sides of the room. It reminded Nell of her old youth club, with the centre of the room cleared for dancing.

She and Julian went to the top of the room and stood side by side with their backs to the kitchen. The DI and sergeant were near the window. Three tables were set out ready for the interviews. Nell spotted the Ramsdens and their farm manager. Her officers all sat together.

Nell said, 'Thank you all for coming. Let me introduce

Chief Inspector Julian McHale of Harrogate CID and his colleagues, Detective Inspector Ian Dennis and Detective Sergeant Angela Ambrose.' She waited, telling herself to take it steadily. Prepare the way for the bad news. 'The chief inspector has a deeply upsetting announcement to make. I will be here to support you all in whatever way I can, as will the chaplain. Over to you, DCI McHale.'

'Thank you, ma'am.' He let the silence last for several seconds. 'It is with great regret I must tell you that Governor Harding died today under tragic circumstances. The death is being treated as suicide. Your deputy governor, Miss Lewis, had the shock of discovering the major's body. I know you will all want to help with our investigation into the circumstances surrounding this sudden and unexpected death. My officers and I will take your details. That way we will know that we haven't missed anyone, or missed an opportunity to gather information. At this stage, we are not taking formal statements, simply asking a few questions that will help us take the investigation forward. If you know of anyone who isn't here this evening, but who may be able to help, please let them know we need cooperation and let us know who we need to contact. Some of you have known the major for many years. I extend my condolences and the condolences of my fellow officers who are here this evening, and indeed from the chief constable and the entire North Riding Constabulary. Please resist the temptation to talk to each other about where you were today, who you were with or what you may know – until you have come up to one of these three tables and spoken to us. An ambulance is expected shortly; it will take Governor Harding's body to the mortuary at Harrogate Hospital, where a post-mortem will be conducted. I know that some of you will be standing by the gate to pay your respects. In church on Sunday, there will be special prayers for the major. The chaplain asks that we now have a moment's silence and reflection to remember Governor Harding.'

'Thank you.' Father James closed his eyes and bowed his head. Everyone followed suit. Nell had not met Mrs Grieves, but that must be her beside him, almost as tall as he, wearing a grey coat and hat.

Nell lowered her head. She pictured the major drinking his glass of sherry, recommending her to stand by the camellias to have her photo taken. In spite of the age difference, Nell could understand how he attracted Theresa. He was diminished by poor health and drink, but Nell had met many men like him, raconteurs with a talent to amuse who, however exalted their position in life, managed to create the illusion that they were here on earth simply to entertain you, now, this moment, and for ever.

When the silence ended, Nell scanned the room. She wanted to see who might be in need of comfort or reassurance. Daisy was crying. Crofty put his arm around her. Jean Markham stood to attention, looking so still and expressionless that she might have been turned to stone. Jeff, Crofty and Daisy were the first to come forward for interview.

The nurse, Theresa Carreras, who was close to the door, may have tried to leave quietly. Her footsteps tap-tapped across the wooden floor, breaking the deadly silence. The door hinges creaked as she left. The chaplain also noticed her departure. For a moment Nell thought he might follow, but he simply caught Nell's eye. It was Kit who got up and slipped out after her.

With the Ramsdens was the farm manager, and two lads

who fitted Jeff's description of Michael and Dave, the borstal boys awaiting parole. Both gatemen, Sam and Bernie, stood with a couple of security men whom Nell had met briefly.

Nell was looking for the person she had yet to meet: Arthur Burnett, the major's visitor who found work on the farm. She came to the conclusion that he was not here. That must be why Julian, without naming Arthur, was appealing for someone to give information about 'anyone who isn't here this evening but who may be able to help'.

Nell went across to meet Mrs Grieves, the chaplain's wife. They exchanged a few words. Nell thanked her for the tulips and the vase. She acknowledged the gatemen and security men, and went to speak to her officers. One of the constables was by the door, making sure no one else left the room without speaking to the police officers. Nell spoke to the constable and then went to the entrance.

Kit was just coming back inside. She said, 'Florence Nightingale has gone back to her flat, ma'am. She can't face talking to the police just now.'

'Do you think she might want to come and stay in the house tonight?'

'I did ask her, but no. She wants to be on her own tonight. I said I'm sure the police will wait for an interview.'

'They'll be back tomorrow, no doubt.'

Kit glanced at the tables where the three detectives were conducting their interviews. Jeff and Crofty vacated their chairs. Kit said, 'Looks like it's my turn.'

She was followed by the Ramsdens.

Jeff came over to Nell and Daisy, who had joined them. He was shaking his head, with that look on his face that signals something is incomprehensible. 'What a loss. I just wish his last months had been better than they were. The governor was part of this place. Say the name Brackerley, and the response would be "Governor Harding". No disrespect, ma'am.'

'None taken. He gave long and distinguished service, not just here but for his country.'

'Will you please do something for me, ma'am?'

'What?'

'Order me not to attend the induction in Durham tomorrow. I'm needed here, surely?'

'That's really thoughtful of you, Jeff, but absolutely not. You'll be starting in Durham in ten days. The induction is necessary, and it will be planned. You know you won't just be walked around the prison, or listening to lectures. There'll be activities, organised according to who's going to be there. You must go.'

Daisy looked pale and tearful. She had worked most closely with the governor, sitting in the office next to his. She fell back on the unarguable voice of the dead. 'The major would want you to go. And what would you do here? Just go. It's the weekend. You're not on duty. We'll see you on Monday.'

Jeff protested. 'There's the service on Sunday.'

'There'll be other services.'

Nell wanted to bring the subject to a close. Jeff would go to Durham, and that was that. 'Why don't we go outside for some fresh air?' She also wanted to be sure everyone would be in place to watch the ambulance take the major from Brackerley for the last time.

Dutifully, the officers trooped out.

Nell went to the kitchen. Pip looked up at her from where Inspector Dennis had placed a mat on the floor for him. She picked up his lead. 'Come, little fellow, we'll be watching your master leave. What will become of you, eh?' She clapped her hands quietly. 'Up you get.'

The inspector followed her in. 'I found a carrier bag in the cottage. I put all Pip's bits and pieces in there, including a marrow bone. It must be fresh, it's only smelling of marrow. I gave it to the officer who came to your door when I rang the bell.'

'Thank you. That would be Officer Friel.'

'She seemed a nice person. She said to tell you she's lit a fire in the staffroom, in case you want to gather when you go back.'

'Thank you.'

Nell clipped on the dog's lead. He looked from her to the inspector, and somewhat reluctantly trotted with her to the door.

The inspector walked with her. 'We've had a telephone call from the constable at the cottage,' he said. 'The ambulance will be here shortly.'

Thirteen

The chief officer was just walking away from her interview with Julian as Nell left the kitchen. They exited the building together, to the sound of the gates being opened. The ambulance entered. Nell waited until the ambulance officer signed the gate-book.

Sam came to speak to Nell, or rather to Pip. 'Hello. A sad day, Pip, for you and us all.'

'Desperately sad,' Nell said. 'The DCI spoke very well, I thought, and I'm glad the chaplain held the moment's silence.' As Sam patted Pip's head, Nell asked, 'Were you able to give the police much help?'

'No, because they asked me about Arthur Burnett. Well, he didn't sign in and he didn't sign out, but it seems that he has not been seen since before teatime. I knew no good would come of lax security.'

'We'll get there, Sam. We'll be secure very soon.'

Chief Officer Markham was standing a little apart from the others. Nell went to join her. They stood in silence, but if brains could make a sound the chief's would clang, buzz and

113

whirr. She said quietly, 'What is this nonsense about suicide, ma'am? He would not have killed himself.'

'The death does appear to be suicide.'

'Never! Please tell me how he died. What I am imagining may be worse than the reality.'

'There is no gentle way of putting this. It was a bullet to the head.'

There was a long silence. A cloud shifted. The moon came into view.

Miss Markham's sigh came from deep inside herself. 'I won't have it that he took his own life.'

'We can never entirely know another person.'

'Yes we can. I met the major in 1944, in Bari, when I was serving with the Auxiliary Territorial Army Expeditionary Force after the invasion of Italy. He was with the Northamptonshire Regiment. After the war, a lot of us joined the Prison Service, not knowing what else to do. I didn't see him again until 1962 when I came here, but I know him.'

The large, tinted bulb above the prison gates shone a glowing circle of pale amber light over the gathering of officers, chaplain and the nurse. The farm contingent, the Ramsdens and two borstal boys, stood apart from the staff. DCI McHale, DI Dennis and Sergeant Ambrose were joined by Sam and his fellow gateman.

The dog livened up when he came close to the taller of the two borstal boys. His whole body wagged. The boy bobbed down, holding out his arms, offering to take Pip. Nell released the dog. It snuggled into the boy's shoulder and licked his neck.

Nell saw that a place had been left for her near the gate,

beside the chaplain who beckoned her. Nell hesitated, indicating to Chief Officer Markham to take that place. Markham shook her head and made way so that Nell stood between the chaplain and the chief.

Stately slow, the ambulance came into view. Mrs Ramsden lowered the veil on her felt hat.

The chaplain, Markham, Jeff, Crofty and Ramsden, who had served in the forces, stood to attention and saluted as the ambulance approached. The driver halted the vehicle for a moment. The chaplain said a prayer. Miss Markham murmured, 'Goodnight and God bless, Major.'

The chaplain turned to Nell. 'Miss Lewis?'

She had not expected to speak but took a breath, and looked from one to the other. 'You all knew the governor best. I met him only once. You have my heartfelt condolences. From such a short acquaintance, I know that Governor Harding is someone you will never forget. We wish him a peaceful goodnight.'

Sam and his fellow gateman each opened a gate and saluted.

Slowly, the ambulance drove into the lane, its rear lights growing dim as it moved towards the bend and then was lost to view.

She turned to her officers. 'Officer Friel has lit a fire in the staffroom. Do go in if you'd like to talk.'

After a moment, people re-grouped. Julian was talking to the Ramsdens. The two borstal boys came closer to Nell, moving into the halo of light from the gatehouse. They wore donkey jackets over their overalls. Their haircuts were identical, short back and sides, Michael's dark, David's a pale ginger.

Nell went to the tallest boy, who still held Pip in his arms. 'Michael?'

'That's me.'

'Thanks for looking after Pip. I'll take him back now.'

'Will you be keeping him, miss?' He set the dog down and handed Nell the lead.

'Yes. We'll take care of him. Good luck to you both for tomorrow.'

'We'll still be paroled?'

'I don't see why not.'

As Crofty and Daisy came to talk to the boys, Julian drew Nell aside. 'I need to interview the lads. They're reluctant to talk. I think they're protecting Arthur, and they don't trust the police.'

'What can I do?'

'Sit in as their responsible adult. You're not police, you're not in uniform and as well as that, you've adopted the dog.'

'I'll do it. Their probation officers won't be pleased if they have to take them to a station for questioning.'

The harsh brightness of the neon lights in the visitors' block created the right sort of atmosphere for a third-degree inter-rogation. Nell played with the switches until she reduced the glare. She joined Julian on the bench opposite Michael and David; Pip was seated between the boys.

'You've met Miss Lewis. She's sitting in this evening because, as your old governor's successor, she wants to ensure fair play. Is that agreeable to you?'

They muttered an agreement, Michael a 'yes', Dave 'I suppose so'.

Julian took out his notebook, saying, 'David Carson, Michael Edwards, to be paroled when?'

'Tomorrow,' Dave said.

Julian made a note. 'The Ramsdens would love to see you staying on. You're good workers, but I know you're eager to be off and I don't want to delay you. When we had a word earlier, you said you hadn't been near the governor's cottage. Do you still stand by that?' There was a pause. 'Think carefully before you answer. Other people have also been interviewed.'

The boys looked at each other. 'We were off to the postbox for Mrs Ramsden,' Michael said. 'Officer Jeffrey told us not to go our usual way because there were girls at Brackerley now. We should walk on the road.'

'And did you walk on the road?' Julian asked.

They each waited for the other to answer. 'We did for a bit,' said Dave. 'We would've stayed on the road but there was traffic.'

Nell waited for Julian to say, In other words, you went along the road until Officer Jeffrey stopped watching you. Instead, he said, 'So you just happened to end up on this side of the wall near the governor's hedge? Did you climb the fence?'

'Well, you don't have to climb it at that point.' Michael scratched behind the dog's ears. 'But we didn't go near the cottage, and we didn't see any girls. Just two women at an upstairs window. One was giving us the come on. We hopped it.'

Julian made a note. 'You've cleared that up. Thank you. Now tell me about Arthur. Did he say where he was going?' He checked his watch. 'He could still be in some pub where the landlord locks the doors. If that's what Arthur's up to, I'll go home to my bed and see him tomorrow.'

Dave tried to be clever: 'He was off to meet a man about a dog.'

'And I haven't heard that one before,' Julian groaned.

'I called on your old governor on Monday,' said Nell. 'He was in good spirits. He told me about Arthur, said he was really pleased to see one of his old boys doing well. Arthur never reoffended.'

Dave folded his arms.

Michael was more forthcoming. 'Arthur was meeting someone who would go in with him on his scrap-metal business. Arthur has the know-how. This chap will sort him out a second-hand van and a trailer.'

'Did he say who he was meeting?' Julian asked.

'Nah,' Michael said.

'Where was he meeting him?'

'Don't know.'

Nell thought Michael looked a little worried at having told this tale. 'Arthur must have liked you both a lot to confide in you.'

'He was a right good laugh,' Dave said. 'But scrap metal? Isn't that like being a glorified rag 'n' bone man?'

'Not at all,' Julian said, putting the notebook back in his pocket. 'There's a lot of money to be made in that game if you do it right.' He stood. 'I'll let you get off, lads. DI Dennis will see you back up to the farm.'

Nell switched off the lights as they left the room. The gatehouse was in darkness.

Michael bobbed down to scratch Pip behind the ears.

DI Dennis was waiting outside in the car. 'Jump in the back, lads. I'll give you a lift to the farmhouse. Try not to wake everyone as you go in.'

Nell locked the visitors' block.

They watched the car go. 'I'll walk you back to your door,' Julian said.

'Okay.' Nell looked up at the sky. 'Don't you just love the dark skies? You forget what it's like when you live in the city.'

'I know. It's amazing. I took up astronomy for a while, but there's so little time in this job. I have my telescope in the attic.'

The outside light was on above the door of the house. Nell took out her key.

Julian said, 'Thanks for talking to the lads with me. It made a difference.'

'I'm glad you asked me. I now know that any hikers treading the Ripon to Harrogate Road might spot a hole in a fence and walk through to the governor's garden. Anything else you notice, would you let me know? I'll be drawing up a long list.'

'I'll set the sergeant on to do you a security check while she's here. Angela would like to do that. Little wonder this place was a colander for the prison contraband cigarette trade.'

'Is that what it was?'

'Suppliers to prisons across Northern England.'

Nell had heard snippets. Ear-to-the-ground Bert Hastings had given her a name, but the service played close to the chest when it came to its own wrongdoers. Once an issue was resolved, a line would be drawn. Staff and public confidence needed to be maintained.

'Do you think the governor knew?' Nell asked.

'I don't know how he could have missed it.'

Nell thought about the whisky, in the cottage, in the pond, and in the barn. If whisky had been at first a treat for the major, then a sweetener, then a bribe and ultimately the silencer, the process would have been gradual. Before he knew it, the major would be an alcoholic, in thrall to the bad guys.

It was too late to talk about this now. She must report to T5. Julian needed to get home. She took out her keys.

'You've come at the right time, Nell. HMP Brackerley turns a corner, eh? Do you want to know who came out the hero?'

'Of course.'

'Brackerley's very own whistle-blower, senior officer Derek Jeffrey. And the major kept his job.'

So I was right, Nell thought. 'Good for Jeff. He's now promoted to principal officer and all set for his transfer to Durham. I'm glad you told me. I was wondering whether there were still any leftover dark secrets.'

'You should be fine now. Any problems, we've a constable by the cottage, he'll hear the phone. Another is on patrol with your security men. We'll have a search team in at first light.'

'And we're still saying suicide?'

'That's what it looks like, until a post-mortem report turns up something to make us think differently. And I know they're busy in pathology.'

'The major dropped hints that at our supper-that-never-happened he might have a tale to tell about doings at Brackerley. It's left me with a feeling of something eluding me.'

'Something eluding me is my permanent state of mind. It will fall into place, like that archive file on Arthur Burnett that you're going to find for me.'

'Leave it with me, Julian. I'm on the case.'

'Er, no, Nell. I'm on the case. Just the file, please.'

'I'll have it for you in the morning. Goodnight, Detective Chief Inspector.'

'Goodnight, ma'am. Goodnight, Pip.'

Nell went inside and locked the door.

Strange how meeting someone again after all these years made her remember a long-forgotten birthday. How well did Julian remember their mutual first posting, she wondered. Someone found out they shared a birthday. They were twenty-two. This was a stronger than usual reason for everyone who could escape the station to drag them to the pub for a joint celebration. Gin and orange tasted like pop. She could not remember very much about that evening, except the heat and the lights and the non-stop jokes, which she pretended to understand. It was Julian who saw her safely home. For years after that, she smelled gin whenever she opened a cupboard door, even when the cupboard housed only a tin of beans and a packet of Ryvita. Scared witless at the thought of turning into her mother, Nell never drank again.

Enough, she told herself.

Arthur Burnett's file ought to be in the archives. Prepare for dust up the nose. First, she would need to find somewhere to settle Pip.

But someone was still awake. There was a light in the hall from the library.

Fourteen

The library door stood open. A reading lamp cast a pool of light on the long table. From across the room, a dim light glowed from a single lamp with a green shade. Nell heard someone talking and stepped inside. Pip pricked up his ears.

The voice said, 'If you know what's good for you, you'll be on your way out of this house now.'

'Hello?' Nell spoke in the direction of the book-lined wall.

A figure rose into view. It was Officer Friel. 'Did you hear me talking, ma'am?'

'I did.'

'The thing is, and you will have been too busy to notice the signs, but I'm giving the mice fair warning to leave the premises. I've re-set my traps.'

'We have mice?'

'Not just mice, ma'am. I've no specialisms, but I don't miss much, though people think I do. I get on with people of high station, low station, or no station at all. And I recognise infestation when I see it.'

As Nell opened her mouth to speak, Betsy Friel got in first as she bent to set another trap.

'Not everyone would have the stomach for it, but I was brought up on a farm.'

Nell made a mental note. No, she would write it down. The way the day had gone it would not be surprising if such an important piece of information disappeared into the ether. She wrote, *Betsy Friel – Farm.*

Nell was curious. 'Did you bring the traps with you?'

'I did, ma'am.'

How did you know you would need them?'

'I'm blessed with foresight.' Betsy Friel bobbed down to place another trap. 'A house in the country, they said. I knew right away who would have got here first and that there are more of them than of us.'

'So we'll be fighting a losing battle?'

'Ah no, we'll outwit them.' She remained crouched on the floor. 'Now who's that?'

Pip was looking under the table at Friel.

'He's called Pip.'

'Come to me, Pip, you little lost soul.' He dashed across to her. She picked him up and then stood, facing Nell across the table. 'Whose is he, ma'am?'

'Pip needs a new home, so I suppose he's ours for now.'

'A Jack Russell is just what we need. Would you have any objection to giving me the care of him?'

'Well, he's taken to you, so you do that for now and let's see how we get on. Sit down a minute, tell me how your interview went, if I'm not keeping you up.'

'Ah sure we're all pulling together.'

'Were you able to help the police today?'

'I was. They wanted to know how we spent the day and whether there was any time at all when Olga and Cherry were unsupervised. Well the answer is no. We were together working in the house and the kitchen most of the day.'

'Did you leave the building?'

'Not until the evening. Olga's knee was swollen. She went into the sitting room to raise it up. It was just going on five before Olga was up to putting a bit of weight on her leg, and then I walked her and Cherry to the garden for a bit of fresh air.'

'Did you see or hear anything unusual at that time, or anyone walking about that you didn't recognise?'

'No, ma'am. Inspector Dennis was satisfied, but he did say that he would still like to talk to Olga and Cherry in the morning.'

'Did he say why?'

'Because of our being so close to what he called the incident. Kit had the same outcome. She was in the cottage with Diane and Linda. So the police want to speak to the four of them in the morning.'

This was just what Nell had hoped to avoid. 'Goodnight, Betsy. Thanks for the good work. If the infestation is as bad as you think, we'll have pest control come in.'

Pip seemed perfectly happy to stay with his new friend.

Nell could leave searching through archives for Arthur Burnett's file until tomorrow, but she had an urge to see it. Going into the basement would be a chilly job. She would go to the flat for her coat and a torch.

She climbed the nearest stairs. The top step creaked. She paused by the door to the women's dormitory. Silence. There was not so much as a gentle snore.

She continued across the landing to the flat that was now

her home. Not that she had paid it a great deal of attention. The place was clean. The bed had no loose springs and a mattress that was not too thin.

She opened the bedside drawer for her talisman torch, the Eveready Daylo flashlight whose wall eye lens challenged moonlight and whose brass case gave it the weight of a small cosh.

It will see you through any blackout, GI Roland Herbert had said. Keep it by you.

She put on her big coat, hoping to be in and out as fast as possible, and to bed and to sleep, if sleep would come. She sat on the bed and changed her shoes. Big coat for warmth, tennis shoes for silence.

Once more, she crossed the landing, moving silently in her soft shoes. This time there were voices from the dormitory. She realised that the first time, she had made a sound. This time, the women did not hear her.

First Olga's solemn, fortune-telling voice. 'I know whereof I speak. There is an unquiet grave in the vicinity of that garden.'

'Put a sock in it!' That was Diane.

Olga would not. 'Someone took a dark secret to the other side and wishes it to be known.'

'Then they should've spat it out before kicking the bucket.'

'I shall need help, a séance.'

'Olga, shut it! You and Cherry were having a cushy time in the kitchen. Linda was cleaning a freezing cellar on her own, scared of the bogey men. I was training to be a bloody window cleaner and then polishing a wardrobe that struck back by dropping two empty whisky bottles on my head. I'm trying to sleep.'

Olga said, 'All right, we'll have the séance another time. Give me a piece of that chocolate you halved with Linda and then I'll go to sleep.'

There was a rule for lights out, but not for mouths shut. It was up to the residents to police themselves, or ask to be moved. Nell now understood why the DI wanted to interview Linda and Diane. It was not just because they were in the cottage but because, for at least part of the time, Linda was unsupervised.

Linda lay awake. It was not Olga who woke Linda, it was Diane, loudly telling Olga to shut up because she was trying to sleep. Olga wouldn't shut up. She talked about doing a séance. Linda pulled the blankets over her head but she could still hear them. Linda thought it might be midnight but felt too tired to look at her clock.

She hoped they would not be going back to that cottage today. If they did, Miss would not send her in the cellar again. It would be someone else's turn, and besides it wouldn't need doing.

The cellar ran the full length of the cottage. Linda was to sweep and damp down the larder part. To reach it, she walked through the coal cellar where a pattern of circles shone on the floor through the holes in the coalhole cover. The pantry with the big stone slab and mesh cupboards seemed hardly used. The stone slab across the wall was empty.

She had to sprinkle water against the dust, and sweep. She did it. She was to wipe the slab. She did it.

Behind the slab was one of those barred windows with the outside visible through the upper part, the lower part looking onto a brick wall. A spider's web decorated the window, its occupier a giant of a thing. Along from the window was an old door that looked as if it never opened. She went to look. She dusted it, coughing. Why didn't Miss Kitteringham come down and inspect? She thought she heard someone on the other side of the door.

She saw a face at the window, a gargoyle face with waving hair and hollow eyes, looking through a web and layers of dirt. She blinked. It was still there. She blinked again. It was gone. She hoped she was not going mad, having hallucinations.

Linda didn't want eyes on her. At Brackerley she was free of the Judas hole through which any passing screw could take a look at her. If she made for the cellar steps, she would be seen.

Under the slab, that was where she would sit, keeping herself small, until Miss came down. She bobbed down and walked crabwise to the slab, squeezing herself into a dirty corner. She could hear her own breathing like a puffing billy train. She should not be afraid, not in here, not now with people upstairs.

One of the shrinks Linda saw was better than the others. He did not pry so much but seemed to know. He talked in stories. He said there was no need to scratch her arms and legs raw. She was a different person now. He said that every seven years we change completely and soon Linda would have been in prison for seven years. Seven was a significant number. All that had been done to her would be gone, without her having to scratch it away. She wondered how he knew. She had not told him. She had not told anyone.

He then seemed to tire of what he was supposed to say and asked her what book she was reading. He was not a young man. His eyes were watery. He said people underestimated fairy tales.

In that cellar, there was no one to spin yarns. Yet it felt like a place where someone might once have told a story, by the set-pot, or by the little fireplace. Linda knew there were eyes at the window. She dug her fingernails into her skin.

Someone called, a man's voice that she did not recognise. 'Are you still down there, miss?'

She heard clattering footsteps on the cellar steps. They had been given boys' lace-up shoes to wear to work. It was by the shoes that Linda knew it was Diane coming down the steps.

Diane said, 'It's me, you skiver.' She bent down and pulled Linda from under the slab, helped her stand up straight and gave her a big hug. 'Gotcha! You're shivering.'

Linda said, 'There was someone at the window.'

They went up the steps, Diane behind Linda, whispering. 'They're all mad. God knows how we'll get through this. Miss Kitteringham seems a nice lass, but she'd be better off doing cookery demonstrations for the gas board. Show no weakness.'

Linda could not stop shivering. They went into the sitting room. Miss Kitteringham was there. There was a movement from the other side of the room. Beyond the scullery, the back door was open onto the garden. The governor said, 'Good thing I came in for matches. Sit the young lady by the fire.'

Miss put a tartan blanket round Linda. The major passed a cup of tea through the scullery door.

Miss then went down to inspect Linda's work.

When Miss came back upstairs, she congratulated Linda on doing a good job. She would take them through the garden and up to the farm because it was such a nice day and they had worked well and it was time to take a proper look round.

Linda thought she must have imagined the face at the window.

Nell continued down the stairs and along the corridor, passing the closed doors of the library, the staffroom, sitting room and the kitchen. She unlocked the door that led to the basement and switched on the light, a single dim bulb.

Nell shone her trusty flashlight to see her way down the narrow steps. At the bottom was another switch. Harsh strip lighting turned the room bright, revealing rows of metal filing cabinets, bookshelves stacked with ledgers and boxfiles, cartons fastened with string. There seemed to be enough space for all the archives that ever were, since the house was built. Discarded furniture filled the corners. On the far side was an external door and a shuttered window. Out of habit, Nell went to check the door. It was locked, but unbolted. There would be no call for anyone to come in here from the outside. She shut the bolts.

A shuttered window rattled. Through a gap, she saw a moving light. Someone was passing with a torch. They stopped at the door. Whoever it was tried the door. They then put a key in the lock. As the key began to turn, Nell banged on the door, 'This door is bolted. Re-lock the door and identify yourself!'

After what must be shocked silence, a voice said, 'It's Crofty, ma'am.'

'Take your key out and go to the window.'

Nell unhooked the shutters and opened the window. Crofty stood there, torch pointing at the ground, cap in hand, his face looked carved from stone, his pale hair a thatch. He blinked when she shone her torch at him, asking, 'What are you doing here?'

129

'Patrolling, ma'am. I saw the basement light.'

Nell felt fumes of anger rising. She spoke so quietly and evenly that the fury did not show. 'There's already a security patrol, and constables posted at the cottage.'

She did not tell him that at first light there would be a search and that he could be trampling evidence and disrupting the investigation. There was a fine line between suspecting foul play and voicing the suspicion before a postmortem was held.

Crofty said, 'I reported to security, ma'am. When we had a full complement of officers, one of us usually joined in a night round, either on overtime or to make up some time.'

'Will you be putting in an overtime claim?'

'No, ma'am.'

'So you are making up time. Is this connected with Monday, when you went for a part for the boiler?'

He hesitated. 'Yes.'

'And why are you carrying a key to the basement?'

'I keep it for handy access to the boiler. I sometimes come at it from the outside.'

'You'll have given the police an account of your movements today. Please do the same for me in the morning, bringing your worksheets for the week, showing where you went for a part for the boiler, and the invoice you were given, and what else you were doing that means you make up time at night by coming on patrol.'

'Yes, ma'am.'

'Now go home and get some sleep. Return that key tomorrow, to be put in the safe.'

'Yes, ma'am. Goodnight.'

*

Nell turned back to the filing cabinets. She ignored the ones that were good quality walnut or cherry wood that looked old enough to belong to former owners. She looked for Home Office metal issue.

Whether it was Daisy or a predecessor, someone had done a good job on labelling file drawers. Nell soon found the 1950s. If Arthur Burnett was demobbed from the navy in 1956, the year of Suez, he must have joined up in 1953. Was he in here for a short sharp shock, or something longer? Nell worked back from 1953. For each year an alphabetical list of names and dates was clipped on the front of the file divider. Arthur's name and number appeared among the 1951 entrants. Folders behind the year divider were in alphabetical order. There was no Burnett. Some folders were bulkier than others. They included date of birth, home address, next of kin. Monthly reports included a note of progress, qualifications gained and prizes for sporting achievements. Nell checked to see whether a folder had slid to the bottom of the file drawer. Next she looked at each folder to see whether Arthur's details had been misfiled. She drew a blank.

She would ask Daisy to come and take a look in the morning.

As she reached the top of the basement steps, Nell was suddenly aware of the cold seeping up through the stone floor. She thought of Linda shivering in the cellar of the cottage while waiting to be told what to do next. Nell knew what she must do tomorrow – begin to get to know the women in her care. They must feel safe here.

Nell went back to her office. Reporting to HQ could not wait.

The phone was answered on the second ring. 'Barnes, deputy director.'

'Mr Barnes, Nell Lewis at Brackerley.'

'Ah, Miss Lewis, how are you after the shock?'

'Coping. The police have left for the night. I set up the visitors' room for their interviews. Governor Harding's body has been taken to the mortuary at Harrogate Hospital. There'll be a post-mortem. The investigating officer is DCI Julian McHale, based at Harrogate. He is regarding the death as suicide.'

'And was it?'

'The investigation is ongoing. We won't be certain until the pathologist reports.'

'Who else knows besides the police?'

'Those who were in the room for the DCI's announcement and to be interviewed: officers, security staff, the farmer and the borstal boys who are due to leave tomorrow. We gathered by the gate when the ambulance left.'

'This could be public knowledge by tomorrow. We'll consider issuing a brief statement about the death.'

'The DCI didn't discuss the death with me. I suppose he can't dismiss the possibility that Governor Harding did not take his own life. The interviews were brief.'

'Anything else?'

'I'll be putting in a report on security. The major had a visitor, Arthur Burnett. He was a borstal inmate in the 1950s and has been working as a casual labourer for the farmer. There's been some misfiling in the archive. If you can let me have his details, that would be a help.'

'Will do. Is he still around, this Arthur Burnett?'

'He may be but no one has seen him since around five o'clock. Apparently he went to meet someone this evening. The police are keen to interview him.'

'We have records in the basement. I'll get the night duty security to bring up Burnett's file. I'll telex the essentials to you.' He paused. She waited. 'Tell me, how did the major seem when you arrived?'

'He was chirpy, talking about his plans for retiring to Filey. His sister was going to find him a house.' It hit Nell what a shock this would be for her.

'I've arranged for the major's sister and her husband to be notified in person tomorrow.'

'Is she his next of kin?'

Barnes hesitated for a moment, as if deciding whether to answer. 'The major has a son. He's a busker, a one-man band. Unless one of us bumps into him on Trafalgar Square and he has "Fred Harding" painted on his drum, I'm not sure how we'll get hold of him. Anything else?'

Nell thought that was quite enough for one night, but she needed to know. 'Just a thought. I wonder if Fred Harding, one-man band, was here at Easter. I'm tightening security and our efficient gateman, Sam Reeves, mentioned that on Easter Sunday, when he was off duty, he heard a band playing in prison grounds. It wasn't the village band and sounded tinny.'

'Could be that Fred visited, but it ought to have been entered in the gate-book. I'm glad you'll be tightening security. Try and get some sleep, Miss Lewis. Sometimes incidents and events are more complex than they seem.'

Nell regarded herself as reasonably fluent in civil service speak, but before she had time to ask what he meant, Barnes said, 'I hope you pass a peaceful night.'

The line went dead.

By morning, the tentacles of news would wind their way up the hierarchy of the Prison Service and the Home Office.

Fifteen

Nell had not closed her bedroom curtains. When she woke at five, the sun had risen. Through the window she saw the maple tree, its uppermost branches swaying in the breeze. The kitchen was tiny. Her bathroom, with a cast-iron bath in the middle of the room, was big enough to host a party. She turned on the hot tap. Miraculously, the water ran warm, and then hot. Whatever Crofty's faults, he must be doing something right in the boiler department. She sprinkled on the rose-scented soap flakes, given to her by a friend from Armley. The bathroom mirror was spotted black from desilvering. Nell looked for signs of dark shadows under her eyes. Fortunately, how she felt on the inside did not show. As the bath filled, she made a cup of coffee. Lying in the bubbles brought her to life. Yesterday's events had shaken her, but she was ready to face whatever would come next.

She dressed and made her way to the office. She put a note on Daisy's desk about Arthur Burnett's missing file. The office telex had been busy. Deputy Director Barnes at HQ had sent on information about Arthur Burnett.

Nell read the potted history. Arthur was born at Hull General Infirmary on 9 May 1935. In 1949, he was sent to Brackerley Borstal for stealing lead pipes. At age fourteen, his only 'distinguishing mark' was a broken nose. His reports were good. He did well in sports and completed a basic course in mechanics. He showed enthusiasm for working on the farm and taking care of the animals. Nell checked his then home address. His family had been bombed out of two houses. Post-war, they settled in a prefab.

On her tour of the premises, Nell had seen the boys' dormitory here. It was like a barracks. Yet to a poor boy who had twice been bombed out of his house, the countryside, a farm, regular meals, companionship and a feeling of safety may have been bliss after a childhood in wartime Hull. Perhaps that was why he came back from time to time. He joined the Sea Cadets. A note added to his file recorded that at age eighteen, he joined the navy.

The place of birth and the date jumped out at her again. Hull, 1935. Where had she seen that recently? Then it clicked. She went to the cabinet and took out Diane Redmond's folder. Sure enough, same hospital, Hull Royal Infirmary, same year, 1935. Diane was born in September. Might they have known each other?

Uppermost in Nell's mind was whether Arthur had turned up at the farm late last night or this morning. The one number that Nell could safely ring at this early hour without dragging someone from their bed was the farmhouse. Mrs Ramsden answered.

'Hello, Mrs Ramsden, Miss Lewis. Apologies if I'm disturbing your breakfast. I'm curious to know whether Arthur Burnett showed up last night.'

'He did not. I went to look in the barn earlier, to see if he was back and sleeping, but no. Either something has gone wrong or he has let us down.'

'Has he let you down before?'

'Not usually.'

'Thanks. I won't keep you. I'll be up later to sign off Michael and David's papers when their transport arrives.'

Nell left her office, locking the door behind her, and crossed the hall to the reception area. Purchases were recorded. Cherry had bought ten cigarettes. Diane and Olga subbed enough for tobacco. No one bought chocolate.

Nell heard footsteps in the hall. It was Kit, looking wide awake.

They exchanged good mornings. 'Kit, you're an early bird.'

'I am, ma'am, and I'm still thinking about where I went wrong with my cleaning party, and also about where Diane got the chocolate that she gave Linda later on. Because no one had bought chocolate or had any with them on arrival.'

Nell was pleased that Kit had checked. She had the makings of a good officer. 'Come in for a moment. Let's have a word.' Nell waved Kit to sit down. 'Have you worked out how things went so wrong that Linda half froze in the cellar?'

The question took Kit by surprise. 'Oh, you heard. I was going to tell you. I divided the house, top and bottom. Linda was to start at the bottom.'

Kit twiddled a strand of her hair. 'The front door was locked, the major was at the back. The place was secure. I was upstairs, showing Diane how to clean windows.'

'Diane is a professional cleaner.'

Kit spoke with a swell of pride. 'Not everyone has the knack of cleaning windows. She took a bit of showing, you know, a drop of vinegar in the water, and a scrunched-up newspaper.'

Nell could picture the scene. 'You were working, she was watching.'

'Yes, but – you don't think she was having me on?'

'Probably. But tell me about Linda.'

'The major stayed in the garden, wanting us to have a free run. He went in to put the kettle on and realised he'd seen me and Diane at the upstairs windows, but not Linda. He waved up to me from the garden. I opened the window. He said, "I just called down. I think that poor girl is still in the cellar." And I thought, what's she doing?'

'Waiting for you to tell her to come up?'

'That was it. She was waiting for me to inspect.' Kit stopped twiddling her hair. 'The major came to the back door, saying to fetch her up, bring an eiderdown, switch on the electric fire.'

'And?'

'He was right. She was still down there. She couldn't speak for shivering. Diane guided her up the cellar steps. Governor Harding filled a hot water bottle and passed it through from the scullery. He made a cup of hot sweet tea and opened a packet of chocolate digestives. I pulled the chair closer to the fire. Diane wrapped Linda in a blanket.'

'And then what?'

'When she could speak, Linda said that I hadn't told her what to do next.'

'Kit, were you at Holloway during your training?'

'Yes.'

'And Risley?'

'Yes.'

137

'Then you know the routines that Linda is used to and how they are never left alone. You had two people in your work party. Working in pairs helps sociability and cooperation. What were you thinking of to send a prisoner alone into a cold dark cellar?'

'There was a light. I just thought of it as sweeping a cold store.'

'It's also about creating confidence and preparing a person for the day when she leaves here and starts her life again.'

'Yes, ma'am. I'm sorry.'

'You're not in trouble. We all have to learn.'

'Afterwards, when we made a fuss of her, she seemed much better. But when she first came up the steps, it wasn't just that she was cold, she seemed afraid. She imagined she saw a face at the window.'

Nell said, 'Kit, you took Linda and Diane for a walk after they had finished cleaning the cottage.'

'I did. I took them to see the farm, just to show them the way, and to see the hens and the pigs.'

'Did you see any of the farm workers?'

'The foreman by the gate, and a chap called Arthur, mucking out the pigs.'

'You had a word with them.'

'Just to say hello. I asked Arthur the pigman did he enjoy his work. When he and Diane started to chat, I thought we ought to move on.'

'Did they seem to know each other?'

'No.'

'Might Diane have got chocolate from the foreman, or from Arthur?'

Kit's hand went to her mouth. Her eyes widened. 'That's the question, isn't it?'

'One of the questions. You don't just need eyes in the back

138

of your head, you need a halo of eyes and an antenna of ears. The chief found a bottle of whisky tethered to weeds in the pond. As you're going round the grounds, look out for anything that may have been thrown over the fence or sneaked in and hidden somewhere. The chief, Jeff and Crofty, they'll know the hiding places. Now off you go, get on with what you're doing.'

'Will you have some breakfast, ma'am. Half an hour?'

'Thanks. I will.' Kit left, closing the door behind her.

In any other area of life, considering the source of a bar of chocolate would be thought slightly mad. In prison, it was different. Had Arthur Burnett and Diane seen and recognised each other's Hull accents? Had he spoken to her and passed her chocolate? Diane, not expecting a custodial sentence, had arrived at HMP Low Newton with her bus fare home and a cigarette. At Low Newton, she had subbed money against pay, just enough to buy cigarette papers and tobacco.

The telephone rang. Nell picked up.

'Morning, Nell, it's Julian. Has Arthur Burnett put in an appearance?'

'Morning, Julian. Mrs Ramsden hasn't seen him and that's where he'd turn up for breakfast. I have his date and place of birth, 9 May 1935, Hull. He served his national service in the navy. His distinguishing marks are a broken nose and a tattoo of a mermaid on his left forearm.'

'Thanks. We'll contact Hull police to see if they have anything more recent on him. I'll be disturbing you again later.'

'I thought you might. You want to talk to the residents.'

'Yes. And the forensics team are still at work. The post-mortem examination is being given priority.'

*

Back from eating breakfast, Nell sat at her desk, glancing at the rule book. Its restrained tone would temper her annoyance. Bloody Crofty! She could have done without having to give him a rollicking at seven o'clock in the morning when the world was not playing fair. The major's tip that 'going for a part for the boiler' was the euphemism for a job on the side had made Nell put up her guard. If everyone in the village regarded Crofty as a spanner for hire, that must change.

At seven on the dot, there was a tap on the door. Nell called, 'Enter!'

Enter he did.

'Good morning, Officer Meadowcroft.' She did not invite him to sit down.

'Good morning, ma'am.'

'I regret having to issue a severe reprimand during my first week. First, well done on maintaining the Brackerley boiler so well.'

He nodded an acknowledgement. 'Ma'am.'

'What was the part for the boiler you went for on Monday, where did you go for it, and which boiler was it for?'

He might bluff. He might lie. She watched him carefully.

He blushed. 'It was the pump and the pressure relief valve. I had to go to Ripon. The boiler is in Sunnyside Nursing Home just outside the village. The old people had no hot water and no heat. I know I shouldn't have done it on work's time, but it was an emergency. It's the truth, ma'am.'

Nell guessed that Daisy had advised him to come clean. 'Sunnyside Nursing Home may be a worthy institution but as far as I'm aware it is not a charity. Doing private jobs on Prison Service time calls for a severe reprimand. Did you do any prison work at all on Monday?'

'I took measurements in the boys' dormitory block, and made a plan for converting it for female residents.' He unrolled a large sheet of paper, holding it up for her to see. It was certainly beautifully drawn. Nell guessed that Daisy made him stay up half the night to do it.

'You have broken the rules. I am a new broom. You may not have expected me to sweep clean quite so quickly, or to recognise a code when I hear it. "Gone for a part for the boiler", sounded fishy. I have no objection to your doing small unpaid jobs in the village for elderly people. We will be good neighbours. But I must know of any work at all, however small, that you are doing away from the prison. If there is any such future incident, that will merit a formal verbal warning, and any subsequent occurrence will lead to a written warning. Is that clear?'

'Yes, ma'am.'

'You must stick to your timetable and worksheets. Officer Jeffrey will be leaving shortly. Your immediate superior will be the chief officer. It is unlikely there will be a need for you to patrol outside normal working hours. Do you have anything to say?'

'Only that I don't like saying no to people.'

'Were you paid for the nursing home job?'

Crofty had the grace to look embarrassed. 'I was given five pounds and the cost of the part.'

'Two things. Learn to say no. Donate that payment to a prison charity.'

'Yes, ma'am. It won't happen again.'

'I'm glad to hear it.

He nodded and bolted, closing the door gently behind him.

Sixteen

Daisy tapped on the adjoining door and brought in the post. 'I went down to the basement. You're right, ma'am, Arthur Burnett's file is missing. It's the only one from the 1950s that is missing. It's a puzzle. Arthur can't have found his way in and taken it himself. He probably doesn't even know it still exists. It's going to annoy me now, wondering where it's gone.'

'Who else has keys to the basement?'

'Chief Officer Markham. There are two keys in the safe for the internal door and two for the external door. There's no reason for anyone other than you or me to go down there. Crofty was allowed a spare key for when he went in from the outside with parts. I've brought it back, ma'am. He'll come in and sign for the key in future, when he needs to enter by the outside door.'

'Thanks, Daisy.' Nell was impressed by her admin officer's professionalism. Crofty would shape up. Nell did not want to lose these two.

Daisy placed correspondence on the desk. 'I've put a note as to what you might want me to do, ma'am. We've had more encouraging letters following the piece about you in the *Harrogate Advertiser*, and a few poisonous and cranky ones.'

'Glad to hear the kind ones outweigh the poison pen letters.' Nell looked at Daisy's note of what she might do, including drafting a reply, thanking the encouraging ones and saying something along the lines of being in touch at a later date. For the poison pen letters, she had jotted that their comments were noted. 'Leave the poison pen letters with me, Daisy. I'll come up with a brief explanation of what we aim to achieve. It probably won't change minds, but we go on trying.'

Daisy passed over two more letters. 'For censoring.'

'Thank you, and something you need to know. HQ is arranging for a counsellor to come. I don't have details yet but she'll be here today. I'll ask the chief to set up appointments but if you could have the timetables to hand and make sure the counsellor has everything she needs.'

'Will do, ma'am.'

Nell looked at the letters Daisy had given her. One was from Linda to her mother, the other from Diane to her family. Nell would need to appoint a censor officer. 'Who was censor officer, Daisy?'

'I did it for two years, ma'am.' Daisy's mouth turned down at the corners. She drooped with the look of a scrawny apprentice who had just been given a hod of bricks to carry. 'Sometimes it made me so sad. There was a boy who wrote home every month and never had a reply.'

'Right. I'll take a look at these. I'll appoint someone else as censor.'

'Thank you.'

There was an instant change in Daisy. Nell thought of her

as one of those people who would never be down for long and would always bounce back.

Daisy put another letter on the desk. 'This came for Olga Tagney, forwarded from Holloway. It's from her neighbour, Hilda Sinclair. I read it, and it's worrying.'

Nell picked it up.

Dear Olga,

I am sorry to tell you the nasty beggars are back. The bailiffs, bang, bang, bang front and back, threatening to break down the door. I set Sidney onto them but he is not here every day so I don't know what to do if they come again and he is not here. The police are not interested. Say it is a civil matter. There is nothing civil about it. A big pile of post for you some in large brown envelopes that I delivered to the gateman at Holloway to pass on to you. Here comes the worst. A white van came. Men got out and changed your locks. I tried to stop them. No luck. I told them that the cat was in the house. The young fellow would have fetched him but the boss made them drive off. I called on young Sol Taylor to go in through a window and fetch Tiger. Sol was well scratched. I gave him two bob for his trouble.

I am sorry to give you such heartbreaking news. There is one law for them and one for us. Don't lose heart. Our day will come. Tiger is well. I sent Sol back to get your crystal ball, Tarot cards, and all to do with your livelihood. Wink, wink.

Your neighbour,
Hilda Sinclair

Nell wondered whether the 'wink wink' meant that Hilda Sinclair assisted Olga in her profession. Olga had been charged under the Fraudulent Mediums Act. That charge had been dismissed by the judge. She was convicted of grievous bodily harm, having broken a man's arm by hitting him with a poker.

Betsy Friel was Olga's personal officer. She would need to talk to Olga before giving her the letter, to prepare her for a shock. 'Daisy, while I'm reading the other letters, will you take a look at Olga's property sheet. I believe she brought some papers with her.'

'I'll do that now.'

Nell turned her attention to the letters. Linda wrote,

Dear Mam,

I hope you are well. This is to let you know that I have moved to a different place, in the Yorkshire countryside, address above. There is a big garden. If the postage is not too dear and it is still there, I should like to have my copy of The Secret Garden. *I want to compare it with the walled garden here.*

I am in a dormitory with three others. The food is good. The library is not up to date but there are hundreds of books. All of Charles Dickens, Walter Scott, George Eliot and Jane Austen are here, and Arthur Conan Doyle's histories as well as Churchill on the Boer War, making it sound like an adventure story with a dangerous escape from prison. Nobody has read these books for a long time, including lots of topo-graphical books about Yorkshire including accounts of battles of the Civil War. I have not yet found a catalogue. I propped a few books on the table, opening the pages and opening the windows. I do not know what to do with books when they are

so musty that opening the pages catches your throat. Please
write back to me.
Love,
Linda
PS I went to see him.

There was nothing in the letter that meant Nell needed to return it to Linda for rewriting, nothing that could be a code. Linda knew the rules: no mention of prison routines, description of the location, naming of staff, and no complaints. The letter suggested that Linda was settling in well. The omissions were interesting, too. No messages or love to relatives or friends, no asking about how others were doing. It seemed to Nell that the letter was written at arm's length, with no personal feelings or hopes of a possible future visit. The tone seemed either oddly content, or resigned. The five-word postscript concerned Nell, and the effect of that visit to her father in hospital. She wondered how Linda might be affected by his death – perhaps not at all. Something inside her was frozen.

Nell returned the letter to its envelope.

She turned her attention to Diane's letter to her children. She had drawn pictures, reasonably good pencil sketches, of the ducks and the pond. She told her children to look after each other, listen to their grandma and auntie and do well at school. She was sorry to have to go away in such a hurry but hoped to see them very soon. They would come and visit, and the time would go quickly, and she would come home to them.

Nell sealed both letters and put them in the out tray.

Time would not go quickly for Diane's children. Time

stretched for ever. It would stretch for Diane, too. Nell knew that all too well.

There were no letters from or to Cherry, who preferred to use the telephone.

Daisy had left the door between their offices open. She appeared in the doorway. 'I checked Olga Tagney's property list. She brought two brown paper carrier bags containing 179 documents, including letters, summonses and bills, as well as the deeds to her house, purchased by her father in 1899.'

Nell heard herself say, 'Right.' Why am I suddenly saying right, she thought, when everything seems pretty much closer to wrong? 'Daisy, one of those offer-of-support letters – was it from the WVS? They have someone who is an adviser at the Citizens' Advice Bureau and would visit if required.'

'Yes. She lives in Ripon, a money adviser.'

'Put a note in Officer Friel's pigeonhole from me, asking her to recommend to Olga that she takes advice. If yes, ring the WVS, thank them very much and take them up on the offer. Let's treat this as urgent. Meanwhile, contact Holloway. See if the mail that Olga's neighbour delivered to the gateman is on its way to us. It would be better for Olga to have a full picture rather than the drip-drip of upsetting news.'

Efficient Miss Markham had set and marked literacy and numeracy assessments and put copies in Nell's inbox. In spite of Olga's intelligence, her extensive vocabulary, her ability to summon spirits and predict the future, Olga had a reading age of ten. She looked set to be homeless when she left prison.

'Will do.'

The phone rang. Daisy answered. Nell knew the police were back before Daisy said, 'Sergeant Ambrose is ready to interview the residents. She also asks if Florence Nightingale is now fit to talk.'

Seventeen

Nell knew that talking to the police was likely to bring back stressful memories for convicted prisoners. She wanted to do something that would prepare them and reduce anxiety or truculence. They would have just finished breakfast and be about to go up to the farm with Officer Friel.

Officer Friel was already by the front door, and Nell saw Cherry coming down the stairs, dressed in overalls. Nell beckoned Friel. 'Betsy, Sergeant Ambrose is ready to talk to the residents. I want to have a word with them before I take them across.'

This sitting room was a room of battered armchairs, a large sofa in a faded plush material, small television, record player, sideboard, a card table set with a game of Monopoly, and the fumes of cigarettes past and present.

'Girls, come and sit in the comfy chairs or on the sofa. I want to talk to you. Officer Friel will be taking you to the farm soon. It's a fine day for it.'

So as to see everyone, Nell sat in a chair by the fireplace with its empty grate. Pip made his way to the rug. 'Does anyone object to the dog being here?' Nell asked.

No one did. Olga came across to pat him.

'I hope you are settling in and getting to know the officers, particularly your personal officer. You can also ask to see me or the chief if there's something you want to discuss.'

She had their attention. They were still weighing up what kind of place this was, and what was she like, this governor, this red-haired woman in the smart suit that you had to stand for and call ma'am.

'I'm glad you seem to be getting on with each other. Sometimes when a person is alone a lot in a cell, it's hard to make sense of thoughts. It will be different here. Don't hesitate to talk. We all think of things we'll say, and we don't say them. We have conversations in our heads. Sometimes there's a reason for not saying, for keeping quiet. But here, speak your thoughts if you want to. Don't be shy.' Nell made one of those pauses, sitting still, ready to creep up on what she must say next. She paused, and could see they all expected a change of tack. 'Sadly, I must tell you that there was an incident in the grounds yesterday. This does not directly concern any one of you, but it was necessary for me to call in the police. Police officers are still here. They want to talk to all of us, just in case we saw or heard anything that will help with enquiries.'

'What happened, ma'am?' Olga asked.

Nell would have liked not to say, to give the excuse of not being at liberty to say, but the news would come out. HQ had arranged for a counsellor to be on hand. The police line of questioning would be revealing. Nell must be straight. 'The borstal governor died yesterday, under tragic circumstances. That is all I will say for now.'

Diane said, 'What if we don't want to talk to them?'

'It is our civic duty to help the police. I'll take you to talk to the officers in the visitors' block – which by the way, we'll improve the look of before our visitors come. Simply answer their questions. When we're done there, Officer Friel will take you up to the farm. I know that helping with a police inquiry isn't something you expected to do here. It will be noted on your report that you were cooperative and helpful. That is exactly the sort of thing that counts towards remission of sentence.' Fortunately, no one asked how much of a reduction. 'Before we go across to meet the police, I want us to do a short conjuring-up exercise, so you don't cross to the visitors' block with a groan in your heart about helping with an inquiry. We all know what goes wrong in our lives. We sometimes forget the things that went right. So, I want each of you in turn to tell us one thing, big or small, that you look back on and think: That was all right. I felt pleased, or happy, about that. It could be a long time ago, or today.'

Nell waited hopefully. The women from Holloway would be used to something like this, a group session that might be called by different names. Diane looked blank.

Olga put up her hand. 'I hope nobody's touched the Monopoly. I'm happy that I bought Liverpool Street and King's Cross stations and picked up a Get Out of Jail Free card.'

Linda, whose life sentence was indeterminate, was first to chuckle.

'Holding my babies,' Diane said. 'And dancing at my wedding to Elvis Presley, "Can't Help Falling in Love".'

Cherry said, 'You were dancing at your wedding while holding babies?'

Diane took a hanky from her sleeve. 'Go on then, Miss Smartarse, what's your happy memory?'

Cherry smiled. Nell thought she would say that it was winning her Young Designer of the Year award. She sat back in her chair and glanced about at the shabby room. 'I designed a perfect dress, to be worn by a beautiful model on a Caribbean island. It has stayed perfect because I haven't made it yet, but I will.'

'Give us a clue what it's like,' Olga said.

Cherry shook her head. 'That would break the spell.' She turned to Linda with a sly grin. 'Come on then, Linda, how was it for you?'

Nell willed Linda to talk. *Please, Linda, find something.* They all waited, looking at her. And then something inside Linda clicked. Her eyes widened, her mouth opened a little and she leaned forward. 'Such a long time ago, before I stopped wanting to do daft things, I went to the feast, with a girl from school.' She looked at Olga and Cherry. 'You two would call it the fair, helter-skelter, coconut shies. We went on the dodgems. We didn't half laugh. I was driving, and then we had another turn and she was driving, and it was all the bumping into people and the screams and the laughing and the madness of it. Best of all was when it stopped, and I felt glad to be in one piece.'

Nell felt a wave of relief. 'Thank you all! What great moments.' From the sound of Linda's moment, it was from a much earlier date than when her life went wrong, it was from 'before'. Nell wondered how old she was, that day when she rode the dodgems, and what had happened between then and the day she murdered a stranger.

'Come on, girls, let's go. You've each got your own memory and three more to keep you warm.'

*

152

Linda did not mind Miss Lewis because she had not pestered for an account of the visit to the hospital and seeing him. She had encouraged them to speak about something else entirely. Perhaps that was what decided Linda to say what it made her feel foolish to say, about seeing the face. Or perhaps it was because, when it was Linda's turn, she went to the woman sergeant who was polite, spoke softly and looked at her without glaring.

Linda had not heard anything resembling a firearm being discharged. She gave an account of her time at the cottage. 'I was sent into the cellar to clean. It was cold and I didn't like being there. The window was dirty and there was a big spider web. I don't know whether it was real or I imagined it, but I saw a face at the window.'

Linda could describe the face when asked because it hadn't gone from her mind. As she described it, she thought it could not be real. 'A perfect shape, like a gargoyle and with that curling hair. The eyes seemed hollow.'

'What colour hair?'

'I think dark, but I can't be sure of anything because it made me afraid and then it was gone.'

The sergeant wrote this down in small, neat writing. 'Anything else, Miss Rogers?'

'No.'

'This will be typed up as your statement. You will be given a copy to sign. Thank you for your help.'

Olga saw nothing. Olga heard nothing. She decided not to tell Inspector Dennis about detecting an unquiet grave in that beautiful garden.

Cherry eyed Sergeant Ambrose's cap. She might do a design based on the bib and braces overalls and a cap. She saw nothing unusual. She did not hear a firearm being discharged.

When cleaning the bedroom window, Diane saw two boys in the garden. She told this, even though Miss Kitteringham saw them too. How much might this little trip to the visitors' centre count towards time off her sentence, Diane wondered. Five minutes, probably. What a miserable place this visitors' centre would be for her kids to sit looking at her across the table.

Eighteen

In half an hour, transport would arrive at the farm to take the two remaining borstal boys to their destinations. Their departure would mark the end of an era. Nell felt regret that it was she who would draw a line under Brackerley's past history as a reform school. It should have been the major asking for signatures, shaking hands with Michael and David and wishing them well.

Nell opened the door to the adjoining office. 'Daisy, I'm going up to the farm. The two lads will be picked up shortly, so I'll wish them luck from us all and sign them off.'

'Oh, right, ma'am. I wondered whether you'd do that yourself.' She reached into her drawer. 'I know it's not much, but the major always did it.' She handed Nell two Mars bars.

'What a lovely thought. Thank you.'

'I don't know what we'll all do as our women start to leave. Perhaps a box of Maltesers or Weekend Assortment?'

'Plenty of time to think about that,' Nell said. Was this Daisy's extremely subtle way of wondering whether she would still be working here, after the 'Crofty's gone for a part for the boiler' incident?

Nell clipped the lead on Pip. The dog looked suddenly eager and began to wag his tail. It struck Nell that he might expect to be going home. She would have to walk him past the cottage. 'I don't suppose you have a dog treat, Daisy?'

She did. Daisy the treasure.

Pip trotted alongside. He turned his head to look at the cottage but showed no indication that he wanted to dash back there. Nell decided he could wait for the treat. As they came closer to the farm and he saw Michael, the dog began to pull on his lead. She let go of him. He ran to Michael and jumped up.

Michael said, 'You can't come with me, little feller. Mi mam has cats.'

'He'll be fine here,' Nell said. 'He's made a hit with two of my officers, and with me.'

The boys' two brown property bags were set on the slatted wooden table outside the farmhouse. 'Looking forward to going home?' Nell asked.

'Looking forward to moving on, ma'am.'

Dave came to join them. 'First thing I'll do is grow my hair.'

Nell smiled. 'Suits you short.' She sat down. 'I've some paperwork for you to sign. Let's do that now, shall we?'

Dave groaned. 'I knew there'd be summat else. Do we have to stop here if we get it wrong?'

'There's nothing to get wrong, just a signature to acknowledge that I've given you your documents.'

When they had completed the paperwork, Nell said, 'The important thing is to keep the appointment with your probation officer.'

'He can't put the kibosh on my plans, can he?' Michael asked. 'I'm going to join the navy.'

'That's a great idea. I'm sure you'll have all the support you need.'

'He's copying Arthur,' Dave said. 'He got half a tale about girls in every port and mermaids singing, and he believed it.'

Michael laughed. 'I didn't believe about the mermaids. Only mermaid was the tattoo on Arthur's arm.'

'Did you know Arthur was in the Sea Cadets?' Nell asked. 'You might look into joining. It would be good preparation for the navy.'

Dave made a scoffing sound. 'Arthur didn't have the bottle to ask for his wages and tell old Ramsden he was hopping it.'

'From what you told me, it sounds as if Arthur had a business opportunity. Perhaps the man who was going to help him brought the van and trailer.'

Michael perked up. 'That'd be good.'

The car that was to take the boys home came winding up the broad drive.

'Arthur might offer you ten quid for the machinery in the barn, miss.' Dave waved frantically at the car, as if he thought it might turn around and drive straight out again, leaving them captive.

Michael said, 'I hope Arthur's mate's come up trumps. He could be back in a few years, driving a Jag and putting in a bid for the farm.'

The car stopped. 'Well, good luck, Dave, Michael. I wish you well in whatever you do next.'

She shook their hands. 'What about you, Dave, any plans yet?'

'Waiting to see how things go, miss. Plenty of jobs around.'

157

Nell put her hand in her bag for the Mars bars. She handed them one each. 'Think of this as coming from your old governor. He would have been here to wish you well.'

The driver of the car climbed out and stretched. His mate vacated the front seat. 'Come on, lads, one in front, one in back, what's it to be? And who's signing our docket?'

There was a flurry of activity, with Dave saying, 'I bags the front!'

Farmer Ramsden chugged up in his tractor to say goodbye. Mrs Ramsden, who had been standing in the doorway, came out with packages of sandwiches. Pip began to yap. Nell signed the driver's form and took a copy.

Suddenly Jeff came haring along the dirt track and through the gateway. He was dressed in overalls and wellington boots. 'Don't think you'd get away without saying goodbye to me, me old sparring partners!'

Dave, who had already sat in the front seat, jumped out of the car to greet him. 'Thought you'd forgotten us, sir!'

'As if!' Jeff shook hands with both of them. 'Good luck, lads. Don't take this the wrong way, but I hope I never set eyes on you again. Go straight.'

Ramsden spoke quietly to Nell. 'I'm going to be stuck without Officer Jeffrey, ma'am. He's off on that course today. He should've set off by now but offered to finish a job for me.'

'We'll miss him.'

'When are your land girls coming up for a look round?'

'Chief Officer Markham will be in touch.'

Ramsden went over to say another goodbye and to talk to Jeff.

Michael dashed back. 'Miss!' He had the slightly shifty look of someone who might be about to tell tales.

'What's up?'

'It's about Arthur.' His words came out in a rush as the driver pipped his horn. 'We played a trick on him, threw his cap on the barn roof for a laugh, right before he was going to meet his mate. Dave told him we did him a favour and he shouldn't go round looking like Andy Capp. Arthur didn't think it was funny. He wasn't happy without his cap.'

'I'm sure he'll find another cap. He'll have done plenty of daft things himself. He'll understand.'

'Anyhow, this morning, I climbed up and got his cap. If he comes back, tell him it's on the hook in the hayloft where he was sleeping.' Michael looked suddenly sad. 'Arthur said it was his lucky cap.'

The boy looked so glum. Nell wanted him to leave in a cheerier mood. 'Well, I think that last night Arthur was lucky without his cap. He's gone off with the fellow who brought him the van. When he does come back to see the Ramsdens, and he will, I'll be sure to tell him where it is.'

The car window was wound down and Dave began to sing, 'Why are we waiting?'

Nell said, 'Off you go now. Lots of luck.'

'Thanks, miss. Bye!'

'Bye! And if the mermaids sing to you, cover your lugs.'

Nell stood with the Ramsdens and waved as the car pulled away.

Once the car was out of sight, Mrs Ramsden asked if she could have a word with Nell. 'Was young Michael worrying about Arthur?'

'Yes.'

She sighed. 'So am I. After what happened to the governor and Arthur disappearing, I hope the police don't have it in for him. As I'm a judge of character, there isn't a malicious bone in that lad's body.' She gave a nod and went back inside.

Ramsden stood for a moment with his thumbs in the tight waistband of his trousers. 'What did young Mick want with you?' Ramsden asked.

'He wanted me to say goodbye to Arthur, when we see him again.'

'If we see him again – now that he's to be the emperor of scrap metal. I hope he hasn't fallen in with a bad lot. That barn full of machinery could be a temptation. I spotted the padlock has been changed. I've no key and glad not to have the responsibility.' He scratched his head. 'It was all cleared with Governor Harding by Crofty and Jeff, and nothing to do with me.'

Why was he being defensive, Nell wondered. 'Nothing leaves the premises until I have authorisation and instructions from the Prison Service works department. Meanwhile, padlock or no padlock, let no one go near that barn.'

He let out a disbelieving grunt. 'It's of no value. Them machines are all from the days of the Marshall Plan.'

'So the machines are twenty-odd years old?'

'That's if they came new, which by the looks of them they didn't!'

Nell pointed to his tractor. 'What's the age of that trusty vehicle?'

'That's different. I know its ways.'

'Keep the farm gates locked. I don't want some dealer finding his way in.'

'The gates is always locked, except when I'm soon coming back.'

Nell managed a few conciliatory words. It may be that

Ramsden, Jeff and Crofty were honest men, but Nell wished the major had given her his full measure of them.

She went back to her office. Next door, Daisy was typing a letter. 'Daisy, when you've a moment, please send a telex to HQ. Ask for instructions regarding the machinery in the barn. Send a copy of the inventory. Cross out the fly press. Say we are keeping it. Send a copy of that inventory to Bert Hastings at Armley.'

Nell went back to her phone and called the Armley workshop number. Bert answered. 'Bert, Nell.'

From his cheery, 'What can I do for you?' Nell realised that news of the major's death had not yet reached him. She would leave him in ignorance for now.

'It's about the workshop machinery. We're sending the inventory to HQ, copy to you so that you can get in quick.'

'I already have, but I'll put in a second bid, in case the first went astray.'

Nell hung up the phone. She had a gut feeling that if anyone paid a midnight call to break into the barn, it would not be Arthur Burnett. Had the promised van and trailer materialised, he would have stayed around to show it off.

She had met men like Arthur, good-natured, unlucky men who thought their next break would be just around the corner. The farm was one of Arthur's fall-back positions. He would not have left without saying goodbye. He never knew when he might need to come back. More than that, he would not have skedaddled without his wages. Nell had the sinking feeling that Arthur had got himself caught up in something that landed him in trouble.

Nineteen

Having let Julian McHale and his team set up shop here to keep them out of the house, Nell now wondered how long this occupation of the visitors' block would last.

Julian was sitting at the Formica table nearest the entrance. DI Dennis was in the kitchen. She could see him through the hatch, using the telephone, holding a pencil in his free hand.

Julian looked up. 'Morning, Nell.'

'Morning, Julian. Thought you'd like to see more details about Arthur Burnett.' She had given Julian Arthur's date and place of birth, now she placed the full telex on the table. 'When Arthur was fifteen, he was charged with stealing lead pipes from a derelict house. That's why he was sentenced to Brackerley Borstal. He was a model inmate, never put a foot wrong. Perhaps the stolen lead gave him a taste for the scrap-metal business. As the lads told us last night, Arthur went to meet a mate who was going to fix him up with a van and trailer.'

'The machinery stored in one of the barns, is it still there?'

'The alarm hasn't gone off and the padlock is on. I checked when I went to sign off Michael and Dave.'

Julian was reading the telex. When they were constables, he had a giveaway habit of biting his lip if puzzled or thoughtful. He no longer did that, but Nell noticed something else, a slight movement around his mouth, a tightening of the jaw. 'Let me show this to DI Dennis.'

He walked up the room and passed the telex to the DI.

When he came back, Nell said, 'You're wondering how much I'll tell you and you'll tell me. I can probably help, so let's be straight with each other.'

Julian sat down. 'I think you wish you'd joined CID.'

'Never! I'm wondering how long the investigation will keep you here. My residents will be meeting their visitors in this room a week on Saturday.'

'You want your prison back.'

'Of course.'

'The sarge said you should have been a social worker. I told him he was wrong. You wanted to change the world. After that, their nickname for you was Joan of Arc.'

'I knew you talked about me. I didn't give a toss. They talked about you too, the eager beaver.'

'And here we are, joined at the hip over Arthur Burnett's distinguishing marks: a broken nose and a mermaid tattoo on his right forearm.'

Nell corrected him. 'Left forearm.'

'Just testing. Do you know what size shoes he took?'

'No! Did the fingertip search this morning turn up footprints?'

'We're still assessing. I don't know what you said to your residents before they came across, but they were helpful. One of them thought she spotted a face at the cellar window in the cottage. There's a size eleven boot print under that window.

Arthur was five foot nine, wiry but strong. That footprint is unlikely to be his, and your officers had no reason to be there. There's a cellar door with wonky hinges. It's been opened recently. Something may have been kept in the cellar, but the floor's been thoroughly mopped so it's hard to tell. DI Dennis is up at the farm now, checking with Mrs Ramsden in case Arthur had to borrow boots. We need to find him.'

A memory from last night flashed through her mind. Michael and Dave had wandered where they shouldn't, looking for the 'girls' that Jeff said had been sent to Brackerley. They wouldn't have got close enough to the cottage to go down the cellar steps, not with Jeff on their tails. Yet something niggled. If Jeff had wanted to keep teenage boys from going out of bounds, the last thing he ought to have said was that girls had arrived.

This was how suspicion worked. She could see how easy it would be for someone to fix on a wrong idea, to be convinced that there was some holding back of information, or lying.

She said, 'I expect you'll ask the male officers whether they were in the vicinity. That footprint could be entirely innocent.'

'Of course it could. And a week ago there were ten other male officers working here. We're following up on them too. DI Dennis has been making enquiries in the village. Arthur was drinking in the Hare and Hounds on Tuesday night.'

'You keep coming back to Arthur.'

'He ingratiated himself with the governor. He's been here before, knows the grounds, the farm, the house.'

'Why "ingratiated"? The governor was glad to see him. I looked up one of my old teachers after I joined the Prison Service. She was delighted to see me. We had a laugh.'

'What made you look her up?'

'She once said that I brought disgrace on the school. I thought it would amuse her to know how I ended up.'

'You have to tell me how you disgraced the school.'

'Miss Duxbury took us on a visit to the Magistrates Court. There was a tiny woman in the dock. You could see she was poor. She'd been caught with black market stuff in her house. Some spiv had a hold over her. He'd taken her ration book. The magistrate tore a strip off her and then sentenced her to three months in prison. When he said, "Take her down", I felt so miserable for her.

'As she was being escorted out of sight down the steps to the cells, she shouted, "What about my kids?" I stood up and said, very loudly, "Yes, what about her kids? It's not fair!" Two ushers removed me from the court.'

He laughed and shook his head. 'I wish I'd been there.'

'I'm only telling you as a way of saying that Arthur may not have been ingratiating himself, just coming to say hello for old times' sake. Ask Ramsden how many times over the years Arthur has come back to work on the farm.'

'I know.'

Nell frowned. 'I'm missing something. If the major's death is being treated as suicide, why are you fixating on Arthur Burnett?'

He went quiet for a moment. 'I told you that the pathologists are busy. They are. Governor Harding was on a downward spiral, no doubt about it. But he was still a notable person, a prison governor with a long track record, a decorated army officer. The chief constable did not want such a man kept waiting in the mortuary. We have a murder inquiry on our hands. I'm thinking that what the major may have planned to tell you cost him his life.'

Nell thought back to what Deputy Director Barnes at HQ had said to her. She repeated the words to Julian. 'Sometimes incidents are more complex than they seem.'

He looked at her sharply. 'What have you been told?'

'Nothing, but I'm beginning to wonder what it is that I don't know.' Nell glanced towards the kitchen. DI Dennis was still talking on the telephone.

Julian said, 'What I'm going to tell you now is between us. There's a full post-mortem being carried out as we speak.' She waited. For a moment she thought he had changed his mind. And then he went on: 'A preliminary examination revealed fresh bruises on Mr Harding's wrist and shoulders, indicating a struggle. The bullet entered too neatly to have been fired by a man who suffered from tremors. Forensics noted a mark on the gun where a silencer had been. My boss has put in a report to Prison Service HQ.'

Nell closed her eyes. It was terrible to think of the major's life ending as it did, but even worse to picture a struggle before he died.

'Was he shot with his own gun?'

'Yes. A Webley. It had been recently cleaned and oiled. He kept it in the back of a drawer in his bedroom, wrapped in a cloth. The cloth is gone but there are oily fibres. I need to question Arthur Burnett.'

Nell lowered her head. She rubbed her fingers through her hair, pressing her scalp, the voice in her head saying, This brain isn't working. What is going on here? She looked at Julian. 'I can't believe Arthur was here to silence his old governor. The major would have seen through him. He was smart. I'm not being self-important, but the major had decided he would talk to me about what had been going on in the borstal. He intended to give me his borstal diaries that he kept in a concealed cupboard in the leg of the drop leaf table. I want to see those diaries.'

'Did he show you the diaries?'

'No.'

'Because we haven't found any diaries. There are no signs of any papers or diaries having been destroyed.'

'Do you think whoever was there, whoever killed him, took the diaries?'

'It's possible. We'll go on looking.'

Nell watched as DI Dennis hung up the telephone. He then came stomping down the room, with the excitement of a man who has solved the case.

'Ma'am.' He gave a polite nod to Nell and then faced Julian. 'Sir?'

'It's all right. You can speak in front of Miss Lewis.'

'Sir, Arthur Burnett is known in Hull, but more for being a local character than a mastermind. In 1959, he was arrested for taking illegal bets. He ended up out of pocket. The charge was dropped. In 1962, he started a scrap-metal business by making weekly payments to an asthmatic rag and-bone man for the hire of his horse and cart. He was picked up for causing an affray and being drunk and disorderly after someone stole the horse and cart. He spent a night in the cells.'

'Not exactly reaching for the moon,' Julian said.

The DI had more to add: 'He hasn't been back to his lodgings. Before he left, he said he was on to something that would put him in the money. He's a popular local figure. Our lot liked him. He'd been a good amateur boxer, but he was unlucky. Last picked up after selling stolen whisky in a pub. He was let off. I think the local bobbies were too busy to bother with him. We have a mugshot and I've a good description. Apparently, he wouldn't be seen dead without his tweed cap.'

'Put out a county-wide alert,' Julian said. 'All forces across Yorkshire to look out for Arthur Burnett.'

'Yes, sir.' DI Dennis retreated to the kitchen.

'His cap's in the barn,' Nell said.

'Hang onto the cap, Nell. We'll get it next time. Arthur might be allowed to wear it in prison.'

The DI picked up the telephone. Nell watched him dial.

Julian seemed so certain that Arthur was guilty. There must be something he wasn't telling her, and why should he? He was the investigating officer, she was the one being as helpful as possible – and not listened to. 'From what the major said, and the Ramsdens, and Hull police, Arthur Burnett doesn't come across to me as a cold-blooded killer.'

Julian said, 'We have oily fingerprints from the drawer where the gun was kept, and on the box in that drawer where Governor Harding kept his medals between two layers of cotton wool. I sent them across to Hull last night. They're a match for Arthur Burnett's.'

Nell could now see why Arthur was Julian's prime suspect. This piece of information seemed damning. Yet she could not dispel her unease. 'What if Arthur was being nosey, or had asked to see the medals?'

Julian shook his head. 'Why would he have hopped it, without picking up his wages?'

'If you're wrong, and it wasn't Arthur, there's someone very dangerous around who knows everything there is to know about this prison.'

Julian smiled sympathetically. 'If I were you, with women

prisoners to take care of and women officers, I'd worry too. We haven't stopped investigating. You may be able to help us, Nell. Talk to the nurse, Theresa Carreras. She was at the cottage every day. We can't get anything out of her. She point-blank refused to go round the cottage with the sergeant to say whether anything was missing. If we press her too hard, she bursts into tears. She'll talk to you. She'll tell you something without meaning to.'

'I intend to talk to Theresa, because she is one of my officers and going through a difficult time.'

Julian stood. 'Thanks for your help. You'll have your visitors' block back. Within twenty-four hours, we'll find Arthur Burnett and be out of your hair. You're right. Burnett doesn't seem the hitman type. But he is someone who could easily find himself in trouble with powerful people who are smarter than he is. When that happens, there's a price to pay, a job to do that will clear the debt. Burnett may have been paid. He may have been coerced.'

'So these powerful people dropped Arthur off, let him get on with the job, and then came back to drive him home?'

'You make a good devil's advocate, Nell.'

'If they're so evil and so determined, Arthur's not alive.'

'There were two sightings. Arthur was seen thumb ing lifts.'

'There are always sightings. For a missing cat there are half a dozen different sightings.'

'Nell, be careful. Try to look like a headmistress of a school for naughty girls who stick chewing gum on the bedpost.'

She laughed. 'I'll do that when you dress as a lollipop man and guide schoolkids over the zebra crossing.'

'What is it you want me to do, Nell?'

Nell could not say that she wanted to help solve the major's murder because of the sinking feeling that her arrival and the major's willingness to talk to her was linked to his death.

'Let me into the cottage to look for the diaries. Bring in dog handlers and a team to search the premises for the body of Arthur Burnett.'

'I can't let you into the cottage – it's now part of a murder scene. We don't have any dogs available, and that's the truth.'

'Then let me bring someone in from the Prison Service. I'm on good terms with one of the dog handlers at Armley. If he's free, I'm sure he'll bring his dog across.'

'I have no objection to that.'

Twenty

Nell let herself into the education block. Having got Julian's agreement to a dog search, she still wanted to think about Arthur. Could she be wrong? She had never met the man. Perhaps he had been a bigger criminal than police records showed.

She walked along the corridor to the workroom, tapped on the door and entered to the sound of music from the radio. Chief Officer Markham was at her desk. She stood and so did the residents. They were wearing the borstal boys' bib and braces overalls.

'As you were,' Nell said. 'I'd like to see how you're getting on.'

The chief walked Nell across the room to where Olga and Linda were seated at either end of a long table. 'Tell the governor what you're doing.'

Nell sensed relief at a break in the monotony. Olga held up a small flat wooden spoon and a paper packet. 'I'm putting the spoon in the packet to go in the ice cream tub that you buy when you go to the pictures, ma'am.'

'Good work,' Nell said.

Her mind was working overtime. If Julian was right, and someone sent Arthur Burnett to kill Governor Harding, they'd chosen the right person. The major had trusted Arthur completely.

Nell moved on to see what Linda was doing. With a narrow brush, Linda stroked glue onto the back of a small satin pad with a design of anemones in a vase. She pressed the pad onto a card that said Happy Birthday. 'I'm sticking these onto greetings cards, ma'am. It has to be exactly centre.'

Nell said, 'And it is exactly centre. They're pretty cards. You've quite a pile there. Well done.'

On the other hand, Nell thought, as she walked towards Diane and the sewing machine, these powerful people that Julian had in mind could also have chosen the wrong person. Arthur may have said yes under duress, but would he be able to pull the trigger? He seemed more the type to throw down the gun, run for it and leave the job to someone else.

Diane machined to the end of a seam and stopped. 'I'm making cushion covers for Woolworths, ma'am. The exciting part will be when we stuff the cushions, ready for a Woolies shoplifter to pick one and stick it up their jumper.'

Nell smiled. 'You're doing a good job, Diane.'

Diane had been convicted of storing contraband alcohol and cigarettes in her cellar, costing her two years of her life. Hull was the connection between Diane and Arthur. Hull, where there would be theft from the docks. Nell suddenly wanted to ask Diane what exactly she had been storing in her cellar, not just this time but on the previous occasions when she was let off with a fine. But that would not be an appropriate question.

The fly press had two balls on top that moved back and

forth, constantly thud-thudding as Cherry pulled a lever every second, causing the press to create round metal discs that fell into a box. Cherry was silently crying. Black mascara streaked her cheeks. She let her arm drop. 'No need to ask me what I'm doing, ma'am. I'm going slowly and quietly mad, that's what I'm doing. It begins with a drift into despair and choked screams that make my jaws ache.'

Cherry had embroidered her bib overalls with a daisy. She wore a colourful belt around her middle. Nell knew that feeling of despair. She said, 'I like what you've done with your outfit, Cherry.'

Oddly enough, this remark wasn't met with derision. 'I'm thinking a cherry should be my trademark, ma'am. Obvious really, isn't it? Either a cherry or a ball and chain.'

'A trademark is a good idea. You'd need to patent it, make sure no one else has exactly the same design.'

'The Beatles have Apple, I'll have handcuffs hung with cherries, and to blazes with anyone who makes a joke of it. That's if I ever get out of here with my brain intact.'

'You will.'

Cherry had been sentenced to three years for bringing five pounds of cannabis into the country. Her defence had been that cannabis was harmless and that the money was to set up her business. That did not weigh in her favour with the judge.

The chief officer glanced at the clock on the wall. 'All change!'

Cherry was still crying when she took over the machining of cushions for Woolworths. Olga moved towards the fly press with grim determination. Linda wiped a dab of glue from her fingers before moving along to the ice cream spoons. Diane took Linda's place.

Nell said, 'You're all doing well. You need an income, the prison needs an income. Keep up the good work.'

The thudding of the fly press, the hum of the sewing machine, and music on the radio enabled Nell and the chief to speak without being heard.

'Has Cherry been crying long?' Nell asked.

'She'll get over it. It's the boredom and utter misery. Operating the fly press numbs the brain. We do it for a small engineering company. There was a job to finish a couple of weeks back. Some of the lads would have done overtime, but there was a boxing match. I decided to put in a couple of hours myself. When I looked at the clock, thinking that's got to be an hour, it was seven minutes. I move the girls on every thirty minutes. Wouldn't suit a time and motion consultant, but it breaks the monotony and protects sanity.'

'You're doing the best you can,' Nell said.

'A little money is better than no money, and a good report for a prisoner counts towards remission. That's what I tell them.'

'Let's see if we can find a way for Cherry to be making use of her talents before they atrophy. It's not rehabilitation if we don't teach new skills, or if we allow the skills someone has to rust over.'

'Cherry got all the sewing machines working again. Sometimes serious tedium can spark creativity. I'm trying to interest her in enrolling on a business course so that she'll find legitimate ways of financing herself and won't have to start from scratch when she leaves here.'

Diane's hand shot up. 'Permission to make the cocoa, miss?'

It was nearly time for the break.

'Yes, go ahead, Diane.'

Nell waited until Diane and the others had gone to the kitchen and she was alone with Chief Officer Markham. 'HQ are sending us a counsellor. She'll arrive today.'

'Yes, I heard from a neighbour in the village, Mrs Shannon. She does bed and breakfast. Elaine McArthur is booked in there.'

'Daisy will set up a room for her. Will you make sure everyone who wants to see her has an appointment?'

'Yes. Will you want counselling yourself, ma'am?'

'No.'

'Me neither, but I think it could be helpful for Kit, Daisy and Crofty. It's sunk in for the residents, too. There was nervousness this morning, and questions about what was going on.'

'Then I'm glad she's coming.'

The chief brought out a flask. 'I stay in here when the residents take their break. The doors are locked. They're free to talk about us if they've no better subject.'

'There's something I've been meaning to ask you, Chief.'

The chief turned off the radio.

Nell said, 'I've been thinking about the bottle of whisky you retrieved from the pond. Do you have any idea who it was for?'

Markham took a moment to answer. She poured tea into the flask top and a cup. 'I have a strong suspicion.'

'I've put you on the spot.'

Markham nodded. 'I can't be certain, but I think it was for the gateman.'

'Sam Reeves?' Nell was surprised. He was the one who seemed so keen on security being observed.

'Not Sam. Bernie Webster. I check various places every

day. The few times I've found a bottle in the pond have been when Bernie was coming on duty. Once I spotted that pattern – if you can call it a pattern – I got up early and went to the pond before 5 a.m. Whoever puts the bottle there does it at night. Someone is evading the night patrol, or the patrol turns a blind eye.'

'Have you told anyone?'

'I told the major. He said he would look into it. But of course, it's the whisky he drinks, or drank.'

Nell had noticed the brand when pouring the major a glass of sherry, on the morning of their first and last meeting.

'You could have told the inspection team of your suspicions.'

'I should have.'

'Why didn't you?' Nell already knew the answer. People who had served in the forces together had the same kind of loyalty as police, and prison officers. Sometimes that loyalty was misplaced.

'The major and I went through the war together. I couldn't give him up. There was so little to go on that I put off confronting him. You're perfectly entitled to report me. I had no proof of wrongdoing at the time, only a strong suspicion that someone was bringing in contraband. I let the inspectorate know in one of those subtle ways. My suspect was transferred, watched, and has now gone.'

'Horace Thompson?' Nell asked, remembering the name given to her by Bert Hastings.

'Yes. I didn't want to turn the major's world upside down. If he had turned a blind eye in exchange for payment in kind, and was found out, he would have been dismissed and lost his pension. I'm telling you now because you asked me. You are asking the right questions. That may mean you'll get to the bottom of it, if there's still something going on. I like to think it's over and that the major just happened to have a couple of bottles left. If I can help, I will.'

Nell wished there was nothing to get to the bottom of. There wasn't a prison in the country that didn't have a certain number of holes where something slipped through. Whatever had been going on would come to a natural end, or she would end it, with a new intake of staff, with careful monitoring. She would schedule that security meeting and grill Sam Reeves as to whether he had any doubts about the honesty of his fellow gateman. All that seemed possible.

What made Nell uneasy was the direction of Julian McHale's investigation, putting a call out instead of searching the area in case Arthur had gone into hiding, or paid a high price for his involvement with powerful people. 'Chief, what do you make of Arthur Burnett?'

'He's torn. He wants to be a city slicker scrap merchant, but every attempt ends in failure. He finds himself at the bottom of the heap. This is where he once felt secure. For the first time in his life, he won prizes.' She straightened the papers on her desk. 'If the police are saying the major was murdered — and he really would not have killed himself — Arthur would make the perfect dupe.'

Twenty-One

Nell went to the visitors' block to make her telephone call. She did not want Daisy or anyone else to overhear.

With luck, her fears were groundless. Arthur was alive and well, driving around the countryside in a van, pulling a trailer, wearing a new cap. She wished she had met him, this rare creature who made a borstal his bolthole in the way some wealthy figure might retreat to a country cottage or a family to their seaside caravan.

She realised that the sense of foreboding she felt might have nothing to do with whether Arthur was alive or dead. It was just as likely to be connected to the dark cloud that had shadowed her since she discovered the major's body.

Julian was looking for Arthur alive, and hoping to find him. Nell would look for Arthur's body, and hope *not* to find him. Chief Officer Markham had swayed her by saying that Arthur would be the perfect dupe, the fall guy for the major's murder. Arthur was no genius, but everyone over the age of ten must understand the importance of not leaving fingerprints at the scene of a crime. Arthur's prints were on the drawer where the revolver was kept, and on the box containing the major's medals. A murderer would have taken greater care, wouldn't he?

Make the call, she told herself, before you change your mind and before trails go cold, or the rains come.

Armley jail had its own dog handlers, guard dogs, search dogs. The one person she knew well, from the prison officers' darts team, was Jimmy Staples, still under training. When she was saying goodbye to everyone, he told her that he was looking for the chance to work with his dog in different situations. Asking Jimmy to come would avoid red tape and save egg on her face if this turned out to be a completely wild idea. She picked up the phone and dialled.

Nell caught Jimmy Staples on his break. He had been putting his dog through its paces in the prison yard. Yes, he would love to come. This was just what his dog needed. Nell took down the number of his van. 'Come to the main gate. You'll be expected. Turn right, pass the cottage, go to the top and park near the farm.'

Nell did not let herself think too hard about this decision. Julian had agreed. As to HQ, Nell was in charge at Brackerley. A person was not appointed governor so that she would begin pleading for guidance to people who were hundreds of miles away from the action. They needed to know, but they needed to know afterwards, when there was something to report.

She went to see Bernie on the gate and gave him Jimmy's registration number. The arrival of the Armley dog van was now part of the police inquiry. No one need know that she had initiated it.

As Nell walked back towards the house, Sergeant Ambrose appeared at the door of the visitors' block.

'I've brought statements for signing, ma'am, including your own, and I'm hoping to interview your nurse, Miss Carreras. She wasn't up to talking to us yesterday.'

'Have you spoken to our admin officer?'

'Yes, she's expecting me with the statements. Apparently, she wasn't able to contact Miss Carreras on the telephone earlier.'

'I'll come in and sign my statement now. I'm going back to the office, so I'll speak to Officer Meadowcroft. She'll arrange for the officers to come and sign. Once that's done, I'll bring Miss Carreras to talk to you.'

'Thank you, ma'am.'

Nell spoke with more confidence than she felt. Everyone was subdued and a little dazed from the shock of the major's death. Daisy had dialled wrong numbers. Jeff had rallied by the time the borstal boys left, but when he had come by first thing asking what he could do to help, he'd looked as if he hadn't slept.

When Nell had read and signed her statement, she went into the office. Daisy looked up as she entered. 'Ma'am, I was hoping to speak to you. The Citizens' Advice Bureau offered a couple of dates for an adviser to look through Olga's documents with her. I took the first date. It will be a matter of putting the papers into some sort of order. Holloway has forwarded the other documents. Catcher has talked to Olga and read the neighbour's letter to her about the bailiffs and her locks being changed.'

'Catcher?'

'Sorry, you haven't heard. Olga's personal officer, Betsy Friel – we nicknamed her Catcher because she set lots of mouse traps.'

Nell felt a slight pang of regret. She had done the right thing in asking for Friel to be transferred because she was too close to her charges, but Friel had much going for her. She had been brought up on a farm. She could catch mice. She liked the dog.

'Did Catcher say whether the letter upset Olga?'

'Apparently not very much. Catcher has a way of putting a good gloss on things. Once Olga knew she would have an adviser, she cheered up. She has the deeds to her house, and that seems to her the main thing.'

'Daisy, Sergeant Ambrose is here with statements to be signed.'

'I'll let people know. Jeff had better be first. He'll be setting off for Durham soon.'

'Try and get people across in the next half hour, to check through their statements and sign. The sergeant will then be interviewing Theresa. Have you spoken to her?'

Daisy answered using Theresa's nickname. 'Florence rang in first thing to say she would be late. She's feeling unwell. I rang a little while ago to see if she needed anything, but no answer. Shall I try again?'

'No. I'll go across there. If anything crops up, that's where I'll be, or in the visitors' block.'

There was a low whine from under Daisy's desk. Pip emerged.

Daisy said, 'He doesn't know what to do with himself and I don't know what to do with him. He's taken to Catcher. She brought the residents back to the education block after their look round the farm. Now she's gone back up there to plan out next week's work with the farm manager.'

Nell picked up the lead from behind the door. 'I'll take him with me.'

The dog trotted happily enough beside Nell as she walked the few hundred yards to the hospital block. She rang the doorbell and waited. The nurse had been so very upset last night that it was worrying. Nell had not yet got to know Florence, who had sat quietly during the brief staff meeting on Monday morning, speaking only to complain about HQ not supplying her with a female anatomical drawing for her surgery. Florence was plump, with a round pleasant face and at thirty-five years old, more than twenty-five years younger than the major.

When Florence did not appear, Nell let herself in through the main door, locking it behind her. Ahead of her was a door marked 'private' that led to the flat. To the right was a door to the waiting area and surgery. Nell unlocked the 'private' door and climbed the stairs.

Nell knocked on the door of the flat. When there was no answer, she knocked again.

After a few moments, Florence opened the door. She wore a red dressing gown with beige spots, her face flushed, nostrils pink from blowing her nose, her eyes red. Nell felt a surge of pity. The nurse's right cheek blazed. Nell pictured her lying on her side, curled up, hugging her pillow and crying.

'Hello. May I come in?'

Florence looked at Nell and then down at the dog. 'I'm in a mess, ma'am. The flat's in a mess.' She bent down and patted Pip's head.

Nell said, 'The flat doesn't matter. You do. I need to talk to you. Do you prefer Theresa or Florence?'

'They all call me Florence.' She opened the door to the sitting room. 'You have the chair, ma'am.'

Nell sat down.

Florence sat on a small sofa and patted the cushion next to her. Pip jumped up. 'I sometimes took Pip for a walk.' She spoke to the dog. 'I can't take you, Pip. You don't belong in a medical block and you'd be too much of a reminder of my stupidity.' She sniffed and wiped her nose.

Nell said, 'We all hate being reminded of our stupidity. That's a big load to put on a little dog.'

'That's the thing about animals. If you say something nicely, they think you are saying something nice. It's not what you say, it's how you say it, eh Pip?'

'Am I allowed to ask what particular stupidity he reminds you of? Because I wouldn't put you and "stupidity" in the same breath.'

'You might as well know, ma'am. Others do. In a novel, the Governor and the Nurse would be a lovely tale. In life, it was a kind of madness.'

Nell thought it probably was, but she was here for a reason. 'I'd be glad to listen, if it helps to talk.'

'But that's not why you're here?'

'You need to speak to Sergeant Ambrose. We mustn't hold up the investigation.'

'I couldn't.'

'You couldn't last night, but you can now. It will be best to have it over and done with, and we must cooperate with the police.'

'Did he kill himself? I heard someone say there was a gunshot. Because if he did, it's probably my fault. But I don't know. That could be flattering myself.'

'The investigation is still ongoing. Don't torment yourself. Speak to Sergeant Ambrose, answer her questions and she'll answer your questions if she can. Wash your face, comb your hair, put on your uniform and be your Florence Nightingale self.' The uniform was not necessary, but Nell thought that wearing it might help.

Slowly, Florence rose. The dog stayed put.

Nell said, 'I'll ring the visitors' block and tell the sergeant we'll be with her shortly.'

By the time Nell had walked the nurse to the interview, and sat in with her, at Florence's request and with Sergeant Ambrose's agreement, Nell knew more than she would have wished about the ill-starred and unlikely romance. The sergeant listened intently, leaning forward, waiting for what might come next, forgetting she had a pencil in her hand.

Florence had visited the major during his illness, checked his temperature, made sure he took his tablets. He began to improve. After his fall outside the Hare and Hounds, she changed his dressings. He was a man full of stories. Florence loved to listen. She watched the major as he polished his medals and cleaned his gun. He dreamed of retiring to the seaside, though he had not yet put in his thirty years in the Prison Service and was enquiring whether his army service might be counted, qualifying him for a full pension. The age difference between the major and Florence was not so great when two people enjoyed each other's company so very much. They made plans, talked about marrying. They went to Filey on a fine day. Nell wondered whether a rainy day might have altered the course of love.

The major would stop drinking when he, Florence and Pip could walk by the sea. They could go fishing. The major's sister Meg found a cottage. Florence bought a car. She was too young to retire, but there were hospitals along the coast she could apply to.

Over Easter week, things began to change, to go wrong. The son arrived at Brackerley, Fred the one-man band, who was Florence's age. He was put up at the farm. Some of Fred's mother's jewellery went missing. The major decided Fred ought to come to Filey, too. They could go out fishing together. It would keep Fred from bad company and smoking weed. A bigger place was needed, such as a bungalow. Florence should have her name on the deeds, they would buy it together, going fifty fifty, and there would be room for Fred, and for Florence's mother if she wanted to visit.

That was when Florence decided her mother was right when she said, 'He's an old man. He wants a nurse and a purse, and he's picked on you.'

Florence saw her pipe dream floating away. She was sad, rather than angry Through habit, she still visited, listened to the major's stories - now for the second, third or fourth time – and slowly realised that he was unlikely to stop drinking. For reasons she could not explain, she continued to do some of his shopping, when he could have put in an order over the telephone. The anger came when, on the afternoon of the day he died, Florence called, thinking she must soon let him down about their plans, but dutifully bringing his tablets. He had been sitting outside in the morning while some cleaning went on. When Florence arrived, he was indoors, at the table, polishing his medals and cleaning his gun, being careful with the polish because he had on his good suit. That evening, he would be going out to supper with his deputy. 'With you, ma'am,' Florence added, in case Nell should be in doubt.

He had never once treated Florence to a meal. When it was her birthday, he wanted her to have a pearl necklace. She would not accept it because it had belonged to his wife.

Sergeant Ambrose listened patiently, and with an occasional look of sympathetic understanding. When Florence's testimony came to an end, the sergeant asked, 'What time was it when you arrived at the cottage, Miss Carreras?'

'One o'clock. I took sandwiches.'

'What time did you leave?'

'Twenty-five past one. I took both sandwiches with me.'

'Because?'

'Because I was annoyed.'

'Do you have an address for the son, Fred Harding?'

'He squats,' Florence said, then immediately clarified: 'Not the kind of lowering himself onto his haunches squat. He and his friends move into empty houses and consider that a political statement.'

'You say the major was cleaning his gun?'

'Yes.'

'Where was the gun when you left?'

'On the table.'

'Did he ask you to put the gun back in its place for him?'

'No.'

'Did he ask you to return the medals to their place?'

'No. They were still on the table too.'

'Was anything said before you left? You were upset, I think, that he had never taken you to supper.'

'Yes. But I didn't kill him.'

'No.'

'I told him that he and his dog and his son could go to Filey on their own. I told him that we now had female prisoners for me to take care of and that making facilities suitable and getting in the correct supplies was taking a lot of my time. I told him that there are nursing agencies in Harrogate and

Ripon. He could call on them for now. When he got to Filey, there'd be some retired nurse who would be glad of a little extra work to supplement her pension. Of course he didn't like that. And he didn't like it when I said that Daisy was run off her feet and here was the telephone number of the Co-op. They would deliver his shopping.' She started to cry. 'I was very cruel.'

'Oh dear,' said Sergeant Ambrose. 'I'm sorry to see you upset. You were very good to him for a long time. Another person might have been more cruel. Another person might have been cruel sooner. Thank you, Miss Carreras, you've been very helpful.'

Florence moved to push back her chair. The sergeant said, 'There is one other thing we'd appreciate your help with.'

Nell watched as Florence almost slumped in her chair. She had psyched herself up for this ordeal. She thought it was done, and now there would be more.

'Miss Carreras, would you be willing to go round the cottage with me, see if anything is out of place, or missing?'

'I can't face that. I won't go back in there.'

'Is there a reason you don't wish to go back in the cottage?'

'Because I was made a fool of, and I made a fool of myself, and I can't bear to think of it, much less look round that place. If I have to walk past there in future, I'll do it with my eyes shut. Ask one of the others.'

'Who do you suggest?'

'Chief Officer Markham shopped for him, so did Daisy. Mrs Ramsden left cakes on the windowsill. I suppose she sometimes went in. When he needed personal help, or help with the stairs, the male officers stepped up — Larry, Crofty, Jeff.'

'Many of the men have left, I believe.' The sergeant picked up her pen. 'I haven't got used to the nicknames. Larry, Crofty and Jeff?'

'Crofty and Jeff, Officers Meadowcroft and Jeffrey. Larry is Officer Bill Lamb, now in Glasgow.'

'Thank you again, Miss Carreras. I have a portable typewriter with me. I will type up your statement now. Where will I find you?'

'Telephone me. I'll answer this time and come to sign.'

They stood to go. Pip looked up at them.

As they went outside, Nell said, 'You did well. You've had a bereavement, not just of the major but the loss of your plans for the future.'

'Oh that! Good riddance.'

'Don't dismiss it. You need time. But you're strong, and you have a lot going for you. You wouldn't have become a nurse otherwise.'

'I'm quite strong,' Florence said, 'but not strong enough to take on P.i.p.' Even though she had spelled his name, the dog looked up. 'Besides, a dog doesn't belong in a hospital wing.'

Nell said, 'He'll come to the house. Do you need to take time off?'

'I will, soon, but I want to be here for the services on Sunday, remembering Governor Harding, before I started to think of him as the major.'

'Don't be lonely, don't be alone. Come over to the house if you'd like to. We can make up a bed. We'll be talking about what we'll do to prepare for the next arrivals. HQ have arranged for a counsellor to come. She'll be arriving this morning. Will you let Daisy or the chief arrange a slot for you?'

'I might do that. It'll save me talking to myself or bending Kit's ear.'

'Good.'

'I meant to ask you, what are your plans for the boys' dormitory, ma'am?'

'To make it or the men's wing suitable for female officers.'

'Ah.'

'What?'

'I thought it might make an excellent mother and baby unit.'

Nell walked Florence back to her door. Here was a woman who had seemed close to falling over the edge, and with cupboards full of poisons available in the surgery. But she was pulling up her socks.

Florence had told all to Sergeant Ambrose. Confession was good for the soul. What was of equal interest to the sergeant and to Nell was that someone else had been at the cottage after Florence, someone who Sergeant Ambrose seemed to think had put away the major's medals and returned his gun to its keeping place. The police would now have a time period during which Arthur Burnett had visited the cottage.

Twenty-Two

Jimmy Staples, tall and broad-shouldered, at twenty-seven the junior member of the dog team, emerged from the van. He had a round face, a ready smile and dark hair with short back and sides.

'I appreciate your coming over, Jimmy.'

'You caught us on a quiet day and it's good training for Samson, ma'am.'

As he called her ma'am, which she still had not got used to, Nell suddenly thought she might never be in a darts team again. That wasn't something a governor did. 'Jimmy, I'm still Nell from the darts team, unless we're visibly on duty.'

'I'll forget. And you'll have to start your own darts team now. Have to get used to your move up the ladder, Nell, ma'am.'

She watched as he opened the van's rear doors. The German Shepherd looked out from a cage. Jimmy opened the cage. The dog came out, wagging its tail.

Jimmy looked down at the German Shepherd with an admiration that was returned in spades.

'What's his name?' Nell asked.

'Samson. He's only eighteen months but he's come on like you wouldn't believe. He's a different dog when he's not on duty, when he comes with me at night. The kids love him.'

Nell walked Jimmy along the drive towards the cottage. 'We're looking for Arthur Burnett, who was working on the farm.' Nell gave a little of Arthur's background, his visit to the governor, the last sighting of him when he had his tea at the farmhouse and sat talking in the barn to Michael and Dave. 'We're going to pick up his scarf, which is on a hook in the cottage doorway, and there's his cap in a barn. I hope Samson may be able to pick up his scent. There's another barn that Arthur may have gone into to take a look at some machinery.'

A thrush flew from the hedge as they reached the cottage. Jimmy stopped on the path. 'A bit of police tape.' He bent down and picked it up.

Nell unlocked the front door. 'That's the scarf Arthur Burnett was wearing when he came to visit the governor.'

'A Hull City supporter.' Jimmy took a pair of gloves from a bag. He reached in for the scarf without stepping across the threshold.

Nell locked the door behind him. 'We'll go to the barn where he slept. There wasn't room in the farmhouse for him.'

They turned back and walked up the drive. 'I heard something on the police wavelength as I was driving over. Is this the man they have a county-wide search for?' asked Jimmy.

'Yes. The police are still here, but they've finished searching the grounds.'

'And you believe he's still here, but you think he's dead.'

'I could be wrong,' Nell said.

'So, it's dead or alive, and who finds him first. Am I breaking any rules by being here?'

'None. You're here at my invitation. Everything that happens in this prison and the grounds is my responsibility, you know that. The investigating officer is DCI Julian McHale. He's glad of your support. Now tell me about Samson and where he's up to in his training.'

Jimmy spoke like a proud parent. 'He can sniff out tobacco. He'll know if someone has booze in a cell. He can follow a scent, hold a prisoner at bay. He's a remarkable dog. I'm lucky to have him. And out of interest, this Arthur that we're looking for, what was he like?'

Nell told Jimmy what she had pieced together about Arthur, his background and his ambitions.

'Sounds to me as if he was on the run from someone in Hull. Got it into his head that he'd feel safe on a prison farm.'

'He left the farm without saying goodbye and without picking up his wages. He didn't have the best start in life and it strikes me that he was . . .' She tried to think how best to describe her impression of the man she had never met.

Jimmy filled in the gap. 'A likeable loser, checks his football coupons every Saturday?'

'I don't doubt it. First out to buy the *Sporting Pink*.'

Jimmy said, 'I'm torn between wanting Samson to have a cadaver experience and wanting Arthur Burnett to be alive and well and watch Hull win.'

They walked in silence for a while. As they came close to the barn where Arthur had slept, Jimmy said, 'What's swaying me to your view is Arthur's sudden disappearance without having collected his wages. But there's another way of looking at it. Arthur found himself in a tight spot with the wrong people. He's given the chance to redeem himself by doing a nasty job. According to the message on the police wavelength, he may be able to help with enquiries into a suspicious death. "Resident of Hull, last seen in . . .", we all know what they're saying.' He shook his head. 'I'm glad I'm with the dog unit.'

'Yes. Good choice.' They reached the barn. 'And this is where he laid his head, up in the hayloft. You should see his cap on a hook. He always wore it, but it was thrown on the barn roof as a joke and then retrieved, so I don't know if that will affect the scent.'

Jimmy went into the barn. 'I'll get the cap and I'll let Samson take a sniff at where Arthur was sleeping.'

'Is there anything you need from me?'

He shook his head. 'Just to be undisturbed. Leave me to it. Give me an hour or so and meet me back here. We'll either find something, or we'll give up.'

Nell walked to the barn where the workshop machinery was stored. She unlocked the padlock and pushed open the doors.

The barn was gloomy, with shafts of light from gaps in the wall and roof. The tough padlock would not have deterred a gang of thieves, but the bulkier, heavy pieces of equipment would. Those machines would need two or three men to shift them. The place smelled of grease and metal. There were twenty items on the inventory and she counted twenty now. Some she recognised, having been given the guided tour by Bert at Armley and Glen at Strangeways. The lathes, saws, presses, milling and drilling equipment looked eerie and abandoned, like monuments to disappeared factory workers. Trying to avoid getting oil on her suit, she stepped carefully between them, a visitor to some strange exhibition of sculptures.

She peered at a crate wedged between the largest lathe and the wall. It was labelled *Spare parts. Drill bits. Spanners.* This was not on the inventory. Such items were usually kept in toolboxes or in drawers or cabinets. Perhaps men did store spare parts and hand tools in a crate, but she had no memory of seeing that. Frustratingly, she could not get to it, not without contortions of bobbing down under the lathe or squeezing through the gap and ruining her suit. Of course the crate might just be full of tools and spare parts, as described. Since Chief Officer Markham had shown her the bottle of whisky from the pond, and she had seen the major with the same uncommon brand, she had wondered who was bringing it onto the premises. There may have been just a couple of bottles. Her suspicion was that someone was using the prison to store contraband whisky and giving out the odd bottle as a sweetener.

As she was about to give up, leave the barn and click the padlock in place, Nell noticed a brown overall hanging on a hook on the back of the door. It was big, it was long enough to cover and protect her skirt. This was madness, but madness that no one would see or know about. She put it on.

Pulling in her stomach, and hoping she would not become stuck, Nell squeezed behind the lathe. It was awkward to get the lid off the crate because of the angle, but her knife helped her to force it. A hessian tool holder lay neatly across the top, its pockets containing spanners, pliers and screwdrivers. Under it was a square of plywood and below that another crate, a crate within a crate. Her suspicions were confirmed when she saw the screw tops of bottles. She lifted a bottle by its neck. It was not whisky but vodka. There might well be just one bad apple who had left this little harvest of vodka behind. Or there could have been a basket of rotten apples providing a stinking windfall across the country in the prisons they had been reassigned to.

Someone at Brackerley must know. Experienced officers like Jeff and Crofty would not leave a crate unopened. Had they really just lifted the lid and thought: Ah, now I'll know where to come for a pair of pliers. If Crofty was involved, so might Daisy be. Jeff had blown the whistle on Horace Thompson. His cohorts had stayed undercover. Bernie the gateman, or even conscientious Sam, might be waving some one through.

Nell set the plywood square and hessian tool pouches back in place and replaced the lid on the crate.

This find, slight as it was, helped Nell make a kind of sense of Deputy Director Barnes's words, 'Sometimes incidents are more complex than they seem'. She had known of very few rotten apples in the Prison Service. Usually they were spotted and either charged or quietly got rid of.

The major might indeed have had interesting revelations for her. If so, why had he not shared his suspicions, or knowledge, with HQ?

The murder of Governor Harding now looked even more sinister, and closer to home.

Twenty-Three

Nell had not spoken to Mrs Ramsden since the night of the major's death when they had gathered to see the ambulance leave. The farmer's wife came to the door when Nell knocked. She had that air of grief after a death that clings to people for days when they have lost someone who has been a big part of their lives. 'Miss Lewis, thank you for calling. Come and sit down, ma'am.'

Nell followed her in. 'I can't stop, but I wanted to see how you are today.'

Mrs Ramsden went back to chopping onions. She gave those wordless sounds and shakes of the head as people sometimes do when a terrible thing has happened and words flit out of reach.

'Shocking,' she came up with. Having found the one word, Mrs Ramsden unloosed a torrent of praise for Governor Harding, distress for his lost future in Filey and the guilt she felt for not having taken him half a dozen fairy cakes last week. As to Arthur, she had known him most of his life and would not hear a word against him.

Nell soothed her. 'I'm sure you did a great deal for the major and he appreciated it. He spoke highly of you and your husband, trusted you entirely.'

'I think he did.'

'Now here's a little bit of positive news. The residents have settled in. Officer Friel worked on a farm. She brought the women up this morning to take a look round and she's talking to your foreman about what needs doing next week. Tomorrow morning, Officer Friel will be here with a work party.'

'Well that's something.'

As she was leaving, Nell said, 'Mrs Ramsden, you might see a prison officer dog handler putting a German Shepherd through its paces. The dog is in training. It's a young dog and easily distracted. We're asked to give handler and dog a wide berth.'

Jimmy Staples was waiting in the barn, seated on a pile of pallets, smoking a fag. Samson lay on the ground beside him. Jimmy stood when Nell came in. He took one more drag on his cigarette, dropped it and crushed the tab under his foot.

'Our man Arthur slept up there.' He jerked his thumb towards the ladder that led to the upper part of the barn. 'There's a sleeping bag. Arthur found a comfortable spot, quiet.'

The dog watched Jimmy, ready for action.

'Is that it?' Nell asked.

'Samson went to the farmhouse and back, several times. He crossed to a field, up and down between rows of vegetables, towards your building, but coming to a stop by a cottage. There's a copse half a mile behind the farmhouse. He picked up Arthur's scent there, too. He was reluctant to leave that spot, but I could see nothing to suggest a shallow grave.'

Jimmy was being annoyingly tantalising. 'Have you found anything?' Nell asked.

'I don't know.' He nodded towards the dog. 'He thinks so, but he would. There's a place Samson went a bit mad over, but we could end up with red faces.'

'No one's looking at our faces.'

'Like I said, he hasn't done any cadaver work before. He went in for a fair bit of scratching.'

Nell felt glad that she had not been successful in persuading Julian that Arthur was still here. If he had brought in dogs and handlers and drawn a blank, he would have had a lot of explaining to do. His only enjoyment would have been to say, I told you so.

Jimmy spoke quietly to the dog. He picked up an evidence bag that contained Arthur's cap, opened it, and let Samson take a sniff. The dog wagged its tail. Jimmy clicked on Samson's lead.

They left the barn and cut across a path. Nell thought that they were going to the perimeter, but the dog led them to a tree and came to a halt.

'I think Arthur took a slash there. We're straight on again now.'

Either the afternoon silence began to hum, or Nell's anticipation created a buzz in her brain. A light breeze ruffled the leaves of an oak tree. She wondered about the lives of the family who had lived here and whether they came to sit under the shade of this tree on a sunny day. Ahead of them was another brick wall. That'll be it, Nell thought. We'll hit a brick wall.

They had arrived at the walled garden, but from a different angle.

'This is the work end of the garden,' Jimmy said. 'The builder didn't bother to make an arch, just straight up and down. The back way in is wide enough for a big wheelbarrow.'

Beyond the entrance was a wild area of garden with buttercups, daisies and dandelions.

Samson began to pull on the lead.

'What's that stench?' Nell asked.

'Fertiliser. Wait here, please.'

Nell watched the pair walk towards a shed. For several minutes, they were out of sight, beyond the shed. The minutes stretched. Nell was tempted to take a few more steps, but she stayed put.

It could not have been more than five minutes, she thought as she looked at her watch, but the wait seemed endless.

When Jimmy came back, he seemed subdued. 'There are two sheds, same size, with a space between. They must have erected one shed, realised it wasn't big enough and put up another. The space behind interests Samson, a muck-spreading spot. He's sure he's found something.'

'You're not sure, Jimmy?'

'No. There's a full bag of fertiliser between the sheds and one that's toppled over.'

'You think that might have been done deliberately, to deter anyone from taking a closer look at what lies beneath?'

'Could be. If someone has done for Arthur, they may have dug a hole first, putting him here for now, re-burying him later. If so, that could backfire. Someone might just shovel up the fertiliser into their wheelbarrow.' He scratched his head. 'I'm thinking about a lecture I attended. Wait here, please.

I've thought of something obvious. If it is what we suspect, the area needs to be approached systematically. But there is a simple test I can do. Stay, Samson!' The dog sat down beside Nell. Jimmy took a trowel and a carton from his canvas bag. He walked off towards the sheds.

Nell knew that this was as far as they could go. The next step would be to report the strong suspicion to Julian. That's all it was, a strong suspicion for Nell and Jimmy, a dead cert for Samson the trainee dog.

Would a spot by the sheds be a perfect meeting place for Arthur and the man he was to do a deal with? A bit cloak-and-dagger, Nell thought. Why not the bar at the Hare and Hounds? But if Arthur was dead, and that was a big assumption, whoever killed him knew his way about. Her idea that Arthur was still here suddenly seemed mad. Julian, his DI, even his sergeant would have thought of that. Arthur was not a big-time gangster who could bring illicit alcohol across by night. He'd thumbed lifts to get here.

Nell felt cold and out of her depth. She was wrong, and Julian was right. Perhaps Arthur's stories about his big plans were a smokescreen and he was hiding from someone who wanted him dead.

Jimmy came back. He patted Samson's head. 'I'm putting my bet on you, lad.'

'What clinches it?' Nell asked.

'I lifted some of the fertiliser that looked as if it had been spilled across that area of ground. The fertiliser had raised the ground, but the elevation was there, beneath the fertiliser. When someone buries a body in a shallow grave, they're putting back the soil they took out. Come and take a look.'

Nell walked with him across the grass. He led the way to

the sheds, and the mound of earth. Jimmy said, 'I'll need to call this in.'

'You better come to my office. I have to telephone DCI McHale.'

Jimmy pursed his lips and made a quiet whistle. 'He's going to love me, marching over his patch with my dog.'

'Will you put Samson back in the van and come with me?' The sooner Jimmy and his dog were off the premises the better, and the less chance of his being spotted by whoever had been digging and spreading. The scene needed to be kept clear until the exhumation could begin.

'I can radio in from the van, and then it's straight back for me. I'll report to my boss. He'll pass it on,' said Jimmy.

Nell was reluctant to move. She wanted certainty, and perhaps there could be no certainty.

Jimmy also stayed put. 'We won't know until we take a proper look.'

'I've put you on the spot.' Nell was certain. She was uncertain. Investigating was not her job. Everything that happened at Brackerley, its grounds, its farm was her responsibility, but this was out of her control.

Jimmy was subdued. 'The mound could be there because of something else. But the ground has been newly turned.'

The dog looked from one to the other of them.

Nell said, 'We are taking the word, the whine, the bark and the sureness of an eighteen-month-old canine.'

Jimmy's spontaneous laugh broke the silence. 'Sorry,' he said. 'It just came out when I thought—'

'What?' Nell asked.

'If we're wrong, and all we've got is a pile of fertiliser behind sheds, this incident could dog our careers.'

Nell couldn't help but laugh. A person could work quietly and efficiently for decades until one false move became the marker for their career. 'That's terrible. What a shocking pun.'

Jimmy scratched his head. 'It's just a pun then, not a prospective blight on your and my records?'

Nell tried to make light of this glimpse into a possible future of being a figure of fun, of being squeezed out, the person who made the wrong call. She said, 'People would hardly give it a thought, except at staff reviews, promotion panels, nights out, Christmas dos and our retirement parties.'

'No gold watch then.' Jimmy handed Arthur's bagged cap to Nell. 'DCI McHale will want this. He'll notice something sewn under the lining. It might be Arthur's emergency fiver.'

'I wouldn't have had Arthur down as the sewing type.'

'You'd be surprised. My dad learned to knit in the army.'

They were still rooted to the spot when there was a sound from the direction of the garden, and a voice, saying, 'Hey up! Who's this then?'

Nell turned to see a man in a baggy jumper and old tweed trousers pushing a wheelbarrow. 'You must be Miss Lewis,' he said.

'Yes.'

'Duncan Reeves, ma'am. You've met my brother, Sam. I'm your gardener.'

'Of course.' They shook hands. Nell did the introductions. 'Jimmy Staples, dog handler, and Samson, dog in training.'

'What does he find so interesting about my fertiliser?' Duncan asked.

Nell explained. 'He thinks something is buried there.'

Duncan laughed. 'Bit more training needed then. I'll be

202

mixing that pile of soil with the fertiliser and spreading it on the vegetable patch. I'd left it for Arthur to do. He was helping me yesterday, but he's done a disappearing act so I'm on my own again.'

So, Arthur had been here. Nell exchanged a look with Jimmy. 'We'll let you get on then, Duncan. I'm glad we bumped into each other. I was hoping to meet you soon.'

Duncan touched his cap. 'Any of your new ladies interested in gardening?'

'I'm sure they will be. One would have difficulty kneeling.'

'She'd suit the greenhouse. There's pots to be attended.' He began to shovel the earth and fertiliser into the wheelbarrow.

There was a second wheelbarrow and spade by the shed. Jimmy said, 'While we have a re-think, let me give you a hand. It was a bit of luck meeting you. Always speak to the locals.'

'Thanks, son.' Duncan paused and watched Jimmy shovel the earth. 'By you're quick. If you ever fancy a change of career, come and see me.' He wheeled off Jimmy's barrow.

Sergeant Ambrose appeared, out of breath. 'Here you are, I've been looking for you, ma'am.'

'What's up, sergeant?'

'Ma'am, we're expecting a visit from the chief superinten-dent. He specially asked to talk to you. He'll be asking what we've found. The DCI will bring him up to speed.' She looked at Jimmy and the dog. 'Anything to report?'

Jimmy kept his lips tight shut.

'Sergeant Ambrose, this is officer Jimmy Staples from Armley. Your person of interest, Arthur Burnett, was at this spot. Your DCI has authorised continuing the search of the grounds and buildings with the help of HMP Armley dog unit. There's full cooperation between the police and the Prison Service. Ring my office when the chief superintendent arrives.'

'Thank you, ma'am.' She sped off.

As Sergeant Ambrose left, Duncan the gardener returned with an empty barrow and a hopeful look.

Feeling sorry for the elderly gardener, Jimmy filled the barrow. Duncan pushed off with it.

'Come on, Jimmy,' Nell said. 'We can do better than this.'

She led man and dog through the walled garden, coming out opposite the cottage. 'The cottage is out of bounds. I'll unlock the male officers' quarters, the boys' dormitory and the gymnasium. Let Samson have a free run in there, before he gets bored.'

'Has Arthur been in any of those buildings?'

'I doubt it, but the chief superintendent isn't going to know that. You're searching the premises. Treat it as practice for Samson.'

'How do I contact you?' asked Jimmy.

'There are internal phones in all the buildings. If you need me, dial 01.'

'And I won't be giving up just yet,' Jimmy said. 'After I've checked the buildings, I'll take the path Arthur walked. It leads to a wood. That'll be worth a look.'

Twenty-Four

Back in her office, Nell looked at Arthur's well-worn tweed cap. It had been a good one, perhaps old enough to have belonged to Arthur's dad. A maker's label said Pure Wool. There was something under the lining. It had been tacked in with the sort of big stitches a sewing mistress would instruct her pupils to pull out and do again because it was sloppy work.

Nell always kept a pair of nail scissors handy. She disliked having a broken nail and had learned to be ambidextrous as far as cutting her own fingernails. She opened her bag, took out the nail scissors, made a snip and pulled out the thread.

She withdrew a yellowing newspaper cutting, undated and without the name of the paper.

TRAGIC ACCIDENT
A twelve-year-old Hull boy fell to his death late yesterday afternoon while playing in a bombed-out house in the Bankside area. He was with a group of children who made this particular spot their den. The boy's family have been informed.

When was this, Nell wondered, and who was the boy? Perhaps a relative. How sad for Arthur. Or perhaps Arthur had a son. But that didn't seem right. The paper was so yellowed. A bombed-out building would have been demolished and cleared by the time Arthur would have had a twelve-year-old child. Perhaps the boy was Arthur's brother, cousin or friend. Arthur would have been too young to take cuttings from a newspaper. Someone else had done it and saved the cutting. Nell's grandmother used to do the same. Nell had Grandma's old dictionary, the pages stuffed with newspaper items: a two-year-old baby stuck in a chimney pot in a back garden, a wild man of the woods, a case of paratyphoid in Mirfield. There was never a date on Grandma's cuttings either.

Arthur's cutting was personal, and important. There must have been a follow-up article. Nell took out a couple more stitches, to see if she had missed a bit of paper. There was nothing.

This called for some archive research, looking back through Hull newspapers. Nell knew someone who could help with that: the daughter she was so proud of. The daughter she could not claim. She checked her watch. Roxana's journalist boss started work late and went home early. Roxana worked until 5.30. There was a good chance she would be in the office alone. This was just the kind of thing she would be able to check by visiting the British Library. The unnamed boy was twelve. Arthur would have been twelve in 1947. Playing out was an all-year-round thing, but more likely kids would be out in the summertime, perhaps during the long school holiday.

Nell rarely rang Roxana at work. She took out her address book and looked up the number.

She dialled.

Roxana picked up on the second ring.

'Roxy, are you on your own? It's Auntie Nell.'

'I know it's Auntie Nell, you don't have to say!'

'How are you?'

'Bored out of my skull, but I'm off to the pictures tonight with a girl from along the corridor. How's your new job going?'

'Very well. I'll tell you all about it when we meet.'

Roxy laughed. 'You will not, you never do. You've signed the Official Secrets Act.'

'Then you'll be pleased to know I have a top-secret research job for you.'

'Go on, I have my pencil in hand.'

'I want you to visit the British Library to locate a short article from a Hull newspaper, most likely an evening paper. I don't have an exact date, but it's likely to be during the summer months between 1945 and 1948. To narrow it down, my best guess would be July or August 1947. It will be on an inside page or the Stop Press column.'

'OK, fire away.'

'It's one paragraph beginning, "A twelve-year-old Hull boy fell to his death late yesterday afternoon while playing in a bombed-out house in the Bankside area."'

'Oh, poor boy. How sad.'

'The boy isn't named. His name must have been withheld, but it's bound to have been released a few days later. I'd like his name, the dates, and names of the friends if they're mentioned.'

'I'll be there when the library opens in the morning. Next time you're in London, you can treat me to a meal at Veeraswamy.'

'You're on!'

'You might tell me what this is all about, but most likely you won't.'

'There'll be a day when I ask you to research something cheerful. Thank you.'

'Happy to help, Governor!'

Nell did not correct her. The title of governor must now be hers, but the joy had gone out of it.

The internal phone buzzed. Nell picked up. 'Deputy Governor.'

'Nell, Julian. Our chief superintendent will be here within half an hour. Obviously, he wants to see you right after I've given him an update. Do you want me to direct him to your office?'

'I'll come across to the visitors' block. Oh and the dog handler has started searching the buildings.'

'Good. The chief super will be pleased to know that.'

The phone buzzed again before Nell got out of the door. She picked up and answered.

'Nell, it's Jimmy. You better come and lock the doors.'

'Where are you?'

'In the gymnasium.' Jimmy's voice was anxious, as if he was out of breath, or being chased.

'Are you all right?'

'I am, but there's something you need to see. Come now.'

His sense of urgency made Nell decide to prioritise Jimmy and Samson over the chief superintendent. She could be down and back to the gymnasium in five minutes.

She picked up her key pouch and went out of the office, locking the door behind her, pausing only to tell Daisy where she was going.

Jimmy was standing in the gymnasium doorway. The only light came from the overhead windows. Samson, standing to attention by the boxing ring, kept his eyes on his master.

'Over here,' Jimmy said. 'It's made me feel a bit sick. I wasn't expecting this, not here.'

Jimmy had put on gloves. Feeling a sense of dread, Nell followed Jimmy to the boxing ring and round to the other side. Why is it called a ring, Nell wondered, when it's square?

Jimmy knelt down. He slid a panel aside and shone his torch into the space below the boxing ring. 'There's got to be ten thousand cigarettes in there. This is dynamite.'

Nell felt slightly dizzy. She had prepared herself for the sight of Arthur Burnett's body. 'Close the panel.'

'What do we do now?' Jimmy asked.

'We go out, I lock the door. I have to meet the chief superintendent. You go on searching the other buildings, as if we've drawn a blank here.'

'We don't talk to the police chief superintendent about this?'

'Absolutely not. The chief superintendent is here to make sure my staff and I have all the support we need, and feel safe. The cigarettes, well that's first and foremost a Prison Service matter. Let me work out how to deal with this. I'll need to report confidentially. We'll put on our best thinking caps.'

'I don't have one. That dog's cleverer than me.' He signalled to Samson, who came across and waited for his lead to be clipped on.

Nell looked left and right at the door. 'Coast's clear. Come on!'

She locked the door behind them.

*

Nell later decided that it was a blessing to have the Prison Service counsellor, the chief superintendent and the coroner's officer all arrive within forty-five minutes of each other. She was able to accept condolences from the chief superintendent, reassure him she had all the necessary support, and thank him for providing extra security. She welcomed the counsellor and gave her a cup of tea before introducing the chaplain and chief officer. The hardest part was going with the coroner's officer to the cottage back garden and giving her account of finding Governor Harding's body.

It was a relief to be able to go back and find Jimmy.

He had brought his van from the farm end of the grounds and was parked on the drive, from where he could see the gymnasium. He had already rolled down the window but now he opened the door.

His right leg was making non-stop rapid movements. 'See that?' he said, putting his hand on his thigh.

'Yes. There's a name for it.'

'It's because I'm too excited to be still. I have to move. I may have to take Samson out, keep moving a bit until I calm down.' He did not speak the words aloud, but his lips moved. 'Ten thousand cigarettes. At least.'

'Yes, a massive find.'

'You'll want to lock the other two buildings, Nell. Samson drew a blank.'

'I'll do that now. You've done well, Jimmy. Keep what you've found to yourself until tomorrow. I'll make sure you get the credit.'

He didn't move. 'I feel sick with excitement.'

'Do you want to come inside, have a cup of tea and something to eat?'

'I brought something with me. And I haven't given up on finding Arthur.'

'Go home now, Jimmy. You've done a great day's work. Let's give the police a chance to find Arthur. If they haven't done so by tomorrow, we can try again.' She shook his hand. 'Thank you. We'll never forget this day. This could be the biggest contraband find in the history of the Prison Service.'

He nodded. His eyes widened. He mouthed, 'Ten thousand cigarettes.'

She watched Jimmy drive away and through the gates. It would not surprise her if he stopped at the woods and continued his search for Arthur. Nell took deep breaths and walked slowly to the men's block and the boys' dormitory. When she went inside she wanted to open the windows and let in air. That would have to wait. She checked that there was no one inside, and then locked the doors.

Julian was by the entrance to the visitors' block, looking glum. He lit a cigarette and then greeted Nell. 'Your dog handler looked happy.'

'Yes. He's relieved not to have found a body. What about you? Any sightings of Arthur, or shouldn't I ask?'

Julian sighed. 'Several false leads. What I need is someone to come forward who's seen Arthur up close and talked to him. The Hull accent is distinctive.'

Nell said, 'The dog picked up Arthur's scent in the work part of the garden, but it was a false alarm.'

Julian took out his card and wrote on the back. 'I ought to give you my home number. If you don't get me, the DI or sergeant at the station, ring me there.'

'Thanks.'

'I'll get off then.'

'Are you in a great rush?'

'What is it?'

'There's something you need to know.'

Julian opened the door. 'Sounds as if we ought to go inside.'

Nell's mind was working overtime. The gymnasium needed to be watched. Jeff the whistle-blower was in Durham. The chief ought to be trustworthy, but she had kept quiet before. Crofty and Daisy were off duty, and she wouldn't trust Crofty, who couldn't say no. If she couldn't trust Crofty, could she trust Daisy? Kit was still a learner. Untrustworthy Bernie Webster was on the gate. One person was completely separate from anything that had gone before: Catcher, Betsy Friel. If it came to putting Catcher on watch with the Jack Russell, Nell might as well invite the one-man band to come and join in.

The assistant governor at Armley knew the ins and out of dealing with rogue officers. He would be the one to go to, but that would take a little time. It went against the grain to involve the police when your own were suspected. But Nell needed to think about the here and now. Murder changes the rules.

Twenty-Five

'Is everything all right, Nell?' asked Julian.

They were in the visitors' block, at the kitchen end. Nell had thought she appeared perfectly calm and in control, but Julian had picked up on her anxiety. 'No. I need to talk to you. To be honest, I'm glad about the extra security. Jimmy and Samson haven't found Arthur, but they found a huge haul of cigarettes hidden in the gymnasium. I've no idea who put them there, whether they've been temporarily "forgotten" or whether there'll be a midnight visitor to wheel them out via the path by the church.'

Julian raised his eyebrows and let out a whistle. 'Have you reported the find?'

'Not yet. I know who would normally deal with this, but we're not in a normal situation. That's why I'm telling you.'

'Because it has to be connected to the governor's death.'

'Yes. If this was what the major intended to tell me about, and was the reason for his death, whoever killed him believed their stash was safe in its hiding place. Do we leave the cigarettes in place and watch? That's what the security governor would do, but you're here, in force. So what happens now?'

He looked at the ceiling and muttered.

'What, what are you thinking?'

'It's our fifteenth wedding anniversary. Joan's booked a big table at a restaurant. If I have to cancel, she'll throw me out.'

'Where, and what time is the table booked?'

'Harrogate, eight o'clock. The order is that I'm home in good time and we go together.'

'Then you and I join forces and you delegate. You've a good DI and the sergeant's keen. How about this – two of your security men in the gymnasium. Constables at the gatehouse, by the church footpath and up at the farm. Crofty watches by the gap in the fence, because he should have mended it. We could have done with Jeff here because he's . . .'

'He's what?'

'An ex-army boxing champion and PE officer.'

There was a pause, and a moment when they just looked at each other, before Julian asked, 'Where is he?'

'In Durham, on an induction course. I told you. He's been promoted.'

Julian ran his fingers through his hair. 'If he's listened in to us on his car radio, he'll know we're looking for Arthur Burnett. Police officers are here solely for your protection.'

Nell said, 'Jeff was the whistle-blower. He's one of the good guys. So is Chief Officer Markham.' Nell hoped that was true about the chief. She had been wobbly once, out of mistaken loyalty to her old comrade.

'And that's why a PE officer, ex-boxer, hides cigarettes under the boxing ring. I'm sure your upright officer was meaning to tell you.'

'We don't know that it was him, unless there's something you've found out and aren't telling me.'

Julian went into the kitchen and picked up the telephone. 'No one will come tonight, Nell, not with all this activity, but you're right. We can't take the risk.'

'Who are you ringing?'

'Joan. I'll tell her I'll meet her at the restaurant and I might be late.'

'Put the phone down, Julian. I just gave you a good plan. Tell it to your DI and sergeant. I'll fetch them.'

DI Dennis was talking to one of the constables who moved away as Nell approached. DI Dennis smiled. 'So your dog handler isn't taking up residence?'

'Jimmy hasn't given up hope of Samson finding a cadaver. Will you come inside, Inspector? Do you know it's the DCI's wedding anniversary?'

'Indeed I do. We've had orders from Joan. He has a new tie in his jacket pocket, just in case he doesn't make it home in time to change.'

'We'll make a joint effort to keep your boss out of the divorce courts.'

'Right. I'll fetch Angela. She's in the car, glued to the radio.'

The four of them sat at the table near the kitchen. Angela had brought a briefcase. Nell saw that Angela was bursting to speak, but waited for the DCI.

Julian told them of Samson's find, and the planned spread of security and constables, adding, 'Ring me at the restaurant if you need to.'

Angela by now was almost rocking in her seat. 'There's news about Arthur Burnett, sir.'

'Go on,' Julian spoke wearily. 'What colour cap this time?'

'He thumbed a lift with an off-duty police officer. The description fitted, he has a Hull accent. He's heading for Durham. The officer realised this was important. After he dropped Arthur off, he went to the nearest station and called it in.'

Nell and Julian exchanged a look. 'Where in Durham?'

'Stanley, County Durham, sir. According to the PC who gave the lift, Arthur Burnett told him that he was evacuated to Stanley. He intended to visit the family who put him up. He was vague about the address, just said he'd find his way from the town centre.'

'Clever lad,' the DI said. 'More than one bolthole. Do we go up to Stanley, sir?'

Julian said, 'Let's locate him first. Stanley's a mining community, close-knit. If Arthur was there as a lad, they'll have adopted him for life. I don't want him to bolt again.'

Sergeant Ambrose pushed up her sleeve. She tapped her watch. 'Sir? The restaurant?'

He nodded. 'What Miss Lewis and I are going to tell you doesn't leave this room. There are cigarettes hidden in the gymnasium. They stay there, we do nothing. We are minding them until the Prison Service can take action. Here's where I want security deployed.'

Nell listened. He had not entirely taken up her suggestions. There was to be no one inside the gymnasium but it would be watched. He was right. Anyone left to sit in the gymnasium all night would have become curious and explored.

When Julian had left and DI Dennis had gone to talk to the constables and security, Angela Ambrose placed an old ring binder on the table. It was labelled 'Recipes'.

'This isn't entirely what it seems. I believe the major told you about a diary, ma'am?'

'Diaries.'

'If there were diaries in the house, they're not there now. This was the only item in the concealed cupboard he pointed out to you, in the leg of the drop leaf table.'

The sergeant carefully opened the ring binder labelled 'Recipes'.

'Some recipes are hand-written. Others have been cut from magazines and glued onto paper. A person looking for something tell-tale wouldn't give this a second glance, which could be why Governor Harding chose to write on the back of some of the pages. Perhaps he thought his diaries might not be safe. He's left behind details of contraband being brought to Brackerley and distributed to other prisons.' She turned pages and pointed out an example.

Nell looked at the writing. 'It's a recipe, in Spanish, Italian?'

'Italian, set out to look like a recipe. Our family name was changed to Ambrose from D'Ambrosio. I could make enough sense of the Italian to know what he was on about. He uses abbreviations, and what appear to be quantities for the recipe, but it's an account of cigarettes being sent to Glasgow.'

'He was taking no chances,' said Nell. 'And it's all a bit Secret Seven-ish.'

'I know. I got the feeling he enjoyed doing it. His Italian isn't perfect, but neither is mine. This ought to be professionally translated.'

'Are you returning this ring binder to me?'

'Yes. We've taken copies.' She turned the pages again. 'Look at this.'

A sheet of paper bore two headings, *Il Colpevole* and *Sospettoso*. Under each heading was a list of four-digit numbers.

'What do the headings stand for?' Nell asked.

'The first column lists the guilty parties. The second lists the names of those who had become suspicious or distrustful, or knew what was going on.'

'But it's just a list of short numbers.'

'I asked our filing clerk at the station to look at it. Alice is one of those very clever women who's secretive about her past and never talks about what she did in the war. Her guess was that the numbers could be part of a staff member's ID, or a significant date, possibly reversed. So, it's over to you and your personnel files for that, ma'am. We need to know the names of the guilty, because this is where our investigations cross over.'

Twenty-Six

Nell sat at her desk, the lamp creating a pool of light. Officer Friel was on night duty. The counsellor had called in to speak to Nell before going to her lodgings in the village. The house was quiet.

His posthumous message of wrongdoing at Brackerley had raised the major in Nell's estimation. It had also given her a headache.

The preliminary translation described a carefully run business, with supplies being brought to Brackerley and delivered to prisons across Northern England.

Nell looked at the digits under the headings of the Guilty and the Mistrustful, or those suspicious about what was going on. These four figure numbers would reveal identities. One number jumped out. It was written in blue ink and was the last number on the Mistrustful list. Everything else was written in black ink. The final number, 9640, had been added later.

She said it aloud, 'Zero four six nine.' It was suddenly so simple. 'That's me.'

Just as Daisy reversed her Co-op divvy number for the safe's combination, the major had reversed her starting date of April 1969 – 04/69 to 9640.

It was as if the major had drawn a line, Nell thought. He left it to me to do something. He knew there was a great deal at stake for those involved. This was his insurance policy; in case he did not live to tell the tale.

She checked her solution against others in the Suspicious list. Another was 2690, someone who took up their post in 1962. Chief Officer Markham had already told Nell that she came in that year. Nell went to the staff files drawer. She took out the chief officer's file. Her starting date was September 1962. Nell slid the file back in the drawer. She took out Derek Jeffrey's file. He had joined in July 1964.

At the top of the guilty list was 4670, July 1964. Nell would have liked to check the number of Horace Thompson, who had ended up in court and in prison, having carried the can for himself and Derek Jeffrey. His file had been removed.

Nell opened the safe. She placed the ring binder inside and then changed the combination, choosing Roxana's birthday, without reversing the digits.

Nell rang HMP Armley and spoke to the assistant governor who investigated corruption. As expected, there would be a cautious, watchful approach, ensuring that matters were dealt with thoroughly and with ruthless discretion. Nell thought of Jeff, on his induction course at Durham, feeling confident about his future. She rang HQ and gave her report.

It was later, as she shut her eyes, that Nell thought of those left behind, the words unsaid, the unasked questions. The major's son, a London one-man-band busker, who did not yet know that he was an orphan. How old must he be? He could be late thirties. He might do well along the theatre queues and with the tourists. There he would be, banging a drum, playing a mouth organ, hitting a triangle with a wand, pretending not to keep an eye on the hat for donations.

Nell imagined a grey-haired old lady, the major's sister, all preparations for her brother's arrival set aside for ever.

She wondered about Arthur – named after a king, or a grandfather? Did he and the rag-and-bone man ever get back their horse and cart? Might he be missed by the barmaid at his local? 'He's no great prospect but he's a nice feller, no malice in him.' And her helpful friend, 'You're right. And there's always a chance he'll make something of himself. It's not too late.'

Nell was relieved that the next day, Catcher Friel would be taking the residents to hoe between rows of vegetables.

Florence Nightingale had booked off Monday and Tuesday. She intended to drive to Filey on Sunday, to visit the major's sister and her husband whom she liked. They were kind, she had said, and with no side to them. It was only fair to let the Barracloughs have first refusal on Pip.

Twenty-Seven

As the residents ate their breakfast on Sunday, Nell came into the dining room, having waited until they had finished eating.

'Good morning, everyone. I hope you enjoyed your breakfast.'

'It's an improvement on Holloway but I prefer a three-minute egg,' said Olga.

Linda and Cherry said nothing. Diane simply sighed, a forlorn look on her face.

'Today we all go to church, to the eleven o'clock service,' said Nell. 'I have everyone down as Church of England so we will attend St Michael and All Angels, which is a short walk along the drive passing the education block and workshops. The vicar is Father James Grieves, our prison chaplain. I'll introduce you to him as we go in.' Nell sensed no reluctance about going to church. They would be glad to break the monotony. 'We will meet by the front door at quarter to eleven.'

After their interviews with the police, Nell had arranged for the women's personal officers to answer questions about the major's death and they had all spent time with the visiting counsellor, Elaine McArthur.

Olga put up her hand. 'I'm a slow walker, ma'am.'

'Set off when you need to, Olga. One of us will walk with you.' She paused. 'There will be prayers for Governor Harding. His is a sad loss.'

Linda had brought a cup to her lips. She took a sip and put it down, waiting to hear more.

Diane said, 'He seemed like a nice man.'

'Yes,' Nell said. 'He will be much missed.' That was as much as she dared say. More information would begin to trickle out one way or another, but hopefully not yet, and not to the residents.

It was a fine day, with a blue sky and white clouds. Nell wore her black suit. At the last minute, she replaced her jaunty peaked cap with a black crocheted beret bought at a sale of work. She led officers and residents along the drive, to the path that led to the church. Chief Officer Markham had set off a little earlier with Olga, who could not be rushed.

'This church marks our boundary,' Nell said. 'In future weeks, you can walk here by yourselves. Church attendance is compulsory, but you have a choice. There is a Methodist church in the village, and you are free to choose to go there if you prefer.'

'In that case, I'll try both,' Cherry said.

'To see which has the shorter service?' Diane asked.

'Because I'm interested and have an open mind. Besides, I once picked up a couple of good costume ideas from looking at what clergy wore, especially the bishops.'

Diane laughed. 'You're mad, you.'

The breeze had blown dying blooms from a camellia shrub onto the grass, creating an attractive pattern.

Cherry looked about her. 'I could get used to the quiet. It's almost creepy.'

Linda spoke for the first time that morning. 'It's lovely.'

As they drew closer, the church bells began to peal.

In the churchyard, Olga made straight for the gravestones, trying to make out the worn inscriptions.

The congregation had begun to go in, saying good morning to the vicar.

'We sit on the third row from the front,' the chief whispered to Nell as they entered the porch.

Nell introduced her residents to Father James. Each had their hand thoroughly shaken as he welcomed them. He's memorising their names, Nell thought. She could almost hear his brain ticking.

The Meadowcrofts and nurse Florence Nightingale were already in the porch. Florence appeared utterly wretched. Her black felt hat sat at an odd angle, not out of attempted jauntiness but from having been plonked on by someone who didn't think, or lacked the energy, to look in her mirror.

The organ began to play.

At the second set of doors, Florence came to a standstill. The chief whispered to her and then moved on. Florence clicked into action like a mechanical toy. Betsy Friel fell into step with Nell.

The oak pews bore the carved mouse emblem that was the trademark of craftsman Robert Thompson of Kilburn. Nell touched the mouse, for luck – or for something.

The stained-glass windows gave a soft light, with rays of sunshine striking through and settling in what must be their

224

usual places, creating a feeling of timelessness and tranquillity. The windows portrayed the Sermon on the Mount and the Virgin and Child. On the largest window, St Michael and All Angels presided over the church that was named after them.

Nell felt fortunate to have arrived in a spot such as this. Brackerley village was a 'Thankful Village', one of the few whose men serving in the armed forces during the First World War all returned.

Everyone in the congregation must have heard about the major's death. There was a straightening of shoulders and a hushed attention as the chaplain stepped into the pulpit.

'Today we welcome the new governor of Brackerley House, Miss Lewis, her staff and residents.'

From along the pew someone turned the start of a scoff into a cough. Probably Cherry, Nell thought. For those who did not want to be here, a welcome would ring hollow.

'We wish you well during your stay amongst us. Be assured that you are in our thoughts and prayers. Sadly, this is a time of shock and deep grief. We gather in great sorrow to mourn the tragic death of our neighbour Governor Harding, who was for many years governor at Brackerley House. The major was a regular attender at this church and known to all of you. He was a familiar and popular figure in the village. We pray for him.'

The prayer followed.

Florence let out a sob, perhaps for her shattered hopes rather than for the man himself. Nell saw that she was seated between the chief and Daisy. One of them would keep an eye on her. This would be her second sitting for prayers for the dead governor, now and earlier at the 9 a.m. Mass at St Kevin's.

Nell realised that she had not told the chaplain about Arthur Burnett's disappearance. Keeping the chaplain abreast of developments was her job. How could she not have remembered to do something so crucial? But it turned out someone else had remembered.

The chaplain continued: 'Mrs Ramsden asks us to pray for the safety and safe return of Arthur Burnett, a young man once resident in the borstal and who often returns to the farm. He was last seen on Thursday evening. Mrs Ramsden is worried about him. Let us pray for his safe return.'

When the prayer ended, Nell whispered to Betsy Friel, 'Straight back to the house after the service. Pass it along.'

To stay behind in the church afterwards would make Nell a victim of introductions, condolences, welcomes and too many questions. As they were filing out, Chief Officer Markham caught Nell's eye. Nell nodded. Someone had to stay behind. Jean Markham knew the congregation. She would field questions without giving anything away.

The counsellor, Elaine McArthur also stayed behind, having been invited to the farmhouse for lunch by Mrs Ramsden, who wanted a listening ear.

At the church door, the group divided. Florence said, 'I'll get moving, collect Pip and set off for Filey. See you all in a few days.'

The chief fell into step with her. 'I'll come with you to the car, check your tyre pressures and windscreen fluid.'

Daisy and Crofty set off for the village.

Diane seemed to be dragging her feet on the walk back. She looked ghastly, her face drawn and pale. Nell said, 'Diane, you don't look well.'

'I feel hot. I feel sick and dizzy.'

Cherry stepped up. 'Take my arm.'

'I'll manage.'

Cherry insisted. 'Your hands are so cold.' Cherry turned to Nell. 'Has the nurse gone, ma'am?'

Diane said, 'I don't need a nurse.'

It's because it's Sunday, Nell thought. Diane is thinking of her children, passing another weekend without her. 'Nurse Carreras is going somewhere, but I'm sure she'll have time to take your temperature and give you a couple of aspirins. It won't hurt to let her take a look at you.'

'I'll hurry along and tell her,' Cherry said, 'and I'll wait with Diane.'

Nell made a mental note to have Cherry's care for Diane entered on her monthly report. She also knew that Florence would come back with them, being that it was too soon for either Diane or Cherry to be fully trusted.

When the group drew level with the hospital wing, Florence was waiting. She looks just as bad herself, Nell thought. Perhaps there's a bug going round.

It was about twenty minutes later when Florence, her patient and Cherry arrived back. Nell had left her office door open so that she could catch them on their return and hear the diagnosis.

Florence came to the door. 'Diane had a temperature and feels sickly. I've given her a couple of aspirins. I told her to go to her room and lie down, and wrap a scarf around her eyes to keep out the light. I should think she'll be all right by teatime.'

'Thank you. Kit has a sandwich and a flask ready for you. I hope you have a good rest in Filey and that being by the sea will do you some good.'

'I hope so too. I'll see you on Wednesday, ma'am.'

She was brave, Nell thought, facing up to what might have been her future and saying goodbye to it. Nell hoped it would stay fine. Misery and pouring rain was never a good combination.

Twenty-Eight

Officer Kitteringham supervised as Olga set the table for tea, with Cherry and Linda looking on. The table setting had to be done correctly so that Olga, or any of them, would be able to apply for a job at a high-class café or a hotel that did silver service.

Miss Kitteringham congratulated Olga. 'You would find work at the Ritz.'

'There was a time when Mother and I regularly took tea at Claridge's,' said Olga. 'One picks up a lot by mixing with the right people, but my favourite place for tea was the Russian Tearooms in Manhattan, where Mother had queues of people waiting to have their tea leaves read.'

Cherry rang the bell for tea. When Diane did not appear, Cherry looked in the sitting room and the library before going upstairs to the dormitory.

They all waited. The tea-maker, Linda, must not make the tea until everyone else was seated, else it would go cold.

Cherry had her lip between her teeth when she came back. 'Diane's gone.'

'Gone where?' asked Kit.

'She's gone.' When Kit simply stared, Cherry said, 'That crimplene dress from the WVS is folded and left on the bed along with her work clothes.'

'Diane is a tidy person. She's gone out for a breath of air,' said Kit.

'Her bag is gone, and so is her lipstick that was on the chest of drawers, oh and her matches. The prison plimsolls are by the bed. Her heels are gone.'

Olga pressed her palms together and closed her eyes. 'When we were in church, I thought I heard a spirit voice calling, "Mummy, come back!"'

Linda had come to listen. She could not make tea until this was settled and everyone sitting down.

Olga nodded agreement with herself. 'Now I believe that what I overheard was an astral cry from Diane's children, calling for her: "Mummy, come back".'

Linda said, 'They're from Hull. They'd say, "Mam! Where've you gone, Mam?"'

'Olga, you didn't mention this after church,' Cherry said reasonably.

This slightly annoyed Olga, but she was used to doubters. 'One cannot be sure of these things until they come to pass.'

Kit said nothing aloud. She spoke to herself. My mother told me I'm not cut out for this. I should be teaching domestic science.

Linda, knowing what it was to be dumbfounded, felt sorry for Kit. 'Miss Lewis is in her office.' When Kit did not speak or move, Cherry said, 'Diane is wearing her plaid jacket and the cream skirt.'

Her eyes betraying panic, Kit mustered her dignity. 'Please

230

set the table, girls, including a place for Diane. Olga, you may make the tea.'

No one pointed out that the table was already set and had been approved and that it was Linda's turn to make tea.

'Be sure to warm the teapot.'

Kit walked along the hall, took a deep breath and was about to knock on the governor's door when she realised she ought to go to the dormitory and check for herself.

What convinced Kit was that three nightgowns were under three pillows. One nightgown, Diane's, was in the washing bin.

Nell was on the telephone. 'It was a mad day yesterday, Roxy. I missed your call and then you missed mine.' There was a knock on the door. Nell opened the door, saw Kit and smiled. 'Give me a moment.'

Kit stepped back, shifting her weight from one foot to the other, swaying slightly as if the room she really wanted was the loo.

'You were saying, Roxy?'

'Yesterday was an early closing day at the British Library. By the time I found someone to help me, I didn't have a lot of time. I found one other small article about the same incident, dated 14 August 1947. I copied it and put it in the post. You should have it by tomorrow. There was a repeat of the information that children were playing in a bombed-out house and that Billy Turner – this piece gives his name – fell from a beam. He was aged twelve. There's his school photograph and details of the funeral at Hull General Cemetery. He was a bonny little chap.'

Nell had hoped for more details. 'No names of other children at the scene of the accident?'

'No.'

'Thank you very much for doing that. I'll see you next time you come home, or I come to London.'

'When will that be, Auntie? Come for my birthday!'

'I'll try! Bye for now.' Nell put down the phone.

The article had been a thread of memory for Arthur, a thread of sentiment. He knew Billy. He may have been one of the other children in the bombed-out house and witnessed the accident. Someone in the Burnett family would have kept the cutting, and then it found its way to Arthur. It might be a comfort to the Turner family to know that Arthur had carried Billy with him all these years, on his head, and in his thoughts.

'Come in, Kit. Sit down.'

Kit came in and sat down.

'What is it, Kit?'

'Ma'am, it appears that Diane Redmond may have absconded. Her things are gone.'

'What things are gone? She arrived in what she wore for her court appearance, and that's what she wore to church. She may have gone out for a walk to shake off her headache.'

Kit frowned. 'In her best high heels, ma'am?'

'Why not, on a Sunday.' Nell remained calm, at the same time thinking that if Diane thumbed the right lift, she could be in Hull in about two hours, home with her kids. There was nowhere else she would go. 'We follow procedure: alerts and searching the grounds and the village. Go into reception, telephone the chief. Tell her that there is a possibility Diane has absconded and ask her to come in. Ring security. Give them Diane's description, say what she was wearing. I'll alert the chaplain and the Meadowcrofts.'

'And Jeff?'

'He's not back until tomorrow.'

'What about Mrs Friel?'

'Mrs Friel will stay here with you. Don't let the telephone go unanswered. Off you go. I need to tell the chaplain and the farm.'

Nell took Diane's folder from the file. She jotted down the address. How big was Hull? Nell had never been there.

She looked up the chaplain's number and dialled. He answered on the first ring.

'Father James, Nell Lewis. It looks as if Diane Redmond may have absconded. If so, I'll be going to Hull to bring her back. I'm instituting the usual searches, so if you'll call the Ramsdens to search their patch.'

'Of course, sorry to hear that. I'll search my designated area and I'll go to the pub in case she's called in for a drink. She's about five foot five and blonde?'

'Spot on, wearing a cream skirt, a tartan jacket with a heather brooch in pewter, black high heel shoes and carrying a black handbag.'

'She could have thumbed a lift?'

'She most certainly could.'

'Do you know the way to Hull, Miss Lewis?'

'Yes. I'll ring the Meadowcrofts now.'

'If they come to evensong and haven't got your message, I'll pass it on.'

'Thank you.'

At least the chaplain did not think this serious enough to require prayers. Nell pictured her road atlas. Hull was south, east, south and east again. Or she could go east and then south. The little globe of a compass rubber stickered to her windscreen would help.

Daisy Meadowcroft answered the phone. She listened to Nell's news, and went quiet. Perhaps as an explanation as to why she wasn't instantly on the ball, Daisy then told Nell they had just finished their dinner. 'Is it the usual search?'

'Yes, that's the starting point.'

Nell heard her passing the message to Crofty and ordering him to the woods.

'That's the direction the borstal boys usually took, ma'am. We always caught up with them.'

'Will you check the village, Daisy? If she's gone for a stroll, that's her most likely destination.'

'You think she's gone home?' Daisy asked.

'Yes, I do, and I'm going after her, but we'll follow procedure.' There would be a report going to T5 later today. Nell needed to cover her back. If there was a procedure, you followed it as quickly as possible, and then did what you knew was the right thing.

Nell hung up the phone just as Kit came in.

'I made the calls, ma'am,' Kit said. 'Everyone's on alert.'

'Good.' It was after church that Diane had looked ghastly. Arthur Burnett's name had been mentioned as missing. The Arthur who was born in the same year as Diane, and who probably gave her a bar of chocolate when Kit wasn't looking. Diane would not go chasing off after a man she knew slightly, would she? Unless they had come to an arrangement. Perhaps Arthur had got himself a van. Diane played sick, went back down through the path past the church, and he picked her up. But that would not fit with the police report of Arthur having been given a lift to Stanley, County Durham.

'I'll be back in a moment, Kit. Fetch the residents to my office, please.'

Nell went upstairs for her coat, shoulder bag and flashlight, not knowing how long this search might take.

A tiny part of Nell still hoped that Diane would come in late, wondering what all the fuss was about. But the voice in Nell's head said, You were looking in the wrong direction. You paid too much attention to the women you thought of as most vulnerable, Linda and Olga. Diane was the one who kicked off, didn't expect to be here, desperate about being separated from her children.

Nell had seen Diane in the hall, taking or making telephone calls to her sister. It was unlikely but not impossible that some relative or friend had driven over to pick her up, without realising they were not doing her a favour.

Twenty-Nine

Officer Friel brought Olga, Cherry and Linda into Nell's office. They stood in a row opposite her desk.

'Thank you, Officer Friel.' She spoke to the three slightly anxious residents. 'It appears that we have temporarily lost Diane.' Nell repeated what the women had been made aware of on arrival. 'If a person absconds, she will be found, spend at least one night in segregation, have additional years added to her sentence and be sent to a closed prison.'

'Are you sending for the police, ma'am?' Cherry asked.

'We send for the police only when a crime has been committed or there is danger to life. Absconding is an offence but not a crime. If we find Diane before nightfall, I'll hear what she has to say. There will be punishment, but because we are going through an extraordinarily difficult time, it may be possible for me to allow her to remain here with you.' Nell had their attention. 'Is there anything you can think of that would give an indication as to what was in Diane's mind? Was there anything unusual going on at home that would draw her back so suddenly, or anything here that had become difficult or even unbearable?'

They gazed at her in silence. Nell tried again: 'What was her mood when you arrived, and by yesterday?'

Olga said, 'I feel sure she is alive and well.'

Cherry said, 'When we arrived, she was pretty fed up, upset that a person can be sent straight to clink when they thought they would go home. But she'd taken an advance on wages and gave Olga and me a roll-up.'

Nell said, 'The more I know, the more likely I am to bring her back. If someone's helped her, I need to know.'

Linda had been looking at her feet. 'Linda?'

Linda looked up. 'After we cleaned the major's cottage, Miss Kitteringham took us up to see the farm. I think Diane knew the man who was with the pigs. She mentioned wanting to see her kids. That's all.'

'Ah!' Cherry raised her forefinger. Something had clicked for her. 'This morning in church, when the vicar said the name of the person who was missing, Diane grabbed my arm and dug in her fingers, like some people do when they're watching a horror film.'

Nell thanked them. 'If you think of anything else, tell one of the officers. We will find Diane. All of you will remain indoors today. This isn't a punishment. It's for the sake of security, until we bring Diane back. Meanwhile, go back to the dining room and enjoy your tea if you can.'

Nell put on her coat. Betsy Friel was waiting by the door. 'Catcher, in case I miss anyone, say I've gone to Hull. I expect to be back by midnight at the latest. Would you make sure there's a security man on the gate?'

'You'll be going to the right place, ma'am,' Friel said. 'She's thumbed a lift and gone home. A Sunday, she'd be itching to put a dinner on the table. She'd have her kids and all the family round her. While she was sitting in the church, she asked the Archangel, "What am I doing here?" When there was no reply, she said to herself, "I'm off home." That's what I think, ma'am. It was an impulse. She'll see sense and be back before bedtime.'

'You could be right,' Nell said, ignoring the fact that Diane would have been relying on someone else in the family to put a shoulder of mutton in the oven, peel potatoes and spoil the cabbage.

Nell went to her car. Chief Officer Markham was screwing a cap back onto a petrol can. There were fumes in the air. 'I've filled her up for you.'

'Thank you.'

The chief cleared her throat in a meaningful fashion. 'I was at HMP Hull for two years. I know the way and I know the city.'

'Thanks. It's a good offer, but I need you here, Chief.'

'I thought you'd say that. I've drawn you a map. Place names in large block letters and straight lines with road numbers. It'll be easier than stopping to consult the atlas.'

There was not normally a gateman on a Sunday. One of the security men spotted that Nell was leaving and went to open the gates. 'Sign out for me please, Chief.' When she paused for the gate to open fully, Nell saw Linda coming from behind the gatehouse towards her. Nell rolled down the window.

'Hello, what is it?'

'About Diane, I was sitting on the other side of her in church. She grabbed my arm, too, when she heard that name, Arthur Burnett. She was tense, shaking a bit. You know when someone can't look left or right, or see or hear, because they're afraid.'

'Thank you, Linda.'

'It's not that I want to tell tales. If she gets in a man's car, you don't know what might happen. She might be hurt.'

'I have a strong feeling she will fine. I'll bring her back safely.'

As Nell drove off, she saw Linda through her rear-view mirror, standing very still, watching her go. In spite of feeling upset by Diane's disappearance, Nell was gratified that the women were looking out for each other.

After two hours Nell arrived in North Ferriby. It should be a reasonably straight, short run from here, she thought. That was when she heard police sirens. It took her too long to realise that she was the one being waved down. She pulled over.

Two officers got out. They would be pleased with themselves. Sunday. Quiet evening. Result.

One officer came to the driver's side. Nell wound down the window. The other officer took up his post by the passenger side, looking in. Did he expect her to do a run for it, or pull out a gun?

'Madam, you were doing fifty miles an hour in a thirty mile an hour zone. May I see your driving licence?' He leaned closer, sniffing for alcohol.

Nell opened her bag, produced her driving licence and her ID. 'Sorry, officer, I wouldn't normally speed.'

'What is your hurry, madam?' He glanced at her licence and her ID.

'Officer, I'm the deputy governor of HMP Brackerley

Open Prison for women.' He looked suspicious. 'It was the borstal until last week.'

He spoke across the car to his partner. 'Brackerley women's prison?'

'Aye, so I heard.'

'Where are you heading, ma'am?'

'One of my residents has absconded. I'm going to bring her back.'

'Residents.'

'Prisoner, but during her rehabilitation a resident. She's a young widow with children. In allowing herself an unauthorised home visit, she's broken prison regulations but not the law.'

'She left you to break the law on her behalf, ma'am.' He smiled at his own wit.

'Yes.' Nell put her hand up. 'Caught in the act. I want to take her back before she makes things worse for herself.'

'You're sure she's at home?'

'In her shoes, that's where I would be.'

'What's her address?'

Nell told them.

'Come on then, follow us, ma'am. And don't speed again unless we do. Better to arrive safe than not at all.'

'Thank you, officers. Much appreciated.'

The officer by the passenger door had come round to the driver's side. He had to put in his two pennyworth. 'Just one thing, ma'am.'

'What's that?'

'If you ever lock up my missus, keep her in.'

Nell would have liked to say something in reply, but in this situation, she kept her mouth shut.

240

'Never mind him,' said the first officer. 'He hates to admit he loves her bones.'

The officers got back in their car, switched on the blue light and sirens and set off, soon reaching forty miles an hour. Nell groaned. All she needed was to arrive at her destination behind a screeching, flashing lights police car. She hoped they weren't radioing in for a second car to form a convoy.

As they drove on, Nell felt glad of the escort. Finding her way through this maze of streets would have been more difficult than crossing the county. She guessed the officers enjoyed the opportunity to switch on lights and sirens. Fortunately, they switched them off before turning onto a cobbled street near an area of waste ground. They parked on the waste ground, at the side of a pub.

Both officers got out of their car. So did Nell, shouldering her bag and locking the door. Even with a police escort, the journey had taken her three hours.

'The house you want is opposite. This isn't the most salubrious area of Hull. Do you want us to stay nearby?'

'I'll be fine now. I'm not anticipating any difficulties.' That was not exactly true. Nell did not know what to expect. With children on the scene, Diane – if she had not already bolted – might have the good sense not to make a huge fuss and upset them.

'We'll back off then. Some of the cellars across there are knocked through. If we've been spotted, your quarry might be halfway up the street by the time you're let in.'

The other officer jerked his thumb towards the pub. 'Put a call in to the station from the Red Lion. The landlord is on the up and up. He'll ring us for you if you need help.'

'Thank you very much. What are your names?'

'Fraser and Tomelty.'

'I keep a diary. You'll be in there with a star.'

Nell crossed to the other side of the street. Diane lived at number 37, next door to her mother and sister at 39. The mother, Mrs Sowerby, was Diane's next of kin. Diane's house was in darkness. At 39, curtains were drawn but not completely closed. A television flickered in the corner. One woman sat in a chair. The other stood at an ironing board, angled to give her a view of the television screen.

Nell knocked on the door. After a moment, a chain was slipped in place. Surely this could not be such a dodgy area, especially for someone who didn't mind taking in smuggled goods.

When the door opened, Nell was tempted to stick her foot in but decided to play softly, softly. No one spoke.

A woman's voice called, 'Don't just stand there, ask who it is and what they want.'

Nell said, 'Anita?'

'Who's asking?'

'Miss Lewis, prison governor. Don't shut the door on me. It will be better for Diane if I can talk to her.'

'She's not here.'

'Then let me talk to you, and to Mrs Sowerby, Diane's next of kin.'

The words 'next of kin' did the trick, the words that sometimes herald bad news.

After a brief consultation between Anita and the woman in the chair, the chain came off.

It was one of those houses where the outside door opens directly to face the stairs. On the left, the door to the sitting room was ajar.

Anita waved Nell in. Mrs Sowerby was seated by the fire in a worn plush velvet armchair, her feet in big pom-pom slippers. Nell put her age at late fifties. Her grey hair, home-permed into a frizzed halo, gave her beatific dignity. Her legs were mottled brown from sitting too close to the fire. A ginger cat sat on her lap. Nell crossed the room to shake hands with Mrs Sowerby. There was no sign of children, no toys or shoes.

'How do you do, Mrs Sowerby. I'm Miss Lewis, governor at Brackerley Open Prison. I'd like to speak to Diane.'

'She's not here.'

The ironing board was up, iron plugged in and a white blouse waiting. Anita went back to her iron. She was the sister whose jacket and skirt Diane had borrowed for her appearance in court.

Nell shook hands with Anita across the ironing board. 'Thank you for letting me in. This must be a worrying time for you. Diane absconded today and that is a serious matter. I am giving her the opportunity to return before the situation escalates.'

They already know, Nell thought. All that surprises them is that I have come in person.

'Sit down, miss,' said Mrs Sowerby. 'Anita, turn that damn thing off.'

Anita switched off the television.

Nell sat down in a chair that matched Mrs Sowerby's. 'You'll know where she is.'

Anita began ironing.

Nell said, 'I need to talk to Diane. Where is she?'

'Not here,' Mrs Sowerby said.

'And the children?'

'Not here.'

'If I can take Diane back with me, she will spend one night in solitary confinement, lose privileges and have extra days added to her sentence. If she does not return willingly, she will be found, face a longer period of solitary confinement, loss of remission and will serve out a longer sentence in a closed prison, probably Holloway.'

Neither Mrs Sowerby nor her daughter spoke, each waiting for the other.

'I need to understand why Diane absconded. I thought it was because of her children, but if so, she would be here with them, and seeing them off to school tomorrow.'

Anita picked up the iron. 'Two men dead at your place and you're trying to understand? I'm surprised you've anyone left in custody.'

Mrs Sowerby yelled at her daughter, 'Don't you go waving that iron!'

Nell spoke calmly. 'Yes, I am trying to understand. I want to know why Diane absconded and why she has gone into hiding. You need to cooperate with me. Belligerence won't help us or Diane.'

After her outburst, Anita was silent.

At least Nell now knew she was searching in the right place. Diane had been here, may still be here, and had told them about the governor's death, and Arthur's disappearance.

Nell said, 'Arthur Burnett is not dead. He left the premises on Thursday evening. This morning's prayers for his safe return were at the request of the farmer he works for.'

'Diane's scared,' Mrs Sowerby said.

'If Diane believes she is in danger, I need to do something about it now. Help me find her and take her back before it is too late. We did have a serious incident on Thursday evening, a death that was treated as suicide. One death. It did not affect the prisoners.' Nell was saying too much, but if she held things back she would never gain their confidence. 'Since that incident, we have better security than Buckingham Palace. No event, however shocking, interrupts the routine of the prison. Look at me. Would I come here to take Diane out of hiding and into danger?'

'You wouldn't know what danger is.'

'Then tell me.'

Anita hung the white blouse on a hanger. She seized a blue blouse, laid it on the ironing board and began to iron the back. 'Some of us have to go to work tomorrow. I have blouses to iron and a skirt to press.'

Go carefully, Nell told herself. They know where she is and that she has the children with her. She would take the children out of fear of harm.

Mrs Sowerby looked Nell up and down. 'You have a smart costume. You don't wear a uniform.'

Nell took out her ID and showed it to Mrs Sowerby. 'A governor wears her own clothes.'

Mrs Sowerby's jaw tightened. She gulped, as if trying to shift the lump in her throat. The cat opened its eyes and looked at her.

'Are you telling us Arthur is alive?'

'Yes.'

It was Arthur's death that shook and distressed Diane. More than that, it made her run for her life.

Perhaps Mrs Sowerby thought the conversation about Diane had run its course. 'You better have a cup of tea, since you've come all this way and have a long journey back.'

'Thanks, but no thanks. I'll be going back when I have Diane in the car. But something set me wondering . . .'

'Oh aye, and what's that?'

'Something that I'm half understanding but not quite getting.'

'Join the club,' said Anita, still ironing.

'Diane and Arthur Burnett were the same age and born in the same hospital. They were friends?'

Mrs Sowerby thought for a moment, not that the question posed difficulty, but she was not prepared for it. 'We were rehoused close to the Burnetts. Mrs Burnett wasn't a well woman. Mr Burnett came back from the war a changed man. Arthur was more in our house than his own. We was all struggling, but I offered to take him in. His father wouldn't have it. He was too proud.'

'So, Diane and Arthur were almost like brother and sister.'

'They were pals. Went about in a little gang. Diane, Gloria and a couple of lads. At the age when lassies and lads still played together.'

Nell remembered Diane's letter. 'Diane wrote to you. Something she said puzzled me. She said that she now had more sympathy with Gloria. Who was Gloria?'

Anita said, 'How do you know what she wrote?'

Being sentenced to prison had taken Diane by surprise. Her mother and sister had not quite grasped it either. Nell was tired of pussyfooting around. 'Prison regulations require that letters sent and received by prisoners must be read for security reasons.'

Anita was ironing a sleeve. 'Diane and Gloria were friends. Me and Gloria were Diane's bridesmaids. I wore a miniature version of Gloria's dress.'

Mrs Sowerby sighed. 'Gloria's done well for herself, in Australia. She would, though. She was a cheeky monkey.'

'She was.' Anita stood the iron on end to tell her story. 'At Diane's wedding reception, Gloria asked all the guests to give her half a crown towards the ten pounds assisted passage to Australia. Diane's husband, Stephen, he gave Gloria a ten-shilling note.'

'Was that out of generosity?' Nell asked, 'or was Stephen glad to see the back of Diane's best friend?'

'Oh, generosity. He was kindness itself.' Mrs Sowerby stroked the cat's head. It had moved onto the chair arm. 'It broke our hearts when Stephen's trawler went down. If I'd gone to court with Diane that day, I would've told them. I would've said to that hanging judge, you don't know what my daughter has been through.'

Nell sympathised, but came to the point. 'Diane has been through a lot. I'm concerned about what she might go through if I don't take her back with me tonight.' Pressing her point, Nell repeated what was likely to happen. 'She will face a longer sentence in a closed prison, farther from home. She can't hide for ever.'

Neither woman spoke. Anita went on ironing.

Nell remained patient, even though she had the feeling of sitting in on an ironing lesson. Domestic science: how to iron a man's shirt. Back-sleeve-sleeve-front-front-cuffs-collar. Nell thought, Anita is much younger than me and they're still teaching it. Useful. But why did the teacher never say, bring in a blouse?

'Anita, tell me more about Gloria.'

'Last Christmas, Diane burned Gloria's letter and stopped writing. Gloria had written that she felt bad about taking money from Diane's wedding guests because afterwards one person gave her thirty pounds hush money.'

'That was a lot. What was Gloria to be hushed about?' Nell was beginning to regret turning down a cup of tea, but the mother and daughter were on safe ground now, leaving Diane out of it.

Mrs Sowerby said, 'I can't remember.'

'Mam, you can't remember because Diane never said, but it was Derek Turner that gave Gloria the money. I saw him. He gave her a wodge of notes that she put down her front, and he gave me two bob.'

'Was he related to the boy who died, Billy Turner?' Nell asked.

Mrs Sowerby said, 'They were cousins who lived with their grandmother. They played together. They were in that little gang. They played cricket, chalked their wickets on the wall by the pub. But how do you know about Billy?'

Nell told them about the newspaper cutting Arthur carried: 'It reported that Billy and some other children were playing in a bombed-out house and Billy fell from a beam.'

Mrs Sowerby reached out to stroke the cat. It bit her. 'It was shocking,' she said. 'Mothers kept their kids in after that, for as long as they could. Of course, then it's forgotten.'

'Not forgotten by Arthur,' said Nell. 'The other children aren't named. Let's name them now. Diane, Gloria, Derek Turner, Arthur and who else? They must have felt so bad, so guilty.'

Mrs Sowerby said, 'Everyone felt guilty. The children's names were kept out of the paper. The police went round the schools, giving warnings. Hull Corporation came in for a lot of criticism over the death traps – that's what people called them.'

Nell looked from one woman to the other. 'What am I

missing? All of us at Brackerley were devastated by our governor's death. Only Arthur took to his heels. Only Diane panicked and ran away. Why?'

Both women spoke at once. Mrs Sowerby said, 'It was nothing to do with that.'

Anita, putting a blouse on a hanger, said, 'She was afraid.'

'Of what?'

'Of whoever killed Arthur.'

'I promise you, Arthur is alive. He's safe. It's Diane I'm concerned about. It's Diane I must take back with me.'

'I told you, she's scared.'

Nell stood. 'Take me to Diane, wherever she is -- in the cellar here, with a friend, a relative. I'll take her back with me. I guarantee her safety. If she is in any doubt, has a reason to fear for her life, I'll arrange a place of safety for her and the children. Otherwise, I telephone the police and they'll put out an alert for Diane Redmond. You run the risk that whoever she is afraid of gets to her first.'

'We don't know anything,' Mrs Sowerby said. 'You're acting as if one of the kids pushed little Billy. Even if they did, after all these years, there'd be no case against them.'

'I'm not suggesting any such thing. That's in the past. You tell me that Diane absconded out of fear, but you won't let me do anything about it.' Nell picked up her bag. 'I've failed here. I thought I could help Diane, but I can't. I'm going across to the pub and I'll ring the police. You'll be required to give statements.'

'Why?'

'Because I suspect the cover-up of a crime. I suspect she has information that would help solve a crime.'

Anita picked up the iron. 'You're threatening us.'

Her mother said, 'Put it down, you daft bat.'

'I've a skirt to press.'

Nell opened the door. 'Mrs Sowerby, there are things I am not permitted to divulge. I fear that Diane and your grandchildren will be easy targets if they stay where they are.'

'They're at Hornsea, in a caravan. Leave them be, just for tonight,' Mrs Sowerby said.

Nell shook her head. 'I've no idea where Hornsea is, but I'm going.'

Anita took off her slippers and slid on a pair of shoes. 'Press my skirt, Mam. I'll have to show her the way.'

'The other kids were Annie Parker, Trevor Harrison and Billy's cousin who was an evacuee who stayed on,' said Mrs Sowerby.

'Why would anyone evacuate a child to Hull?' Nell asked. 'They might as well have sent him to the East End of London.'

'That's what we all said, but his grandma had a big house, and it stayed intact. They were lucky.'

Anita was having second thoughts. 'Why should we trust you? You speak nicely, you wear a good costume, but you're a guard, a warder – you're not on our side.'

'I know what people think of prison officers. I joined because people fall through the cracks, and I try to catch them. Help me to do my job.'

Mrs Sowerby and her daughter exchanged a look.

Finally Anita said, 'Shoreline Caravan Park. The caravan belongs to my boyfriend's parents.'

'Thank you,' Nell said. 'You'll have to show me the way.'

Anita knew the way to Hornsea, but as a passenger. She would only think to say turn right, or turn left, after they passed the turn. Fortunately, the road soon became straight, with a fine view of the Atlantic on their right. When Nell lowered the car window, she could hear the waves crashing.

'It's beautiful. What a lovely place to have a caravan.'

'Yes, the kids were so excited to come. I hope they don't make too much mess. My boyfriend's parents are a bit picky.'

Nell thought picky caravan owners fretting about their big tin can would be the least of Diane's worries. She would make short work of a bit of muck. Running for her life might take priority.

'How did Diane seem when she arrived back?'

'She was relieved and pleased to have hitched a lift almost all the way home. I'm the one who could have cried, seeing my new skirt and jacket already wanting dry cleaning. I don't think she's had them off.'

The pounding waves and the blur of sea and sky did nothing to alleviate the air of unreality that Nell was beginning to feel. Before they set off, Nell had thought of calling at the Red Lion and making a telephone call to Brackerley, saying where she was and what was happening. Yet that would risk losing Anita's trust. There would be a payphone at the camp site. She had to both protect Diane and her children, and not panic Diane into making another run for it.

Thirty

Nell turned into the Shoreline Caravan Park entrance. 'The car park is to the right,' Anita said, for once giving directions in good time.

Nell drove in. There was plenty of space. On the other side of the fence from the car park was a farmer's field. Someone had lit a small bonfire too close to the fence. Sunday evening, weekenders were leaving. There was no queue to come into the caravan park, but a queue to go out. A bearded man was taking the cover off a Mini while the woman with him fastened a child into a seat.

'My future in-laws cover their car,' Anita said. 'Salt air damages the paint.'

Just beyond that Mini was a familiar car, a white Rover with a Hull number plate. Nell had seen it before. It belonged to Derek Jeffrey. She was now hyper-alert. Yes, he could be driving this way back from Durham, but why would he? When he tried to get out of going to HMP Durham for the induction course, he made it appear that it was because he thought he could help by staying at Brackerley. His reason for wanting to stay now became suspicious. With a high-level investigation going on, he wanted to safeguard his property – keep an eye on the cigarettes under the boxing ring.

Nell wanted to bring back Diane quietly. It wouldn't do for Diane to think that Nell had brought in reinforcements. Not that she would have brought Jeff. The finger of suspicion about contraband cigarettes didn't now just point at him, it poked him in the eye. Nell wished she had taken notice of Jeff's number plate, other than spotting it was a Hull plate, as was this one. She got out to take a quick look. If it wasn't Jeff's car, it belonged to someone who smoked the same cigarettes. There was a packet of Gauloises on the dashboard.

Nell drove past it and along through the car park to the bottom end.

'This is a good place,' Anita said. 'We're quite close here.'

Nell pulled in. She turned off the engine, opened the door and went to the boot for her car cover and plastic mac.

Anita watched her shake out the car cover. 'My boyfriend can't be faffed with putting a car to bed under a plastic sheet. He doesn't believe it makes a difference and you can have a re-spray anyway.'

'Your boyfriend is probably right, but since I have a cover – Anita, grab that end, would you?'

Nell did not say that covering the car was not due to fear of salt air damaging the paint but to avoid making her presence known. She drew the sheet down and tied the tape to the bumper so as to obscure the number plate.

She put on her plastic mac.

Anita said, 'It's not raining.'

'It might.' A woman wearing a smart black suit in a caravan park might stand out, and be recognisable. The Rover may or may not belong to Prison Officer Derek Jeffrey, but it was better not to take a chance. At the very least, he might plonk his two big feet in her delicate prisoner recovery operation. At worst, he might be up to something that she'd like to keep an eye on without being seen.

They set off walking. 'I love the caravan,' said Anita. 'The trouble is that I share the bed with Henry's mother. Henry sleeps at the other end with his dad.'

In Anita's place, such an arrangement would have struck Nell as too high a price. 'Do your future in-laws know that Diane is here?'

'Only Henry knows. Diane was upset and scared, wanting to be out of the way. We couldn't just sit, waiting for a knock on the door.' Anita was having second thoughts. 'I hope Diane isn't going to have my guts for garters when she sees you.'

'I'm sure she won't.' Nell turned and pointed back. 'Is that white car often here?'

'I've seen it before. Henry's dad knows the driver. He owns a few of the caravans and the garage in Beverley where Henry's dad takes his car for service.'

Not Jeff's then. Nell realised she was being too cautious and need not have bothered with the car cover. 'When we get to the caravan, you tap on the door first, Anita. It'll give your sister too much of a shock to see me.'

They walked past rows of neat arc-shaped cream caravans. Most were now shut up after the weekend, curtains closed, buckets and spades lying under the caravans to be picked up again next weekend.

Nell heard the sound of children's laughter, and 'Caught you out!'

'No! I caught you out.'

'That's them,' Anita said.

Nell saw the little boy first. He was blond and skinny, lying on the ground on his side and rolling with laughter as he pointed to the other side of the caravan.

Anita called to him and he came running, jumping at her. She grabbed him in a hug.

'We were playing this game and the rule is one of us hides and the other comes looking, but you're not allowed to look under the caravans because then you see their feet!' He began to laugh so hard he couldn't stop.

A girl emerged from the other side of the caravan. She was laughing, too. 'You cheated!'

'So did you, or you wouldn't have seen me.'

The boy said, 'Have you brought us sweets?'

Anita ruffled his hair. 'No, because I didn't know I was coming.'

Nell stepped to the side of the caravan door to be out of sight while Anita knocked. The door opened.

The children went inside.

Nell heard Diane's voice. 'I told you to stay close, where were you?'

She didn't hear the children's reply.

Anita followed. 'Diane, you have a visitor. Don't blow your top.'

Nell stepped into the caravan. 'Sorry to startle you, Diane. May I come in?'

Diane looked from Nell to her sister. 'It's for the best,' Anita said.

Nell took a bar of chocolate from her bag. The children stood side by side, looking up at her.

'My name's Miss Lewis, what are your names?'

'Ruby.' They eyed the chocolate.

'Albert.'

'Ruby, Albert, through that slatted door, is that one of those beds that comes out double and you can jump on it?'

'Yes.'

'Off you go and jump then, is that all right with you, Mrs Redmond?'

Diane said, 'Yes. Get jumping, kids. I might come and join you.'

Anita went to the slatted door. 'Don't eat that chocolate while you're jumping. Don't get any on the bedclothes.' She closed the doors and turned to Diane. 'Henry's mum and dad won't be pleased.'

'Bugger them,' Diane said. 'You won't stick with him anyway, if you've the sense you were born with.'

'Diane, will you tell me why you absconded?' Nell spoke quietly.

Diane lit a cigarette. Her hand shook. 'Who else is with you, ma'am?'

'I came alone.'

Diane got up and closed the curtains. 'No one else from the prison?'

'No. Talk to me. You're not in big trouble yet. I can take you back tonight. Otherwise, you could be transferred to a closed prison for a longer stretch.'

'I'll never be safe now.'

Nell said, 'Yes, you will. Trust me.'

Diane took a drag of her cigarette. 'Well, it's a long story, and we've no milk, and I daren't go outside.'

Anita went to sit beside Diane. 'I thought you'd feel safe

here. You can't stop here if you're going to sit shaking. And never mind milk. I can go for milk if the shop's still open.'

There would be a telephone in the shop. Nell would call Brackerley and tell the chief she had located Diane and would be bringing her back.

'Shop will be shut now. I was going to get some milk earlier, but I saw his car.' Diane reached for an ashtray decorated with a seagull and the words Hornsea Pottery.

'Whose car?' Nell asked.

Diane shook her head. She didn't want to say.

Being inside the caravan behind closed curtains created the feeling of being cut off from the rest of the world. The children had stopped jumping, there was no sound from outside. There was only one car from the prison that Diane would have seen, and only one car that Nell recognised, and Anita had said that it belonged to a garage owner.

'I think I know which car, but you must tell me. Give me the name,' said Nell.

Diane whispered, 'The white Rover, Officer Jeffrey.'

What was he doing here, Nell wondered, taking a scenic route? Stopping overnight in a caravan? No, he was up to something.

'When did he arrive?'

'I saw it earlier this evening.'

'Is there a telephone outside the shop?'

'No. It's inside. The next nearest public phone is in the pub along the lane about half a mile away.'

The jumping resumed, the caravan rocked again.

Nell said, 'I'm going to tell you something. You are going to tell me something. You are coming back with me and you will be safe. Now you tell me, what is your connection to Officer Derek Jeffrey?'

'He wasn't always Derek Jeffrey.'

'Explain.'

'He came to Hull when he was little. He was sent here. He had one relative, his grandmother, Mrs Turner. She already had his cousin Billy. Billy was her blue-eyed boy. But the authorities brought Derek. He was on the school register as Derek Turner because that's what his grandmother told them. She didn't like Mr Jeffrey, her daughter's husband, so she wouldn't have that name under her roof.'

Nell began to think Diane was making this up, spinning a yarn to hide a darker story. 'Are you saying that Officer Jeffrey has two identities?'

'No. A few of us knew his name but the teacher called his name as Turner and he answered. Eventually, when we were in the seniors, he brought in his ration book and school had to change it and send for a birth certificate and someone went to see his grandmother. By then, Billy was dead. Old Mrs Turner stopped caring what Derek called himself.'

'She must have been devastated when Billy died.'

Diane looked in the direction of the jumping Albert and Ruby. She lowered her voice. 'It said in the paper that Billy fell while he was walking across a beam in the bombed-out house where we used to play, our den. It had been blocked up but there's always ways in. Billy fell. He fell because Derek pushed him.' She was crying now. 'He lay there, on broken bricks and cracked tiles.'

Anita stared at her. 'You were mad. Why play in such a dangerous place?'

'It was a good place on a rainy day. We'd all walked across that beam, that was what you had to do, to be in the gang. Derek came up with a new game. He would walk from one side of the beam and Billy from the other and then turn around and go back. We all knew Billy didn't have a lot of nerve, but he had to do it. The two of them, Derek and Billy, they met in the middle. Billy froze, and then we watched him fall. Derek said he was trying to help him. It was a push. We all knew it. Gloria was the one who said it aloud.'

The pause seemed endless. Nell said, 'Is that why Derek gave Gloria thirty pounds to go to Australia, to keep her quiet?'

Diane looked at her sister. Anita shrugged.

Diane said, 'I think so. Gloria was drinking a lot at my wedding.'

'She was,' Anita said. 'She was so jolly, so funny.'

'And then her mood would swing, so you never knew what she would say next.'

Nell wanted to be absolutely sure. 'Diane, are you certain that we are talking about the same person, Prison Officer Jeffrey?'

'Yes, ma'am. You had Officer Meadowcroft and Officer Jeffrey pop into the library so that we would recognise them as officers. I kept my head down. I had to look up and say hello, but I pretended not to know him.' Diane paused to light a cigarette. 'On Sunday, when the chaplain said a prayer for Governor Harding and in the same breath said that Arthur was missing, I thought everyone would see me shaking.'

'Diane, Arthur is safe. He was seen thumbing a lift, like you did. Nothing bad has happened to him. Go on with what you were telling me.'

'After we cleaned the governor's house, Miss Kitteringham walked us up to the farm. We went to see the pigs. Arthur was there, mucking out the piggery. We knew each other straight away. Miss Kitteringham asked him did he enjoy his job. He said he liked it well enough but would be going back to his own occupation, dealing in scrap metal. A business partner would put up the capital. Miss Kitteringham said something polite and encouraging, and then a pig came up to look at her and she started to scratch its ears. Arthur gave me the wink, slipped me a bar of chocolate, and he mouthed the name, "Derek Jeffrey", and "he's here". Of course, by then, I already knew. Arthur asked me what did I think of Brackerley. Miss Kitteringham stopped stroking the pig and turned and looked at me, to hear what I'd say. I said that I missed my kids and didn't know when they'd get over to see me.'

Anita interrupted: 'Henry will bring them over.'

'No, he won't.'

Nell said, 'Go on, Diane. Did Arthur say anything else?'

'He said, "There's bound to be someone who'll arrange for them to come across. Some old friend." I knew who he meant.'

'Diane, what happened to the grandmother? Is Mrs Turner still alive?' Anita asked.

'They moved to Beverley. She died on Derek's eighteenth birthday. She fell down the stairs.'

Nell had heard enough. She tapped on the louvred door. 'Ruby, Albert, come out with me. I want to show you a game.' The children were out in a flash. If Nell could find out Diane's whereabouts so easily, so would Jeff. Nell picked up her bag.

If Jeff knew which caravan they were in, he would have a row number, and the rows were clearly marked. 'We won't be long.' The children leapt out onto the grass.

Nell stepped out. 'Lock the door behind me. We'll rat-ta-ta-tat on the window when we want to come in.'

Diane said, 'What are you going to do, ma'am?'

'I'm going to buy a pint of milk and make sure the coast is clear for us to leave.'

'Shop's shut.'

'I'll find someone to open it.'

The little voice in Nell's head said, What if Diane is lying? If she is telling the truth, everything she has said could be denied or challenged.

What Nell needed to do was get Diane, Anita and the kids away from here and make sure that Jeff stayed put. She would disable his car.

The children were waiting to hear about the promised game. It might be that Jeff was here for the night with his lady friend. He had said he would be back at work on Monday morning. Or, he could be here because he had found out where Diane was hiding. If so, he would need to know which caravan she was in.

'Here's the game,' Nell said. 'All those little flags at the end of each row of caravans, pull them out and make a pile of them somewhere no one will find them.'

'You're not allowed,' Albert said.

Ruby was more practical. 'We won't find our own way back.'

'Yes, you will. Put something under the end caravan, a spade or a bucket or a big stone. Afterwards we put it all back. If anyone sees you, run back to your caravan really fast and hide underneath. There'll be a shilling each for you.'

They were off.

Nell lifted the hood of her rain mac and covered her hair. She walked back in the direction she had come, moving along the caravans, cutting through, noticing how many owners and renters had now gone home. Here and there, an elderly couple sat on deckchairs outside their caravan, reading the Sunday papers.

By the time she reached the white Rover, the last rays of the setting sun cast a gleam over the bonnet. Nell took out her Swiss army knife first. It was not as easy as she imagined, slashing tyres. One had to give vandals a certain credit for energy and skill. No doubt there would be a spare in the boot but that would still leave three beyond repair, she hoped. It would be better to take no chances. Driving without side mirrors was illegal and very difficult. She put away the knife and took out the torch. Of course, it might make a noise, but she only had to do it twice.

In the strength of material stakes, the 1940s flashlight outweighed the 1960s side mirrors. Nell did not linger to admire her handiwork. She took off the plastic raincoat, folded it and pushed it in her bag. She then walked along the rows until she spotted the camp shop, the Shoreline Caravan Park Stores. It did not matter what fancy name a place was given, it would always be a holiday camp and this was the camp shop. The sign on the door was turned to Closed. She could see a light in the back.

Nell knocked on the door. When no one answered, possibly because no one heard, she went round the side and looked through a window. It was a stock room. The shelves across from her were stacked with holidaymakers' staples, tins of baked beans, spaghetti in tomato sauce, Fray Bentos and spam. Three people sat at a kitchen table. One of them was Jeff. Even with his back to her, she recognised him. He turned his head to speak to the woman next to him, a glamorous creature who might be the mysterious lady friend.

They looked out of place in a holiday camp shop. He'll go far, Nell thought to herself. He's in his element in the Prison Service, and here too. It would not surprise her to learn that he owned the place. A grandmother dying when he was eighteen gave him a better financial start than most teenagers could dream of.

Not wanting to walk half a mile to use a pub telephone, Nell tapped on the window.

The owner, or manager, whatever he was, raised his hands and made crossing motions to indicate they were closed. The other two ignored her. She tapped again, had his attention, and called, 'Fire!' Whether he heard her or not, he read her lips. She bobbed out of the way as he rose from his chair and went back round to the front of the shop.

'Where?' he said, as he opened the door.

'Top end, near the car park.'

'Lizzie!' he shouted as he ran out. 'Call the fire brigade!'

Nell sighed. That had not been her best idea. She went back round to the side window. Jeff was gone, and so was the woman. All she had to do was wait, and hope Jeff would not lock the shop door as he went after the owner, which he would be certain to do. Catching arsonists and putting out fires would be just the ticket for a man who, by his own estimation, went at a hundred miles an hour. The boys would be the action men.

Nell went back to the main door. Looking between the rows of caravans, she saw two men, running, one very fast and in the lead, a fire extinguisher under his arm, the other a portly man, stopping for breath, putting the fire extinguisher down for a moment, his shoulders heaving, and then picking it up and carrying on.

The woman was on the telephone, nodding, and talking, and nodding.

Nell waited outside the telephone booth. The door opened. 'How did you get in?' she asked. It was a polite question, but so it should be to a well-turned-out woman of five foot six, hair nicely coiffed, wearing a Jaeger suit and carrying a beautifully made leather satchel.

'I'm sorry, I realise the shop must be closed but I have to make an urgent telephone call.'

'We know about the fire.'

'I suppose I ought to talk to the caravan park owner.'

'Can I help?'

With no way of knowing who this woman was or whether she could be trusted, Nell decided against taking her up on the offer. 'Some vandals have been damaging cars,' she said.

'Has your car been damaged?'

'The worst was a big white car. Someone must have taken a sledgehammer to it.'

'What sort of white car?'

'I'm no good on cars.' Nell paused, as if trying to remember. 'Very elegant, a strip along the side. Rover, that's it.'

'At the top end of the car park?'

'Yes.'

The woman turned pale. 'That's ours! I'd better go see.'

'How awful,' Nell sympathised. 'Would you mind if I ring the breakdown people? I'll be quick.'

'Go ahead. Will you stay in the shop till we get back, and keep the door closed?'

'I will.'

Nell rang 999. To the familiar question, Police, Ambulance, Fire, she answered 'Police, Hull police.'

She was connected quickly. 'Hello, my name is Helen Lewis. I'm prison governor at HMP Brackerley and I am at the Shoreline Caravan Park at Hornsea to take back an absconding prisoner. Officers Fraser and Tomelty can vouch for me. They pulled me over earlier today. I'm unfamiliar with the area and am escorting not just my prisoner but her sister and two children. I should be most grateful for an escort back to Hull.'

If she were wrong, this would be the most appalling gaff in the history of . . . Nell's imagination failed her.

'Where are you calling from, madam?'

'From a telephone box in the Shoreline Caravan Park's store.'

'Are you able to stay where you are?'

'No. I have to go back to the caravan. It's on E row. There's a standpipe at either end of the row. It's the fourth one down, cream, with blue and white check curtains that are closed.'

'Go back to your caravan. Don't open the door until a police officer shows you his ID at the window.'

'Thank you.'

Nell rooted for her purse and put a coin in the slot. She dialled Brackerley. The Chief answered.

'Governor here, Chief. I'm in Hornsea with Diane, her children and her sister. We're safe. Call Harrogate CID. Urgent message for DCI Julian McHale to come to Brackerley. I'll be back in around two hours and I have information for him.'

'Received loud and clear, ma'am.' Nell thought that such a pithy phrase ought to be said over a short-wave radio in a room where people wore earphones.

She answered in kind: 'Over and out, Chief.'

She picked up a pint of milk, put payment by the till and quietly left.

As she walked back to the caravan, a clanging bell announced the fire engine. She watched as it hurtled into view and came to a stop in front of the store. Nell edged closer, in time to see a fireman with a puce face stride towards Jeff and his lady friend, asking in a booming voice, 'Who rang the fire brigade?'

Nell slipped on her raincoat and put up the hood. It could be unpleasant when people raised their voices, and quite unnecessary. The exchange between the fire brigade chief and Jeff and his lady friend was becoming heated. Since the police were on their way, there may have been no need to disable Jeff's car, but it was better to err on the side of caution.

The officer who tapped on the caravan window and showed his ID was Fraser. Tomelty stood beside him.

Back at her car with Diane and the children, Nell untied and removed the cover she had placed over it. Diane got in the back with Ruby and Albert. They had to wait for Anita, who was still in the caravan, trying to do a quick tidy before locking the door and hurrying to join them. 'What a mess we've left. His mam and dad will go mad.'

Nell followed the police car, now with lights flashing but no siren, back to Hull. Tomelty parked the police car on the waste ground by the Red Lion.

Nell continued to Mrs Sowerby's house and parked outside. The day's events cost Nell two shillings, and a story to Ruby and Albert about why there was no need for them to put the caravan row number flags back into the ground. Anita sat quietly beside Nell.

Mrs Sowerby heard the car draw up and came to the

window. Nell waited while Diane, Anita and the children went inside. After five minutes, Diane came out and got in the back seat.

Fraser and Tomelty, blue lights flashing, led Nell and her prisoner along unfamiliar roads to the outskirts of York, well beyond their patch. They pulled over under a streetlamp. Fraser got out.

'What is he up to?' Diane asked.

'He obviously wants to talk to me.'

Nell got out of the car and walked to the pavement.

'You'll be on a straight road to Harrogate from here, ma'am.'

'Thank you, officer.'

'So, we might get two stars in your diary?'

'At least.'

'Tell me,' he asked, 'did you happen to notice a white Rover in the caravan camp car park?'

'I particularly noticed it when we arrived because, unless I'm mistaken, it belongs to one of my officers, Derek Jeffrey.'

'It had been vandalised, or disabled.'

'Not when we arrived it hadn't.'

'Do you happen to know what might have brought Officer Jeffrey to Hornsea?'

Nell glanced in the car at Diane, raised a hand and smiled to reassure her. 'I don't know what brought him to Hornsea, officer. He will be transferring from HMP Brackerley to HMP Durham next week as principal officer. He was there this weekend for an induction. He must have decided to call at Hornsea on the way back.'

'And how is your absconder?'

'She's going to be all right. We've had a difficult first

week at Brackerley. I had to call in the police. I can't go into details, but DCI Julian McHale from Harrogate has been on the premises.'

'I'm sorry to hear of your trouble, ma'am.'

'We'll pull through.'

'I'm sure you will. Ma'am, you may not be seeing Mr Jeffrey first thing tomorrow. He is helping us with certain enquiries. Now, we're going to take you just that little bit farther to the roundabout where you'll see the sign for Harrogate.'

They were ten miles from Brackerley when Nell said, 'Tell me, Diane, after you exchanged a few words with Arthur Burnett and you got the idea that Prison Officer Jeffrey might do you the favour of arranging transport for the children to come and visit, did you speak to him? Officer Jeffrey, I mean.'

It took five more miles before Diane answered.

'I nearly didn't. But I wanted to see the kids. Wanted them to know I haven't vanished off the face of the earth.'

'What happened when you spoke to him?'

'I went out early for a quiet smoke, between the gatehouse and the visitors' block – no one can see you there. I'd been out a couple of times, hoping to spot him. He didn't see me, so I called to him. He looked about, checking whether there was anyone nearby. I wasn't nasty, threatening, not hinting about anything. Why would I? Nobody could touch him now. All I said was, did he know anyone who was coming this way on a Saturday who might bring Anita and the kids over to see me. He came up really close, toe to toe. He said he refused to be blackmailed. If I so much as looked at him the wrong way, I'd regret it. He said that he knew I'd lost my house. The landlord wasn't a charity, and neither was he. I couldn't answer. I tried to walk away, but he was blocking me. He said, "I expect your kids have moved in with your mam and Anita." He told me he'd always liked my mam. He remembered that one day she gave him a boiled egg, and he couldn't believe his luck. He said, "Those were the days, eh? But those days are over." If you'd seen his face, his eyes, you'd know why I'm afraid.'

'I'm so sorry you've had such distress.'

Diane hugged herself, rubbing her hands up and down her arms. 'Olga said things would get worse before they got better. But it's not over. Why would anyone take my word against his? Lock me in my room if he's still at Brackerley.'

'I believe you, Diane. You're going to be safe now.'

Diane was right to be anxious. The police had Jeff in custody, helping with enquiries, but he was a slippery customer.

Crofty was in the gatehouse. Nell caught sight of him in her headlights as he came out to open the gates. He brought the gate-book and a pen to the car so that she would not have to get out.

'Ma'am.'

'Thanks, Crofty.'

Nell drove the few yards to the house. 'A few things puzzle me, Diane.'

'I'm in a maze myself, ma'am.'

'Why did you invite Derek Jeffrey to your wedding when you believed that he'd pushed Billy to his death, and you suspected that he killed his grandmother?'

'I didn't invite him. He came with a girl I was in the youth club with. After we stopped bothering with the youth club, we used to go dancing together. She'd just got engaged to Derek, on the rebound.'

'Are you still in touch with her?'

'She died. She drowned in a swimming pool when Derek

took her to Spain on their honeymoon. He made a big fuss. It was in the paper. He tried to sue the hotel.'

Nell parked her car by the door. Lights were on in the admin office and the reception area. She took her keys from her bag, but someone had been watching out for the car. The front door opened.

Nell got out. 'Come on, Diane.'

Chief Officer Markham stood in the doorway. 'I haven't been waiting behind the door for several hours, ma'am. Hull police gave us your ETA. Welcome back, Diane.'

Kit appeared. She stepped forward to take charge of Diane.

'Miss Kitteringham, please search Diane, give her a cup of cocoa, a slice of bread, and then take her to segregation,' said Nell.

Diane did not move or speak. She stood rooted to the spot. Kit put her arm around her to escort her. Diane struggled to free herself. 'I can't be on my own!'

'You won't be,' Nell said. 'An officer will be watching you. She'll have an alarm that the security patrol will hear.'

Nell watched them go, and then turned to Miss Markham. 'Chief, debriefings?'

'All quiet. Mrs Friel has volunteered to watch Diane. She and I will do three hours on, three hours off, if that's agreeable, ma'am.'

'Thank you.' Nell unlocked her office. 'Give me five minutes. We'll compare notes.' She looked at her watch, remembering that she had told Diane's dormitory mates that she would let them know when Diane was back.

She went upstairs. The dormitory door was slightly ajar. Olga was talking in a whisper. Nell tapped on the door and said quietly, 'Who's awake?'

Olga said, 'All of us.'

'You can go to sleep now. Diane is back, in one piece.'

'When will we see her?' That was Cherry.

'Goodnight, all.'

Nell went back to her office.

The chief had brought in a tray with cheese sandwiches, a pot of tea and two cups. Until now, Nell had not noticed how hungry she felt.

The chief poured milk in the cups. 'DCI McHale will be here in the morning. He telephoned from home. I believe he was ready to come straight over, but I sensed a domestic situation erupting in the background while we were talking.'

Nell felt glad that Julian had not come this evening. Enough was enough for one day.

The chief poured tea. 'Did Diane spin you a yarn?'

'A very good yarn. I believe her.'

Nell felt a draught, which must be the cool air of her chief officer's scepticism. 'Chief, what is your honest opinion of Officer Jeffrey?'

'He is a superb hundred miles an hour officer. I don't know where his money comes from and I don't trust him. It crossed my mind that he may be moving to Durham because he has friends there, on the other side of the bars. And I didn't say any of that to you just now, because I have no evidence.' They sat in silence for a while. The chief topped up their cups. 'I told the major my suspicions. By then, he was ill. He didn't want to believe me at first. Jeffrey kept the major in whisky. They'd chat. Boxing. Football. They took some of the lads fishing. There was a day when the penny dropped and the major saw Jeff for what he was.'

Thirty-One

On Monday morning, an outside money adviser was coming to talk to Olga about her financial affairs. Olga and Linda had permission to be in the library for the meeting.

Officer Meadowcroft had placed a sign on the library door: MEETING IN PROGRESS.

Olga could not help viewing Officer Meadowcroft as a slip of a girl, a very efficient slip of a girl. Her office was next door to the governor's so that must count for something.

Olga and Linda came into the library early, so as to set out Olga's papers on the long table.

Linda could see that Olga was nervous. She was saying, 'Remind me what that pile is,' and 'Shouldn't all the red bills go together and the black summonses go together?'

Each pile of papers had a neat piece of stiff paper on top, cut from porridge oats packaging, and was tied with string using a slip knot. In the centre of the table were the deeds to the house.

To accompany the bundles of papers, Linda had made a list of dates, such as when Olga's gas and electricity were cut off.

Some dates had VE for Visitor Enemy, the neighbour who persistently knocked on Olga's door, offering to clear her debts in exchange for the keys to her house. One of these dates had a tick, to mark the day Olga hit VE with the poker and broke his arm in two places.

Olga went to the window and tried to open it. 'A bluebird might fly in and bring me luck.'

'The window won't open,' Linda said, 'and we don't have bluebirds in this country.'

'Yes we do. There's a song about them.'

A bird thudded against the window. Olga looked out. 'I can't see it. It must be all right.'

There were bills from a locksmith who repaired two broken locks and supplied new keys.

Some of Olga's clients had written her notes of thanks for her predictions and reassurances. Linda labelled these Olga's Testimonials. This was Olga's favourite bundle.

Loans Olga had taken out were listed in a payment book. Letters showed the amounts of interest due, figures that Olga felt sure must be wrong.

Linda had read about forgotten bank accounts, unclaimed inheritances, old stocks and shares. 'Is there any money in a bank or a building society, anything at all that is due to you?'

'Only my pension, which feeds me and the cat. I was robbed of my earnings when I was warned to stop contacting my clients' lost loved ones.'

Olga produced another package.

'Where did that come from?' Linda asked.

'My good neighbour took it to Holloway and they sent it on. She's doing her best, but the vultures are circling. I need this advice person to sort them out and send them packing.'

They were early by half an hour. Olga couldn't keep still. She said, 'Did I tell you the story about the prisoner on Dartmoor who hatched an egg in his cell? I didn't know him, but I was told the story by someone who did know him. He was a housebreaker.'

'No, you didn't tell me that one.'

'From Dartmoor working parties would go out on the moor. One day, out with a working party, this man, the housebreaker, he took an egg from a nest. He carried it under his armpit to keep it warm. He kept the bird warm until it hatched and then he fed and cared for it. It would fly out of his cell from between the bars and come back. Sometimes it would bring him a little treat such as a worm.'

Linda edged the papers about to make sure Deeds to House was dead centre. She said, 'What warders would allow a prisoner to hatch an egg and keep a bird with him?'

'The warders didn't know until the fledgling hatched. The housebreaker knew the chick was still alive. He had been taught how to put the egg in water and see which way it tilted.'

Olga picked up the Testimonials papers. 'The adviser can sit on this side. We'll have my testimonials where she'll see them.'

'It's the financial matters she'll be looking into,' Linda said. 'And about Dartmoor: the warders would have known that a bird was flying in and out of the housebreaker's cell.'

'That was allowed,' Olga insisted. 'Thanks to Queen Victoria who gave permission.'

'If you knew this man who knew the prisoner, wasn't Queen Victoria dead by then?'

Olga gave a triumphant little sniffle. 'Ah, but Queen

Victoria decreed that men on Dartmoor could keep birds in their cells.'

Linda conceded defeat. 'Good for her. A pity she didn't decree they could have glazed windows instead of just bars.'

'They may have been warmer with proper windows,' Olga said, 'but it would have been a poor show for that man's tame bird if it couldn't come and go.'

There was a tap on the door. Officer Meadowcroft opened the door and introduced them to Sylvia Davis. Olga had seen a play called *Who is Sylvia?* She had liked that play. She also greatly admired Bette Davis. The name augured well.

Olga was relieved to see that the adviser person was grey-haired, perhaps the same age as Olga, though you never could tell. There were Peter Pan sorts of people whose lives had not been battered by misfortune and malice. This woman might be older than she looked, which would be to the good. There were cat hairs on her brown coat.

Sylvia Davis took out a notebook and pen.

Linda's notebook and pen were already on the table.

'This is my friend Linda. She helped me with the papers,' said Olga.

'Are you happy for Linda to sit in?' the adviser asked.

Olga was happy.

Officer Meadowcroft left, saying she would be in her office if needed.

The adviser looked at the documents on the table. She opened the package that had come from Holloway and spent a long time looking at each document.

'Miss Tagney, there are two kinds of loans, secured and unsecured. You have both sorts. Your debtors can take you to court for the unsecured debts.'

'They already have.'

'Your property is at risk when you take out secured loans. Was that explained to you?'

'It may have been, or I may have thought it was something that wouldn't happen. I have the deeds to my house.'

The adviser looked at the deeds. 'With your permission, I will take some of these papers to your admin office to be copied. It's possible that the firm of solicitors your father dealt with is still in existence and could act for you in the sale of your house.'

'No! You can't sell my house.'

'I can't, but you can. That may be the best way of clearing your debts and leaving something over for you. It would be best to act quickly before the interest and costs increase and before your debtors lay claim to the house. They are entitled to do that.'

'I don't want to part with my house.'

'Of course you don't, but that might be the best option. Will you bear with me while I ask whether your admin officer has a London directory? I can find out whether the solicitors who acted for your father are still listed, or I can find out from another source.'

'A solicitor would want paying,' Olga said.

'Yes, out of the proceeds. You would then be making a decision based on hard information, rather than hazarding guesses. What I'll do is gather the facts. Do you agree?'

'I suppose so. What do you think, Linda?'

'It's up to you, but it sounds the right thing to me.'

'Very well.' Olga took a sip of water. She had hoped for some encouraging words, that everything would be all right, that she could pay five shillings a week or something of that sort.

Sylvia Davis left them sitting there, looking at each other.

Olga took out her roll-ups. Her hands were shaking. She went to the fireplace. Linda took the matches and lit the cigarette for her. Olga inhaled. She blew smoke into the grate.

Linda poured her a glass of water. 'Take a few sips. You'll come out all right. I have a feeling. From everything you've said, that house has been a millstone round your neck.'

She went to the windows. 'This one opens. Come and get some air, take deep breaths.'

Olga took a breath. 'I don't like fresh air. It makes me dizzy. I can't breathe when I'm away from London.'

'You'll get used to it.'

'Oh God.'

'What?'

'I'll end up a hopeless case, like the old women who throw a brick on Christmas Eve to get into Holloway for Christmas dinner. I'll be a bird with no nest, nowhere to fly to.'

Sylvia Davis came back. They all sat down at the table.

'The solicitor is still in North London. Here's the new name.' She passed Olga a note. 'There's another partner. They will be willing to act for you. You're a historic client and they won't let you down. Solicitors can be human. Let me find out as much as I can. Do you have any questions?'

Neither Olga nor Linda could think of any.

The adviser offered Olga her hand. 'I'll do my best for you and will be in touch soon.'

'Do I have to part with my house?'

'I'm sorry to be so blunt, but I won't raise false hopes. It will be entirely up to you what action you take, but if you don't take that first step you will lose control altogether. House prices have increased considerably since your father bought the property. Let's see what can be salvaged. When a house has taken a heavy toll, people sometimes feel much freer when it's gone.'

Linda began to put the papers back into the carrier bags.

Olga stayed put. She stared at her hands, palm down on the oak table. She spread her fingers. 'Sometimes you see yourself differently,' Olga said. 'It happens suddenly. These hands aren't mine. They're my mother's hands.'

Olga did not like the smell of this library. It reminded her of musty attics, and her own junk.

Linda said, 'You should take your papers back to reception.'

'I will in a minute.'

'See you later.' Linda now had the notebook in her pocket that was full of Olga's business, her personal information. It ought to be somewhere safe. She had no private place. The chief officer appeared in the hall. Linda thought she might ask her where she could put something private, to be safe, but Miss Markham got in first.

'Linda, there you are. Has your meeting finished?'

'Yes, miss.'

'I'd like a word. The library?'

'Olga is still in there.'

The chief officer opened the opposite door. 'In here then.' It was a room with too many chairs and a snooker table. Miss Markham sat and waved Linda to join her. 'Linda, the chaplain would like to speak to you.'

'What about, miss?'

'He'll tell you.'

Linda already knew. She bit her lip. The chaplain was the person who broke the news when a prisoner's relative died.

Thirty-Two

In the visitors' block, Nell and Julian took seats on either side of a table, prisoner and visitor fashion. He lit a cigarette. 'I was glad you pulled me into the loop so quickly, after you spotted Derek Jeffrey at the caravan park.'

'I'm not aware that I pulled you into any loop.'

He gave a small smile. 'If you didn't, I'm not sure how Hull CID knew who to ask for. They're talking to Mr Jeffrey about certain items, missing from Hull docks and found in the boot of his car and in storage in the cellar of a caravan park shop in Hornsea.'

'So Jeff had combined his induction weekend at HMP Durham with an inspection of his new storage facilities.'

'The caravan park owner was only too ready to talk. He'd had a bad day. Hull police have had Derek Jeffrey on their radar a long time. He always came out squeaky clean. Being in the Prison Service gave him a good cover and kept him beyond reach. Coppers only come onto prison property when invited. I'll be working with Hull CID. They're going over his house in Beverley with a fine-tooth comb and going back through their records. Mrs Turner, Jeffrey's grandmother, was a healthy old lady, steady on her pins. Her fall down the stairs was suspicious. Jeffrey, her beneficiary, was supposedly fifty miles away. Arthur Burnett believed it was an accident. He gave Jeff an alibi.'

'So Arthur was blackmailing Jeff?' Nell said.

'That's how Jeff saw it. Arthur's a simple soul. He'll have seen Jeff's response to a request for a favour as an old mate doing him a good turn. The off-duty copper who gave him a lift said Arthur was shocked and scared.'

'Why?'

'I'll come to that in a minute.'

Nell stood. 'Julian, let's go for a walk as we talk about this. The residents will be in here soon with a couple of officers. We're going to smarten the place up before next Saturday. Diane is expecting visitors. She wouldn't be in prison if she'd known who was pulling the strings behind what she stored in her cellar.'

'She's low down the food chain, just like the man who asked her to do the favour on Jeffrey's behalf.'

Nell remembered that she had felt iffy about Jeff's cockiness when she first met him. In spite of that she, and everyone else, had him down as a good guy, for a while.

Trust your first instincts until proved wrong.

'How's Diane Redmond today?' Julian asked.

Nell knew what was coming. 'She spent last night in solitary. She'll be there a few more hours.'

'Oh.'

'Oh what?'

'This case needs to be watertight. I need another statement from her. I have her mother's and her sister's statements.'

They walked up towards the farm. Nell wanted to give the Ramsdens the news that Arthur was safe and well. They reached the cottage. It would be a while before Nell went back in there. She turned towards the garden. 'Let's go sit down. I want to hear what else you have to tell me before we get to the farm.'

She led the way to the far end of the garden, passing the magnolia tree where the major had suggested Nell have her photograph taken. 'Another week and Jeffrey would have been transferred to Durham.' Nell sat down on the bench.

Julian joined her. 'That may be where he ends up, but without his prison officer uniform.'

'Just make sure he stays locked up, Julian. I don't want him anywhere near my prison. I hope you're building a strong case.'

'Let me try it out on you.'

'I'm all ears.'

Jeff's motive for murder was to make sure the major did not unburden himself to Nell. He knew that his governor had grown sick of his involvement and was ashamed of being drawn in so deeply. When caught, the bad apple, Horace Thompson, had kept silent about Jeff having masterminded the operation. There must have been a quid pro quo: in return for Thompson's silence, Thompson's family would be taken care of, and there would be a nest egg at the other end of his sentence.

'Is Horace Thompson talking?'

'We're leaning on him,' Julian said, 'and looking into the Thompson family bank accounts. Jeff will be in no position to keep his promises now.'

Nell realised that just by being at Brackerley, Arthur

became a persistent nuisance to Jeff, a reminder of the past, always hoping for favours. 'What about Arthur?'

'We have his statement. Angela drove up to Stanley in County Durham. She has relatives up there and I knew she would do a good job. Arthur had called on the governor during his midday break. Your major had been cleaning his gun and his medals. He was tired. He asked Arthur to do a couple of little jobs, which he did. He changed a light bulb. He carried a few things back upstairs, including a dressing gown, the gun that had been cleaned and oiled and was wrapped in a cloth, and the chocolate box the governor used to store his medals.'

The tone of Julian's voice told Nell that Arthur had been believed. His account would explain the fingerprints found upstairs.

Julian continued. 'Arthur told Governor Harding that Jeff was going to back him, help him set up a scrap metal business and put up the money for a van. The major gave Arthur a fiver, which was all he had in the house. He ordered Arthur to finish what he was doing at the farm, so as not to arouse suspicion, and then to leg it. He said that Jeff would be going to prison for a long time, and that the next time Arthur visited there'd be a lady governor in the cottage and he must say hello.'

They both fell silent. The buzz of a bee became intensely grating. As she thought about the major talking of her future, Nell suddenly lost the strength to rise from the bench. She watched as a blackbird alighted on a nearby branch. It began to sing, a fluty song, ending on a squeaking note. A breeze stirred the willow tree. It was as if everything in nature had something to say about what may have been Governor Major Harding's last conversation.

Julian suddenly rose from the bench and held out his hand to Nell. 'Come on then, stir thyself.'

They walked on, passing the sheds, re-tracing Nell's steps with Jimmy and Samson.

'Julian, it sounds as if you've put Arthur in the clear. You have strong evidence about Jeff's dealings, but what about the murder?'

He scratched his head. 'It's all there. We're piecing it together. His was the footprint by the cottage cellar steps. He was careful about not leaving fingerprints, but not careful enough. The gun had been oiled and wrapped in a cloth. A couple of oily patches on Jeffrey's clothing are being examined. His fingerprints are on the deckchair. He used the cloth that the gun had been wrapped in and then must have shoved it in his pocket. We found it in his car. I won't go into any more details, but we'll get there. And of course, his name is at the top of Governor Harding's "Guilty" list.'

They did not speak again until they reached the farmhouse gate. 'There was one other thing,' Julian said.

'What?'

'While you were at the caravan park, did you see anyone vandalising, or disabling, a white Rover? Derek Jeffrey was more upset about that than his own alleged breaches of the law.'

'Is a charge pending, if they find the person?' Nell asked.

'A reward, I think.'

'I'd certainly give them a reward. I wouldn't have wanted him to follow me and my passengers from the caravan park.' Nell quickly changed the subject. 'If I give you a package for Arthur Burnett, containing a cap and a note, would you see that it's sent on to him?'

Thirty-Three

On her way to see the chaplain and to hear from him what she already knew, Linda got a stone in her right shoe. Somehow, the stone in her shoe made her feel fed up with the world. She could not muster the energy to bend down and take off the shoe. It must have been a small stone to have found its way in. By the time the church came into view, the stone felt huge. When she reached the church gate, she leaned with her back against the gate post. She took off her shoe and shook out the stone. Sorting Olga's papers had taken Linda hours. After paying attention to Olga's money adviser, and making notes because Olga wouldn't remember, Linda felt weary that nothing seemed to go right. She still held the shoe in her hand as the chaplain came out of the side door of the church. He came towards her at a brisk pace.

'Miss Rogers, let me.' He took the shoe from her, bent down and placed it on her foot.

'Thank you.' Linda thought this would be the nearest she would come to a prince charming moment. He had on a cassock with eighteen buttons in three groups of six.

'Will you come to the vicarage, or the church?'

'The church,' she said, having it in view, and not knowing where the vicarage was. She followed him in and wished she had accepted Miss Markham's offer to come with her, but she found sympathy hard to bear and even the sympathy of someone as practical as Chief Officer Markham would bounce Linda off balance and make her feel awkward and aware of her lack of feelings.

How will he break the news, Linda wondered, as they entered the church.

He walked to a pew three rows from the front and stood aside to let her go first. She walked all the way to the other end of the pew so as to be able to get out quick if needed.

He kept a suitable distance. 'Linda – if I may call you Linda?'

'Yes.'

'In some ways you will be expecting sad news because you visited your father in hospital.'

'Yes, Father James, I am expecting to hear that my father has died. I know that it falls to you to tell people.'

'We had a telephone call from the hospital,' he said.

The chaplain said what a shock it can be when a parent dies and how it affects people in all sorts of ways and there is no right or wrong way to respond.

Linda thought he would say something of that sort.

When he said, 'Shall we pray?' she said yes rather than, 'If you like', because that was his job after all. Rain or shine, people have to get on with their job.

He said a prayer for the dead. She liked the words 'plentiful redemption', which for no reason in particular made her picture a big basket of fruit tied with a ribbon.

When they were done, he walked her to the gate and shook

her hand. 'I'm here for you, if you want to talk. Shall I walk you back?'

'I'll be all right, thank you, as long as no stone jumps into my shoe.'

'I'll pray for you, and for no more stones.'

There had been a boxing match on the television while they were continuing the Monopoly game. As she walked back, Linda pictured herself in shorts and a vest and gloves punching her father until he fell and was out for the count, which now he was. She was upset because it was not her punches that had knocked him out.

When she got back, Linda went up to the dormitory. She thought she would kick off her shoes and lie down. No one could object to that on a day such as today.

Cherry was in the dormitory, sitting on the floor by her bed with what Linda thought was a big scrapbook. It wasn't a scrapbook. Cherry was pleased with herself. 'I have my portfolio back. It was sent on to me. My so-called boyfriend and his sister had it. Penny sorted it for me.'

Penny was a highly regarded Holloway prisoner with contacts on the outside who could fix things.

Cherry said, 'I promised to design her a dress and I will. I'll make it for her too. Do you know when she gets out?'

Linda did not know. She lay on her bed.

Cherry went on talking. When Linda did not answer, she asked, 'What's up?'

'Oh, I just had to listen while the chaplain told me that my father died.'

Cherry stood up and came over. She sat on the bed next to Linda. 'I'm so sorry, and here am I wittering on.'

'It's all right.'

'No, it's not!'

'I haven't seen him for years. He didn't come to my trial or write.'

Linda could look back now and say, I wouldn't be here if not for him. 'I heard from my mother that he was demoted at work on the day I was arrested. He probably held that against me.'

'Not to be ghoulish, but will you be going to his funeral?'

'I don't know.'

Cherry got up. She picked up her portfolio and put it back in the envelope. 'I'm putting this behind the chest of drawers. If anyone so much as touches it, I'll chop their hands off.'

'No one will know it's there. I won't tell them. I need a private place for a notebook.'

'Put your notebook behind the chest of the drawers on the other side.'

Linda lay looking at the white painted ceiling. She could see the brush marks. It was soothing to listen to Cherry, who was so completely absorbed in herself that she would ask nothing of a person. And then Cherry surprised her. She said, 'Linda, you could do me a big favour.'

She paused. Linda did, after all, have to prompt, and say, 'What kind of favour?'

'I need to do something other than make cushions and go mad. Let me design you an outfit for your father's funeral. I'll do your hair and your make-up.'

'I've never worn make-up.'

Cherry stood. 'I'd better go back down before I'm missed. But I mean it. You'll go to that funeral and knock 'em all dead.'

Thirty-Four

Nell and the officers were aware that preparations for Linda to go to her father's funeral brought a new lease of life to the residents. Cherry announced that though the velvet curtains from the staffroom were in such a poor state that she would be lucky to get a bolero out of them, the linings were very good and had washed and ironed well. Without consulting Linda as to what she might prefer to wear, Cherry created a two-piece. This consisted of culottes and a short jacket, trimmed with braid. Linda would need tights and new shoes. Given that Linda had spent none of her prison earnings, she was taken into Ripon to make her choice of shoes and a bag. Cherry gave way on the blouse, agreeing that Linda could, at a pinch, wear the striped grey and white Bri-Nylon blouse with a bow that had been donated by the WVS.

There was something else going on, too. Linda was talking more. The four of them would make for their dormitory on the dot. There was a different atmosphere, slightly electric. Linda did not look like a young woman in mourning. It was more as if she was about to set out on an adventure. Cherry's older cousin had sent a portable record player. One night, when Nell went upstairs to get something from her room, she heard them all singing along to Thunderclap Newman's 'Something in the Air'.

On the day when Linda's outfit was ready, all fittings completed, she came downstairs to show everyone. Nell was invited to see the show. It was more like bridesmaids preparing their bride than a person dressing for a funeral.

There were oohs and aahs, except from Cherry.

'What's up?' Linda asked. 'It fits me.'

Cherry pulled a face. She turned to Nell. 'Ma'am, permission for Linda to go to a hairdresser. It's the cut that matters.'

Nell said, 'That's up to Linda.'

Cherry turned to Linda. 'Spend your money, Linda. He'll only die once. This outing isn't for him, it's for you. Make the most of it.'

Nell parked a little way from what she thought must be the main gate to Undercliffe Cemetery. There were no other cars. Nell looked at her watch. 'Better early than late. There's a place where we'll gather, the lodge I think.'

Linda looked straight ahead. 'I don't want to gather. I can find the grave.'

'Won't you want to walk with your mother?'

'I told my mother I would be by the grave.'

'You know your way?'

'Yes.'

They walked along a well-kept path where the branches of trees on either side reached out and just missed connecting with each other.

Linda walked on without speaking.

Nell was used to cemeteries of reasonable proportions, and to large cemeteries where it was hard to find the way back to a grave where you once were on a long-ago day. She had been to cemeteries where there was a Polish section, a war graves corner, a gloriously decorated area of travellers' graves and paupers' graves that were chock-a-block, with room on the headstone for nothing but names. She was used to cemeteries of manageable size where conformist and non-conformist were neatly divided by a broad path and where a local council would surreptitiously decide to move certain worn headstones, tidy the place up, so that a person might go back, taking flowers, and say, Who has moved the stones that were here? Who has moved your stone? Will you know that I remember you if I can't read your name aloud?

Undercliffe Cemetery was like no other Nell had visited. The people buried here knew they would be remembered. They expected no less. On either side of the paths, Gothic monuments reaching for the clouds might have given inspiration to the architects of skyscraper cities. Crosses, obelisks, solemn angels, Grief in the form of a woman in Grecian robes with curling waves in her stony hair, and an Egyptian temple guarded by snakes and sphinxes.

Nell noticed how different Linda looked, stylishly turned out, in black culottes with a wide waistband and a short jacket. No one would have guessed the outfit was made from curtain lining. Her hair had been cut and blow-dried, though she had drawn the line at make-up. Linda walked with more confidence. Nell thought this might be because she had to brace herself for her father's funeral, but the attention she had received from Cherry, Diane and Olga must have helped.

At a fork in the path, Linda hesitated, trying to get her

bearings. 'We have plenty of time,' Nell said. 'They won't have left the church yet.'

The path narrowed. Fallen leaves had been trodden into gulleys. They stepped over brambles. 'Over there,' Linda pointed towards a wall a little way off.

This was an area of modest headstones in permanent shade where weeds grew wild by the wall. On the grave of Alfred and Mabel Pickles stood a jam jar of wilting flowers.

The newly dug grave neighboured that of the Pickles family. Soil piled up at a sufficient distance for mourners' standing room.

No millowners, mayors or bankers rested in this part of the cemetery. Nell put her hand in her pocket and brought out a bag of sweets. She held it out to Linda. 'Officer Friel gave them to me, for you. Pear drops.'

Linda took one. 'Miss Friel says that with pear drops, the taste is consistent. There are none to be fond of and none to strongly dislike.'

'She was your personal officer in Holloway?'

'Yes, ma'am. I am glad she is not here. She would have been upset on my behalf. Upset is not what I am.' Linda held herself stiffly, clenching her fists. Although it was not a cold day, Linda shivered. Nell kept a black stole in the car, an emergency in case of breakdown in the cold. The stole was a present, given to her by a friend who had visited New York. It bore a Saks Fifth Avenue label. Nell put it around Linda's shoulders.

'Sometimes we don't know what we feel until long after an event,' Nell said. She was asking herself how best she might offer support without saying the obvious things. Linda had been coming out of her shell, at least with the other prisoners.

'There is no need to call me ma'am today, Linda, in front of your family and the mourners. I'm here to see you through.'

'Thank you.' She paused. 'The girls call you Miss Jaeger. I could call you that, but I'll call you Miss Lewis.'

'Miss Jaeger?' Nell smiled.

'Cherry told us the brand of your suits. She said you set a good example. We should buy a few quality outfits rather than lots of cheap clothes.' Linda went to stand with her back to the wall. She said, 'There may be people here that I can't bear to be near.'

'Then give me a prod if you want me to come between you and some other person. You'll stand by your mother?'

'Yes.'

'And I'll stand by you.'

'Yes.'

The vicar came to stand by the side of the grave. Four pall-bearers placed the coffin near the mound of earth. The thin, upright woman in black must be Linda's mother. She wore a small hat with a short veil. 'That's her,' Linda said. Mrs Rogers was flagged on one side by a middle-aged couple and on the other side by a woman with an angular face. 'My aunt and uncle and godmother.' Linda edged her way forward. The godmother with the angular face smiled and made room for Linda to stand beside her mother. Briefly, the mother clasped Linda's hand, and then let go. The godmother reached out and patted Linda's arm. The uncle made a point of walking up to Linda, nodding to Nell as she made way for him. He squeezed Linda's shoulder. 'Good lass for coming.' He moved away.

Linda, who had never had a visitor in all her time in prison, was now flanked. Nobody had her back. Nell stood behind her, briefly putting her hands on Linda's shoulders to let her know she was there. Why had no one visited?

Three men stood on the opposite side of the grave, one an elderly hollowed-out man outdoing the others in an expression of infinite sadness. He gave Nell the impression of being a professional mourner, scanning the local paper deaths column for names of an old workmate, or a second cousin once removed, whose family would put on a decent funeral breakfast.

The other two men were in their late fifties, a tall, pale man in a brushed down black suit, the other a portly moustached man in pinstripes.

The vicar began his eulogy. 'We are gathered here today to say goodbye to Frank Rogers, in the sure and certain hope of his resurrection in Jesus Christ Our Lord.' He cleared his throat. 'Frank was husband to Evelyn, father to Linda—'

On hearing Linda's name, two of the men opposite stared at Linda, as if suddenly recognising her.

Linda grasped the edges of the stole and drew it tighter.

The vicar turned the page. 'To every thing there is a season, and a time to every purpose under heaven: A time to be born, and a time to die; a time to plant, and a time to pluck up that which is planted; A time to kill, and a time to heal—'

Linda's head was bowed, but when the vicar said, 'A time to keep silence, and a time to speak,' she looked up, and stared at the men on the other side of the grave.

The man in the black suit moistened his lips.

The moment came when the coffin was lowered.

A small dish of earth was passed round. It went first to Linda's mother. The aunt and uncle and godmother all dipped in. It then came to Linda who took a handful of earth and dropped it onto the coffin. Nell took her turn and then handed the dish to a pall-bearer who took it to the men at the other side of the grave.

'Look at their hands,' Linda whispered, gesturing in the direction of the men who stood side by side.

Nell was not sure what she was looking for, but as the man in black turned his hand to drop earth on the coffin, she saw a tattoo of an eye on his middle finger.

The vicar brought things to an end, with references to dust, and to the spirit travelling upward. He shook hands with Mrs Rogers. The relatives shook hands with the vicar. Linda kept her distance.

The uncle came close and said, as much to Nell as to Linda, 'Will you come back to the Institute for the meal that's laid on?'

Nell's black stole was long. Linda wrapped it around herself twice. 'No thank you, Uncle. I won't go back with you.' She looked across at the two men, side by side in black and in pinstripes.

Linda took a deep breath. 'There's a time to keep silence, and a time to speak. I don't know when that time is, or was. Perhaps it is now. Those two men, the long streak of whitewash and Mister Moustache, with the tattoos on their fingers, are here because they were friends of my father's.' She had started to shake. 'I wish I'd never set eyes on them.'

'What? What about them?' her uncle asked.

'Holloway gave me the words to say what I went through. I didn't have those words when I was thirteen, or when I was eighteen. The older prisoners called it being interfered with. The younger women had lots of other names for what those men did to me. I won't say them all. Abuse will do.'

Her aunt came up alongside her, reaching out for her. 'I told them. I said something was wrong, something was going on.'

Linda stood stock-still. 'I thought no one knew.'

For a moment, Nell had the experience of being in some sort of tableau that was coming to life. Linda's mother, pale, with an expression that might have been horror, or disbelief, the aunt in tears.

Linda turned to Nell. 'I'd like to go back to prison now, Miss Lewis.'

Nell took Linda's arm. As they walked away, voices floated after them.

The uncle said something to the men.

Moustache said, 'Don't you slander me!'

The long streak of whitewash called, 'She's a little liar!'

Linda turned back.

There was a cry. Nell looked back and saw that the uncle had punched one man and then the other.

The godmother came hurrying after Linda, saying, 'What, what did they do to you, my little love?'

'It's time for us to go, madam,' Nell said quietly. 'You can write, or visit, if Linda wants a visit.'

They walked back the way they had come. Nell experienced an odd sense of the grand memorials taking sides, dividing between stony disapproval of and solid applause for Linda. It was not until Nell and Linda were back in the car, and had been sitting in silence for several minutes, that Linda said, 'It just came out.'

'Yes, I thought so.'

Nell brought out the bag of pear drops. They each took one. Linda's hand shook.

Nell said, 'It might be a good thing that it came out.' She decided against saying there might have been a better moment, because that would not be true.

Linda was still shivering, in spite of having double-wrapped herself in the stole. As Nell drove, the car warmed up. Linda stopped shivering. They stopped at a bakery with a café attached, confining their conversation to the beans on toast, until Linda said, 'I've spoiled things for my mother. She'll never get over it.'

'Perhaps, perhaps not. Mothers can be resilient.'

When they arrived at Brackerley, Linda unwound the stole. She folded it and handed it back to Nell. 'Thank you, ma'am. It didn't just keep me warm. It was like a cape you would read about in a fairy tale. It didn't give me invisibility, it gave me strength.'

Later that evening, at about nine o'clock, Nell was walking along the corridor, passing the library. She heard a sound and stopped to listen. Someone was sobbing. She looked in. At first, she did not see anyone. There were no lights on. The curtains were drawn. The sound came from the corner of the room where an empty chair stood by an unlit lamp. As she came closer, Nell saw a pair of shoes, feet, legs. Someone was sitting, hunched up in the corner, behind the chair.

Nell moved closer. Linda was crouched on the floor, rocking back and forth, her knees drawn up, arms crossed around her chest. Nell moved the chair, bobbed down beside Linda and put her arms around her.

Even in the dim light, Nell saw that Linda had been digging her nails into her skin, making vivid scratches on her upper arms as she rocked.

'Linda, what is it? What's the matter? You did so well today.'

For the longest time, Linda did nothing but sob. Finally, the words came out between her sobs. 'The sight of them. They make me feel dirty, disgusting. And now everybody knows.'

Nell shushed her, rocking her saying, 'You're going to come through. Talk to me. Tell me. It won't go any further, I promise.'

Thirty-Five

In the run-up to the Brackerley Summer Fayre, to be held in the prison grounds on the third Saturday of July, debates took place among the residents about something that might not happen: what should they say if someone imagined that paying his or her entrance fee entitled them to ask why you are banged up. Answers varied, from Piss off and It's none of your bleeding business, to Cherry being prepared to say precisely how much cannabis she attempted to import in order to jump-start her business. There was also the question of celebratory themes. Only Olga was for something royal, such as a picture of the Prince of Wales. Cherry thought a fashion show too important to be squeezed into a summer fayre. Playing records was thought a good idea but none of the original four wanted to be DJ. A new girl was coerced into it, and rewarded with ten Silk Cut.

Linda did not join in the conversations. She chose to be the seller of soft drinks in the green marquee. The light would be dim, not that she looked the same now as in those photographs published at the time of her arrest.

The day came.

Nell was pleased that she had been brave enough to go on with the summer fayre in the wake of all that had happened. She had kept it simple, inviting the villagers to hold their produce show as part of the fayre, choosing a visiting day so that relatives could come.

It was good to do this before a date had been set for Derek Jeffrey's trial for the murder of Governor Harding. A few reporters had telephoned. Daisy dealt with them. A photographer turned up outside, carrying a long lens camera, but with improved security could not find a way in and was sent packing. Nell hoped that by the time of Jeffrey's trial, Brackerley would have established itself so thoroughly as an open prison for women that the connection with the bad old days would be diminished.

The allocated number of tickets for the big day sold out.

Linda angled her soft drinks table so as to be in shadow. There were volunteers here, Friends of Brackerley and villagers, all carefully checked. An outsider could not be sure who was a prisoner and who was not. This was a comfort for Linda.

In a soft drinks trade lull, after a family of five had quenched their thirst, a woman of about Linda's age walked slowly to the soft drinks table. She was neither tall nor short, fat nor thin. Her shining light brown hair reached shoulder length. Her amber eyes fixed Linda in a not unfriendly stare.

'Linda, I'm Annette. Lemonade, please.'

Linda wondered how the woman knew her name, but did not ask. She poured the lemonade. Annette paid. She took a sip. 'You don't know me, but we have something in common.'

Linda waited. She had a feeling this woman might be a

journalist looking for a sensational story. That would be it. Everything would begin again. Linda placed her hands flat on the table. She forgot to breathe.

When a couple with two children came to the table, Annette moved away.

The mother bought four orange juices. The father carried the paper cups. The mother directed them to go outside and sit on the grass with their drinks. She paid, and thanked Linda with a smile and in a manner that seemed to Linda to say, I am being very nice to you because you are banged up and even though you look smart today, you are probably entirely pathetic.

Annette came back. Linda concentrated, telling herself that she must breathe, remember how to breathe. Linda would not ask the stranger, What is it you want with me? What do you imagine we have in common? She would not give her an opening. Besides, she was remembering the letter Miss Lewis showed her. She was remembering the name.

Annette looked about. They were alone now. 'You killed my father, Simon Saunders,' she said softly.

'I did murder someone of that name,' Linda said quietly.

The answer sounded to Linda ridiculous, as if she killed many people but that was one she particularly remembered. It was something to do with the matter-of-fact way the woman talked. It rubbed off.

'How is your own father, Linda? I remember the eye tattoo on his finger. Red.'

'He's dead.'

'So that's two down and two to go.'

Linda did not reply.

'You know that only death or infirmity will stop them.'

'Probably.'

'I know the names, approximately where they live, what else can you tell me so that I don't kill an innocent bystander? It is likely to be a motor accident.'

Being unable to think what to say, Linda said nothing.

'If I stand here talking too long, I'll look odd. Smile, tell me about the lemonade.'

Linda said, 'It comes in a big carton. We transfer it to jugs.'

'Thank you. There is no need for you to know my surname. I changed it. I didn't want his name. You should do the same.'

She is trying to trick me, Linda thought. I don't believe her.

The woman said, 'Thank you for not seeing my mother. She prefers not to know. I don't know what she expected of you. To be honest, when she said she would write to Holloway and ask to see you, I was tempted to say, "Mother, never mind pestering that poor girl. Why don't you ask me?" I tried to tell her. Some people can't listen, can't hear.'

Linda said, 'In answer to your question, the streak of white-wash is a self-employed painter and decorator. Moustache is an insurance agent.'

Annette nodded. 'If anyone asks, we were talking about the weather, and how sad about the Beatles splitting up. Is there anything else you can tell me now? There may not be another opportunity.'

'My mind has gone blank.' Linda thought about her god-mother. She was on Linda's side now that they had met again by the grave. Her new counsellor had brought Linda round to saying, 'It's not me who should feel the shame,' although she did feel it, wondering would she ever slough it off. Probably not.

Annette took a straw hat and dark glasses from her bag. She

301

put them on. 'We may not speak again. It would be better that way, though I might come back next year for another glass of lemonade.'

Linda again remembered the letter from Mrs Saunders that Miss Lewis had shown her. 'Your mother said you finished your degree.'

'Two degrees, at different universities. Psychology and then Law. You should do the same.' She nodded in a gracious manner and was about to move away when Linda spoke.

'What you have in mind isn't a good idea. Murder never is. They should be the ones with the shame. Instead, it's me. It's you. Find another way.'

Linda served two more lemonades. When she looked, Annette had gone from the tent, Linda was left thinking that the conversation may have been a waking dream.

It was Linda's turn to be relieved from selling soft drinks, so that she could walk about the stalls. Linda bought a raffle ticket for a dress from Cherry. She bought a small iced cake from Diane.

There was a long queue for Olga's fortune-telling booth. Annette was at the end of the queue.

Linda pretended to join the queue. 'Something I wanted to know. Mr Saunders frightened me when he came to my room with your suitcase. Were you and I to have shared?'

'No. He followed you. The prosecution would have called it a deadly mistake, but you pleaded guilty. I'm sorry. And thank you.'

Thirty-Six

Nell prepared for the meeting at HQ by telling herself that things could be far worse. She had been in post for three months. After everything that had happened, she had feared the expected new arrivals would be put on hold. She had teetered on the edge of wondering whether this might be the most short-lived governorship on record, and the shortest life of a women's open prison. They could all be turfed out of Brackerley and posted who knows where. The site could be sold for redevelopment.

When the summons came for a meeting at HQ, she felt let down. Someone ought at least to have come north to see what she had made of the prison, rather than calling her in for a command performance. It would have been easier to show the transformations than to photograph and write reports. But taking photographs and writing reports was what she did. She would dare them to say thank you and goodbye after looking at her achievements.

Nell drove to London for the eleven o'clock meeting, had difficulty finding a parking place and ended up hurrying, carrying her bulging briefcase with its evidence of Brackerley being the foremost example of good practice.

Before the meeting, she had a quiet word with the chairman, knowing he would begin with a moment's silence for Governor Harding.

He agreed, 'And how are you, Miss Lewis?'

That was when Nell realised. This is not about the prison and whether we can move on from all that has happened. This is about me. It is about whether I am up to continuing or ready to throw in the towel.

Nell's reports, in multiple copies, were on the table. Nell now blushed at the thought that she had gone completely over the top with her enthusiasm. In the report on the fabric of the building she had included photographs of her pride and joy, the tiled floors and the ballroom floor. No one would want to look at floors. Before the meeting opened, the chap from admin was already flicking through. He asked what floor cleaning equipment they had used. Perhaps he was doing up a house.

After the moment's silence for Governor Harding, the chairman thanked Miss Lewis for her sterling work over the past weeks and asked her to give her report.

She chose to begin with 'everything that had happened' and praised her staff and the local community for their support – referring them to the list of organisations and contacts made, including the piece on herself in the *Harrogate Advertiser*.

Nell showed a photograph of the sapling willow tree, planted on the spot where Governor P. W. Harding, MBE had died and of the grave in the churchyard, planted with flowers.

She began with her report on education, and the enrolment of a resident, Linda Rogers, on a psychology course at the newly formed Open University. Linda was also undertaking a training programme with the Citizens' Advice Bureau. Cherry Davenport, a talented young designer, was working in a boutique and following a business studies course.

She linked the painting and decorating course to the refurbishment that was going on. She smiled. 'We are ready for an additional intake of residents. Residents have spruced up the rooms in the house that will become dormitories. Next, they'll move on to redecorating the prison governor's cottage.'

Nell was expecting what came next. It was a deputy director who asked the question. 'Miss Lewis, you have your female governor's suite of rooms.'

'Yes.'

'What use do you have in mind for the governor's cottage?'

'Thank you for asking. The suite of rooms in the main building will be a dormitory for seven residents – the best use of space. The governor's cottage will house two residents who have jobs and go to work each day, Cherry at a boutique in Harrogate, Diane demonstrating cookery for the gas board.'

The chairman leaned forward. 'And what about you, Miss Lewis, if you are not occupying the suite of rooms or the cottage?'

'I'll be buying a house in Brackerley village. It will show my commitment to the local community, and create a slight degree of separation from my place of work.'

Nell left the meeting assured of her own and HMP Brackerley's future. It was time to go back to her hotel and kick her shoes off for a while, before going out for the evening to Veeraswamy, taking Roxy out for that promised meal.

Acknowledgements

I am indebted to retired prison governors Veronica Bird and Judy Gibbons for generously sharing their experiences and answering my queries. *Veronica's Bird*, written with Richard Newman, is an engaging account of Veronica's thirty-five years as a prison officer. Thanks also to Kellie Reeve, HMI Prisons, and to Fionn Gordon. Thank you to Viv Cuthill and Michelle Hughes for their valuable insights into police procedures. Any mistakes are mine.

The Story of a House, published in 1997 by Yorkshire Art Circus in association with Askham Grange, edited by Brian Lewis and Harry Crew, offers an insightful close up of Askham Grange Women's Open Prison.

Many thanks to the team at Piatkus, especially editors Emma Beswetherick and Hannah Wann who complemented each other's work so brilliantly. Copy editor Anne O'Brien was spot on. Thanks, too, to agents Judith Murdoch and Rebecca Winfield for their unfailing support.

Thank you to Jean Coates, formerly of CLINKS, for the loan of books, to Lynne Strutt for her superb back-up, and last but not least, for the usual reasons, to Pat McNeil and Sylvia Gill.

Discover the Kate Shackleton
mysteries by Frances Brody

To find out more visit www.francesbrody.com

Don't miss the latest novel
in the Kate Shackleton series

It's the spring of 1930 and Private Investigator Kate
Shackleton responds to a call for help from the owner of
Barleycorn Brewery in the North Riding of Yorkshire.
The brewery's books don't add up, but when the one
employee who may know what's really going on meets
with a fatal accident, Kate's investigation intensifies.

On the day of the brewery garden party, amidst celebrations
for the newly crowned Yorkshire Brewery Queen, Kate opens
the wrong door and finds herself staring at another body.

It's clear there are secrets somebody would kill to keep
buried. And with the Brewery Queen's growing reputation
bringing Barleycorn further into the spotlight, Kate's wit,
skill and passion for the truth are tested to the limits.

Available now in paperback, ebook and audio